Misty Falls

Also by Joss Stirling

Finding Sky

Stealing Phoenix

Seeking Crystal

Storm and Stone

(published as STRUCK in eBook)

Misty Falls

Joss Stirling

OXFORD
UNIVERSITY PRESS

OXFORD
UNIVERSITY PRESS

Great Clarendon Street, Oxford OX2 6DP

Oxford University Press is a department of the University of Oxford.
It furthers the University's objective of excellence in research, scholarship,
and education by publishing worldwide. Oxford is a registered trade mark of
Oxford University Press in the UK and in certain other countries

First published 2014

British Library Cataloguing in Publication Data

Data available

ISBN: 978-0-19-273735-9

1 3 5 7 9 10 8 6 4 2
Printed in Great Britain

Paper used in the production of this book is a natural,
recyclable product made from wood grown in sustainable forests.
The manufacturing process conforms to the environmental
regulations of the country of origin.

For my editor at OUP, Jasmine Richards. Without your enthusiasm for the Benedict boys, they would never have been published.

Thank you.

Chapter 1

'On the Misty scale of disasters, one to ten, where would you put it?' Summer asked me.

I stared miserably at my two best friends as they clustered together on the screen of the laptop. Summer looked sympathetic, Angel amused.

'It's an eleven,' I admitted.

'Surely not?' Summer twirled a lock of dark hair, dusting her cheek absent-mindedly as she reviewed my record. 'Misty, it can't be as bad as the time you told Jenny Watson that she was a lying cow with all the character appeal of a cow pat.'

'And Misty was righteous to do so,' said Angel firmly. 'Jenny had split you up from Tom, Summer, so you had to agree with her.' While giving the impression of being a fairylike waif, Angel had a surprisingly husky voice. It had shocked me when we met at our first savant summer camp together three years ago but, fortunately, she had forgiven me for declaring that before everyone and gone on to become a loyal friend.

Summer kept to her plan of making light of my most recent mishap. Being sweet-natured, she always wanted everyone to feel better, which had made me even angrier that Jenny had picked on her. 'OK, I agree that Jenny Watson is a no-good boyfriend-stealer but most of us don't say this in front of an audience including her very influential school governor of a father at Speech Day. That has to be worse: Misty had to transfer to another school.'

'I didn't like that one anyway,' I muttered. 'They should have known better than to put me in front of a microphone.' Jenny and her friends had mocked me unrelentingly after that incident and I was more than happy to leave.

'So what could be worse than the Jenny Watson Misty moment?'

Time to confess. 'Remember I told you I thought Sean in Year 13 was *so* hot?'

Angel bent closer to the screen. 'We saw the prom photos and we agree. But you said you weren't going to do anything. It's not as if he's a savant like you so he can't be "the one",' she made quotation marks in the air, 'and you said he was way out of your league in any case.'

I propped my forehead on my finger and thumb, elbow resting on the dressing table. 'I know, I know. The ones I like always are out of my league.'

'Don't run yourself down, Misty. They would be lucky to be your boyfriend.'

I love my friends. 'Thanks, Angel.'

'So what happened?' prompted Summer.

I sighed. I had to force myself to say the words aloud. 'I went up to him yesterday to wish him a good summer—you know, that kind of thing.'

'Uh-huh.'

'And it just popped out.'

'What popped out?' Angel had a cheeky twinkle to her eye as her gaze dropped to my shirt.

2

'Nothing like that. No wardrobe malfunctions. Geez, remind me why I'm your friend again?'

'Because you think I'm great.'

Summer elbowed her to let me finish. 'Go on. You need to tell us so you can get past it.'

'OK, OK. I intended to say—coolly—"Hey, Sean, have a great holiday," but out came "You have the most gorgeous bum".'

Summer clapped her hands to her cheeks. 'You didn't!'

'I'm afraid I did.'

'And what did he say?' asked Angel.

'He said: "Thank you for sharing that with me", laughed and went off to tell his mates.'

'The rat.' Angel was trying not to smirk. She really didn't understand what it was like to live with my gift.

'I spent the rest of the day having boys come up to me to ask if I thought their bums were attractive too.'

Angel dipped off the screen. She was probably rolling around on the floor in a fit of giggles.

'You poor thing,' said Summer. At least one of my friends knew how to react appropriately to social death.

'I can't face them again. I'll have to move schools.'

Summer sighed. 'Misty, you can't do that. You've been to three schools in the last five years already because you were bullied for being different. You've got to stick it out for Sixth Form. And just think, you've the whole of the summer for them to forget about it. They won't remember in September.'

'You sure?'

'Of course, I'm sure.' There was a faint tingle of a lie to her words as if she wasn't entirely convinced but I let it pass. 'Sean will have left, won't he, as he's done his A-levels, so you won't have to see him or most of his friends.'

I brightened up at that thought. 'You're right. I'm getting panicked about nothing.'

'You'll be in South Africa for a month so you'll have time to forget about it too. When you get back for camp, we can talk more.'

'Thanks, Summer. You can tell Angel to stop laughing now.'

Angel came back on screen. 'I wasn't laughing.'

I rolled my eyes. 'You can't get away with lying to me.'

'Sorry. I feel your pain.'

'Yeah, right.'

'And Sean does have a gorgeous bum.'

I smiled as I ended the call. 'Ain't that the truth, girl.'

The flight to Cape Town climbed towards the top of the display screen. Boarding gate was now listed. I had already said goodbye to my parents and my three sisters and two brothers a few minutes earlier—the little ones were too much of a handful to wait until I went through to departures. My Aunt Crystal had stayed with me to check I made the plane.

'You'd best go through.' Crystal bent down and kissed my cheek, her mop of curly dark-blonde hair tickling my face as it swung to envelop me. 'Give my love to Opal, Milo, and the little ones, won't you?'

'Will do.'

Crystal squeezed my hands. 'I'm so envious, Misty. You'll be there to see Uriel track down his woman.'

I squeezed hers back. 'It'll be epic.' I couldn't wait to get away and put the embarrassing last few days at school behind me. We looked over to the two brothers, Uriel Benedict, my fellow traveller, and his younger brother, Xav, Crystal's fiancé. They were standing close together, Xav displaying none of his usual teasing as he murmured encouragement. As two insanely good-looking guys, they attracted more than their fair share of admiring glances from the girls queuing at the check-in desks.

It had to be a relief for my amazing aunt that she matched Xav in the looks department, with her catwalk height and unusual features, dark brows and film-star mouth.

Crystal shook her head, an amused glint in her eyes. 'Why do they both act as if Uriel is going off to war?'

She was right: Uriel was running his hands through his golden-brown hair in a nervous gesture I'd not seen before as he was usually so calm and self-contained. Blessed with classic bone structure, he reminded me of St Michael, the warrior angel as depicted in a stained-glass window I'd seen in Italy, all competence and athletic goodness, dispatching dragons with one hand and justice with the other. He wasn't quite as tall as Xav but almost, so the pair of them stood out a head above the milling crowds pushing trolleys around the brotherly pep-talk on the concourse of Terminal Five.

'They're too macho to admit it, but it looks like Uriel is terrified and Xav is worried for him.'

Crystal laughed. 'You're right. Poor little scaredy big guys.'

'Have to say, it's a big deal heading off to meet your future partner. You did tell him enough to take him to her door?'

Putting her arm around my shoulder, Crystal steered me towards the security check. 'As much as I could without holding his hand all the way to the first face-to-face. My gift tells me she's in Cape Town. I can't get too exact from such a distance but I see white buildings—crowds of people. Opal is fairly sure that means one of the hospitals and she even has a shrewd idea which of the savants in that part of town might be the match. She's arranging a get-together so they can meet.'

I hadn't realized that preparations were so far advanced. 'Is she tipping off her target?'

'No, just in case she raises hopes that then get dashed. If she's wrong, I'll fly out next month and see if I can get a closer bead on Uri's girl.'

Of course, Crystal would come to the rescue if necessary. She would do anything for family and now Xav's six brothers were all included in the term. Crystal was only a couple of years older than me, making her more like a sister than an aunt, but she took her responsibilities seriously. My mum, Crystal's oldest sister, always said the baby in the family had been given the heaviest burden with her gift.

I brushed her arm. 'But you can't fly out for every soulfinder you locate or it would break the bank.' That was also something my mum said. Crystal had been busy since her gift was discovered in the autumn, helping family and friends find their savant counterpart. It was not a simple process: she could give a direction and a sense of place but people had the annoying habit of hiding out in big cities full of potential matches or they moved about, following a pattern that made perfect sense to them, no doubt, but to a soulseeker like Crystal was infuriating.

'You sound just like Topaz.' Crystal frowned slightly, thinking hard. 'I wish I could afford it but I don't believe it'll be necessary this time. The direction I've sensed has stayed pointing to South Africa. Uri would've gone sooner if he hadn't been locked into a work commitment but luckily she stayed put.'

I wondered what could be more important to Uriel than meeting his soulfinder but with a gap of twelve years between him and me it didn't seem my place to ask. I was still at school and he already had a doctorate from Denver University in the United States.

'It's a total bummer,' admitted Crystal, 'that I can't now go with him as Xav and I have to be in the US next week so we can hunt for a place to live in New York. He has to start at uni soon.' She pulled a face. 'And we're saving up to help Victor and Will. I've got a feeling Victor's one is going to be a really expensive hunt.' She looked a little harassed for a moment, lining up all the tasks she had to do before the beginning of the university year. Then her face cleared. 'So it's down to you, Misty, to look after my brother-in-law-to-be.'

I was thrilled she thought me up to the job. She was one of the few in my family who didn't treat me like a screw-up. Mum and Dad had spent much of the last decade clearing up the messes I made at home and school with my blunt talk; it was a pleasant change to be trusted. 'No pressure then.'

She gave me a hug. 'No pressure. Enjoy your holiday.'

'It's going to be interesting, I know that much already.' I tried to lighten her mood. 'And I can't change your mind about telling me where my soulfinder is?'

She raised her eyes to the ceiling at my familiar plead-ing, hands on hips. 'No—and you know that I'm not lying so don't bother to argue. No soulfinders before you're eighteen. You tell your little brothers and sisters the same thing. Gale's already been nagging me. You all need to have a normal life until you join the rest of us in that stuff.'

'Aw, spoilsport!' I mock-pouted but I knew she was serious. She'd explained before that her gift of finding our counterparts came with a cost. Life could be cruel and not all matches would be successful. She firmly believed that the people she linked should be mature enough to cope with any disappointments or disasters. All of us savants, like Summer, Angel and I, are born with special mental powers, but we have to face up to the negatives about our gift as well as the benefits. Look at me: I'm a poster girl for the downside. I have a problem with the truth. Thanks to my savant gift, I can't get away from it. Best friend with dodgy taste appears before me in new purchase to ask my opinion. She circles with a pleased smile just waiting for me to bolster her self-esteem. I line up my white lie: *Hey, don't you look great!* but, oops, out pops *Sorry, but you look fat in that!* It is as though I have Google translate in my brain: feed in a fib and it gets straightened out into the unvarnished truth. Worse still, if I lose control, it can be infectious; people end up telling the truth around me, even when they don't intend to do so.

My friends have to be very understanding.

Savants come in all shapes and sizes. Nearly all of us are telepathic and can move things with our mind. On top of that, some get awesome gifts. Uriel can sense the events of the past attached to place, object, or person. My mum can see through solid objects when she concentrates. It makes being a teenager in her house particularly difficult, trust me. Her brother, my uncle Peter, can change the weather. Even Gran can make you fall asleep, which means she is much in demand as a babysitter.

But best of all is Crystal, as her ability allows her to locate our savant counterpart, our soulfinder, and so she can solve the central problem of our lives. You see, when one of us savants is conceived, somewhere on the globe the person who is to be our other half in a very real sense also starts life. They have half our gifts and together we can be even more than we can be apart. So, roughly nine months later, two people destined to be drawn to each other are born. But have you seen how big the world is? Talk about needle-in-haystack! That's why Crystal is so special: she can send you right to the doorstep of your destiny. What she can't guarantee is the reception. Your soulfinder might fall headlong in love with you but it is also possible their emotions will be violently against you, depending on how their experience has shaped them. Savants have a huge capacity for feeling for their soulfinder but whether they are filled by love or hate is beyond Crystal's control. When I was little, I concentrated more on the fairy-tale potential of the prince in my gran's tales of soulfinders, but now I realized that those tales contained an equal number of trolls and witches so, for all my testing of Crystal's red line, I was in no rush to meet mine.

For the hundredth time, Uriel checked his boarding pass

and ticket were in his carry-on bag. He knew that this gamble was what was in store for him at the other end of the plane journey. At twenty-eight, he was more than ready to meet his soulfinder. No doubt he was praying it would prove to be as successful a match as those of his own parents and his four brothers who had found their girls. Among the Benedicts, only Uriel, Will, and Victor remained unattached.

I could see Crystal was biting her lip as she watched Uriel. I gave her a hug, which was harder than it sounds as she is almost six feet and I'm an ordinary five foot four.

'Not your fault if it goes wrong,' I whispered as I pulled her ear level with my mouth, 'but you can claim the credit if it turns out well.'

She chuckled as I hoped. 'Good philosophy.' She straightened up and gave an impressive whistle. 'Hey, cupcake, let your brother go or he'll miss his plane!'

Xav looked across at us, his eyes alive with laughter. Next to the fair St Michael Uriel, Xav was more a dark-haired Lucifer, or, changing mythologies, Loki with a wicked twinkle. 'OK, Beauty, message received loud and clear.'

Uriel picked up his carry-on bag and squared his shoulders for what came next. 'Got everything, Misty? Passport? Boarding pass?'

I opened my mouth to make a joke but Crystal nudged me before I could protest at his mother-hen act. 'It's doing him good to worry about someone else. Takes his mind off it.'

I smiled at Uriel sweetly. 'Yep. All present and correct.'

Xav gave me a hug (my heart went pitter-pat as he was so swoon-worthy) and shepherded me to the barrier with a brotherly hand on the shoulder. What was it about these Benedict boys that made them want to order us around? I rolled my eyes at Crystal but she just grinned. I guess she'd come to like that side in her man.

Just after I had waved a final time to Crystal and Xav, the first Misty moment of the trip struck.

'Miss, I'm afraid you can't take liquids over a hundred millilitres in your hand luggage.'

I looked up at the security guard who had unzipped my bag. There at the top were all the bottles I had intended to transfer to my suitcase but forgotten in the excitement of the morning.

'Oh, sorry. I am such a scatterbrain.'

I could feel Uriel beside me frown. He must have been thinking that I was a total baby not to know about the restrictions.

'You'll have to leave them here.' The guard took them out one by one.

I watched sadly as my curl-taming lotion, favourite shampoo and conditioner were consigned to a bin. He looked closely at the suntan lotion before deciding that too infringed the rules and chucked it in the rubbish.

'There you are. Ready to fly.' The guard passed over my now much lighter bag.

Uriel glanced at his watch. 'I'm afraid we'll have to run, Misty. No time to replace your things at the shops.'

'It's OK. My fault.'

'Yes, it was.' Uriel looked disconcerted. He had been intending to say something kind and consoling but instead had blurted out the truth. My grip on my gift had to have slipped. Again.

'That was me,' I muttered, cheeks burning. 'My control is a bit iffy.'

He gave a funny-sounding laugh. 'Yes, Xav warned me about that. I'll have to take care around you, won't I?'

Behind us I could hear a woman confessing, to her own great surprise, that she was attempting to smuggle drugs through security. Policemen were descending. Uriel arched a brow. I nodded.

'Maybe I should leave you here. They wouldn't need a scanner.' Uriel took my bag and added it to his. The loudspeaker announced that our plane was boarding. Uriel handed me the tickets to hold. 'Come on. I don't want to be late for my future.'

On the flight, I watched crummy films while Uriel worked quietly away on his laptop. We had excellent at seat service thanks to his all-round hunkiness; the cabin attendants couldn't do enough for him and I was the happy recipient of the overflow of their goodwill.

I nudged him after we had yet another refill. 'It's not fair, you know.'

He looked up from his screen. 'What's not fair?'

'You good-looking people. You don't realize what it is like to be the rest of us.'

He opened his mouth, then paused, trying to sense if my gift was under wraps or roaming free.

'It's OK. You can lie if you want. It's in here.' I tapped my head.

'I wasn't going to lie exactly.'

'But . . . ?'

'I was going to say that I didn't notice, but I do. And it's stupid.' A little huff fluttered his golden-brown fringe. 'I don't see myself like that. It's what's inside that counts.'

'Yeah, but us moths are attracted to flame and you and your brothers are like candles.'

He grinned. 'Was that an example of your inability to lie?'

'I suppose, yes. I'm blunter than most people as I can't be any other way. I tell it how it is.'

'Then let me say that no one in your family is exactly homely.'

'Homely? Is that like American for butt ugly?'

His eyes twinkled. 'A better translation would be plain. Crystal is stunning.'

'Yes, she is.'

'Diamond is beautiful.' Diamond, the next sister up in age from Crystal, had married the oldest Benedict brother, Trace. She was the epitome of elegance, sleek and coordinated.

'I know.'

'And you are very cute too.' He winked.

I checked my lie detector but nothing he said had set my teeth on edge, the usual sign of a fib. Uriel thought I was cute? Aw! I honestly believed myself to be a bit of a mess in the looks department. I had inherited the same wildly frizzy hair as Crystal but several shades paler. Without my hair lotion I would be wandering round Cape Town looking like an alpaca in need of a shearing. I had pale skin and freckles, weird long blonde eyelashes and eyes that had settled on an unremarkable grey. I should not press him for any more compliments as he would have reached the end of the road of his honest opinions.

'So what are you working on?' I asked in a none-too-subtle change of subject.

Brought back to his task, his smile dimmed. 'Please don't read the screen.'

'Sorry.'

He could tell from my tone that I was feeling shut out. 'It's nothing to do with the trip and it's not that I don't want to tell you; it's more that I can't.'

'I don't get it.'

He sighed. 'You know I work in forensics?'

'Yes, Crystal mentioned it. You're doing post-doctoral studies, she said.'

'I undertake investigations for the American authorities into crimes that seem to have some link to the savant community. Victor brings me in when he needs me.'

Victor, Uriel's younger brother, worked for the FBI.

'Oh, I see. So it's like a state secret or something?'

'More like it's too grim for you to see. Post-mortems aren't exactly vacation reading.' He closed down that document and called up a map. There were red dots scattered over the globe, clustered in North America, Australia, New Zealand, and several countries in Europe. 'I can tell you, though, that I'm looking into some connected deaths.' He angled the screen for me to see. 'Twelve we know of so far—a serial killer who preys on the savant community. We're searching for a way to stop there being another victim. My job is to tug the thread loose that will trap our murderer.' He rubbed his hands over his face. 'I'm a little obsessed with it—haven't been able to put it aside since the first murder last year.'

My truth power was perhaps encouraging him to confess more than he normally would, or maybe he just needed to offload, but it gave me an insight into what the last few months had been like for him.

'Twelve—that's terrible!' I suddenly wished I wasn't so far from the ones I loved. I'd have to text them on arrival to take special care.

Uriel's expression was really grim. 'Each one an unspeakable loss for the family involved. I can't bear the idea that there will be more.'

'And that's what's kept you from flying off to South Africa?'

He gave a hollow laugh. 'Yeah. I wanted to solve the case so it didn't tarnish this moment. Victor finally told me it was time to take a break. He thinks I'll see things more clearly once I get the soulfinder business over with.'

I lifted an eyebrow. 'Business?'

He shook his head at his own clumsy phrasing. 'I hope not. Pleasure: I hope it is going to be a hundred per cent pleasure.'

'Don't worry, I'll be there to help.' I crossed my fingers that he hadn't heard too much about my Misty moments or he'd be even more worried.

He snapped his computer screen closed. 'Thank you. Now, you've reminded me that this isn't supposed to be work. I should arrive with something other than murder on my brain, agreed?'

I nodded.

'Game of cards?' He pulled a pack out of his pocket. 'What do you want to play?'

'Go Fish?'

His smile was wry. 'How appropriate.'

My Auntie Opal was waiting in arrivals with my three cousins, Willow, Hazel and the toddler, Brand. Willow and Hazel had crayoned a banner for us, an amazing drawing of a lion roaring a welcome. Both had inherited a savant gift for capturing images in all sorts of forms—for Willow it was drawing, for Hazel sculpture in any material—paper, clay, cardboard, wood. What they saw they could reproduce with amazing accuracy and artistic flair. I doubt anyone on the concourse suspected that the excitable five- and seven-year-olds were responsible for making the banner unaided. I had last seen them at Diamond and Trace's wedding in Venice in December where they had run wild with my younger sisters, Gale, Peace, and Felicity only pausing to pretend to be angelic bridesmaids for an hour. Not that anyone in the family was fooled.

'Misty! Misty!' shouted Willow as if I couldn't see the party waiting for us.

I waved, only to be taken aback by a lion's roar that came, no, surely not, from Brand? The huge noise from a tiny boy caught many by surprise. I saw the hordes of taxi drivers looking nervously around in case a wild creature was prowling the concourse. My aunt went into a flurry of distraction activity and handed Brand a drink to prevent a repeat.

'Sorry about that. His gift has begun to show,' she said as she kissed me and then hugged Uriel.

'What kind of gift is that?' I asked, eyeing with suspicion the squirming bundle of black-haired toddler. 'Does he turn into a lion or something?'

'Not as bad as that.' Opal started with the pushchair for the car park, expecting us all to follow. She always acted like mother duck, no matter the age of her ducklings. 'He's a natural mimic. It might even be a gift for animal languages, we're not quite sure.'

I sensed there was more to tell. 'But?'

'He seems to have long conversations with our dog.' She wrinkled her brow. 'In fact, I'm not sure if Brand doesn't think he is a puppy, as he likes playing fetch for hours.'

'It's nice that he likes playing with the dog,' said Uriel kindly, catching the bottle the little boy had dropped as he bobbed up and down in his seat.

'No, I meant Brand likes us to throw *him* a stick; the dog doesn't get a look in. And he gnaws things, trouser legs mostly.'

I laughed as Willow and Hazel giggled. Uriel handed him back his bottle and Brand gave a bright yip, which suggested he was following more of the conversation than a two-year-old could usually be expected to understand. He promptly dropped his drink again.

Uriel snatched it up before it hit the tarmac. 'I think I'm being taken for a ride. He's playing bottle-fetch.'

'Welcome to my family,' I said to Uriel. 'We are all certifiable.'

He offered his hands to the girls to hold for crossing the road. 'Makes me feel right at home.'

Chapter 2

After a shower and time to unpack, we convened in the kitchen for our council of war. My family home back in the UK was in a leafy suburb of London; Opal's house was in a similar area in Cape Town: the Zwaanswyck district, an affluent neighbourhood with fabulous houses and gardens, south of the centre. Cape Town has one of the world's best climates so everything looked fresh and green, except for the rocky flanks of Table Mountain that dominated the skyline. A cloud-cloth covered the top, formed as the moist sea air bumped into Africa. Her husband and soulfinder, Milo Carr, worked as a dental surgeon; Opal was a lawyer but was taking a career break to be with the children. Their house was a lovely place to spend a holiday: a long low building with sprawling lawns and a circular pool, though during the cooler and wetter winter days, only the hardiest swimmer would take a dip. That would be me. Coming from England, I was going to take advantage of the slightest glimpse of sunshine and had laid out my bikini in case it warmed up later.

But first things first: Uriel's big moment.

Opal put coffee cups on the kitchen table in front of us and then carried over a plate of homemade biscuits. Through the picture window behind her I could see the girls playing on the swing hanging from the silver oak at the far end of the lawn; Brand was sitting in a playpen having an earnest conversation with Nutty, the family's chocolate Labrador. The girls' pictures and models decorated every spare inch of the kitchen cabinets: a random collection of unicorns, family faces, butterflies, and safari animals. Pot plants exploded in happy blossom on every spare ledge and windowsill. I thought the whole place had a friendly messiness to it, which had to be Milo's relaxing effect on my aunt as she was famous among her brothers and sisters for being a neat freak, a good practical example of soulfinders balancing out each other's gifts.

I picked up a biscuit and took a bite. 'Hmm-hmm—chocolate chip! You made these?'

Opal finally took a seat, hauling a large file with her, which wafted the crumbs as she dropped it down in front of Uriel. The surface of his coffee ringed from the centre out in the shockwave. 'Hardly, Misty. I don't have time to cook. I've been too busy with this. Willow made the cookies with her dad last night.'

'Compliments to the chefs,' said Uriel. He tapped the file. 'What's this?'

'My research.' Opal took a sip of coffee. 'On your potential soulfinder—I've trawled through those with the right age who fitted Crystal's hints. They're only the ones known to the Savant Net but I had to start somewhere. To save you time, I've narrowed it down to one front-runner.' She frowned slightly, reviewing her material. 'Of course, we can't rule out that there is another candidate out there who doesn't know about us.'

'You are very thorough.'

'Legal training.' Opal shrugged as if that explained it. She also had a savant gift for restoration, returning things to their original condition, which went well with her compulsion to see to the detail. She would have been knockout as a picture restorer but had surprised the family by choosing law. She explained that she preferred restoring justice to lives than flecks of paint on old masters. 'My favourite is the one at the top; there isn't really anyone else in her league of suitability. You'll see I've gathered a lot of information on her, educational background and professional qualifications. She works at the Groote Schuur Hospital in the paediatric department. I got to know her a little when she treated Brand for a bad chest infection.'

Normally so controlled, Uriel's hand was shaking very slightly as he opened the file to the first photo. 'Francie Coetzee.' He studied the picture, his finger tracing the edge, then put it down, expression puzzled. 'Strange, I was expecting something, I don't know, *more* when I saw her.'

Opal gave him an understanding smile. 'It isn't always a bolt of lightning, Uriel. Milo and I weren't sure until we connected telepathically.'

'And then?' I asked, curious to hear this part of the story.

She grinned. 'Zap!' We laughed as she blushed.

'Well done, Uncle Milo!'

'Yes, well.' Opal cleared her throat, too late to hide her embarrassment at letting that out. 'I've asked Francie if I can meet up at the hospital café after her shift. I mentioned I was bringing savant guests who were visiting Cape Town for the first time.'

'What's she expecting from us?' Uriel asked.

'I said that Milo and I were very boring hosts with the kids limiting our partying and wondered if she could introduce you to some younger locals. She's got a group together for tomorrow night. Is that soon enough for you?'

He swallowed. 'Yes.'

Opal patted his hand. 'Look through the file. She's a lovely girl, brilliant at her job.'

Uriel nodded, but I could tell he was disappointed. It was probably just jet lag so I told him so.

'You're right. I should sleep on it.' He picked up the file. 'Is it OK if I take this back to my room?'

'Absolutely. I'll let you know when it's time for lunch.' Opal whisked some crumbs into her palm in a nervous tidying gesture.

We waited for him to leave the room before letting our eyes meet.

'Oh dear,' said Opal. 'Do you think I should phone Crystal?'

'Let's not panic, auntie. It's just the first candidate.'

'I think I convinced myself I'd done a good job finding the right woman but now I'm not sure.'

Brand started whimpering because Nutty had left him to join the girls. Opal used her telekinetic powers to make his teddy bear do a jig in front of him. He switched to a throaty chuckle.

'He's gorgeous,' I said. 'So sweet. He is going to have all the little girls in kindergarten after him.'

'That's savant boys for you. Heartbreakers, all of them. I just hope Francie is tough enough to take it tomorrow. She must have suspected I was up to something.'

'Why?'

'Her gift is to read minds. That's why she's so good at what she does: she can pick out the thoughts of even the most confused little person who doesn't understand what's making them feel bad. I'm afraid she'll be expecting something momentous to happen.'

I felt a moment of déjà vu. Hadn't I had a similar conversation with Crystal? The women in my family all seemed to feel they were responsible for everything. 'It's not your fault, auntie. You've done your best. Anyway, I'll be there to help you both find out the truth.'

Uriel pulled out all the stops for his first encounter with his potential match; he emerged from his bedroom shaved, groomed and dressed in a carefully picked green T-shirt with a tree on the front and faded jeans that showcased his yummy golden skin and cyclist's lean fitness. I emerged from my room looking like I'd had a close encounter with a hedge trimmer. I'd made the mistake of washing my hair before going to bed, forgetting that my curl-taming lotion was back in a Heathrow bin.

I held up my hand as Uriel and Opal caught a glimpse of me. 'Don't. I know.'

Hazel cartwheeled into the kitchen. 'Hey, Misty, what's happened to your hair? You look funny.'

Just then I felt a hot resentment of Hazel's neat black plaits. Opal had escaped the plague of the frizzy hair that had been inherited by some members of our family and so her children were free of the jinx.

'I do not look funny, Hazel. I'm just channelling my inner alpaca.'

Brand made a sound like a high-pitched donkey bray.

'What was that?' I asked.

'I think he's imitating the alpaca alarm call,' said Uriel, bending down by the little guy. 'That's so cool. Where did you learn that?'

Brand howled like a wolf.

'Discovery Channel,' said Opal. 'He gets Nutty to fetch him the remote when my back's turned. He loves nature programmes. And you wonder why I've not yet gone back to work? Think what he would do at nursery.' She laughed and shook her head. 'Milo, we're leaving!'

Uncle Milo came in from the garden, Willow riding piggy-back. A short, rounded man with a high forehead, Opal's soul-finder was built for comfort rather than speed. He had a gift for making things grow and bloom so was usually very restful to be around. But not today. Instead of calming with wise words, he looked anxious. 'I hope it goes well, Uriel. We'll be rooting for you.' He reached out and shook hands with his American guest. Here was another one treating it like a major battle.

'OK, guys, let's go then.' I headed for the door before Uriel got too spooked.

Mercifully, the drive to the hospital did not take long. Opal swung into a bay in the visitors' car park and we got out onto the damp tarmac. The evening was turning sunny after the earlier rain showers; long shadows stretched out before us so we looked like an alien landing party. Nudging Uriel, I put my fingers by my ears and waggled to make antennae, hoping to make him laugh.

'What on earth are you doing?' Opal asked, locking the car with a click of the key fob.

Normal people would make up a lie at this point, something about massaging their temples, but I can't. 'Making a Martian?' It came out with a question mark as I realized how stupid it sounded.

'If you can't take this seriously, Misty, perhaps you'd better stay in the car.' Her tone was more irritated than justified by my goofing around; nerves were getting to her too.

Uriel smiled at me. 'She's fine, Opal. She's making me relax. I feel a little fish-out-of-water. You know, Misty, you remind me of Xav—in a good way.' He slung an arm around my shoulders and we walked together to meet his destiny. 'He's our family clown.'

We sat with our drinks around a mosaic-patterned table near the door to the café. Coffee beans fought with the anti-septic smell of the hospital foyer—caffeine just winning. I stirred my raspberry frappuccino, enjoying the marbling effect through the clear glass. Opal kept checking her watch every minute.

'She's late.'

'I imagine that she can't just down tools at the end of her shift doing what she does,' Uriel said quietly. His leg under the table was jigging nervously. I had to do something to make him relax or this would be one awkward first-day-of-the-rest-of-their-lives.

'OK, Uriel, if you could be an animal other than a human, which one would you pick?' My mind was still pondering that alpaca thing so this was the first question that came to mind. I liked 'what if?' conversations as they didn't involve lies and there was nothing to set my teeth on edge.

'Misty.' Opal sounded so like my mother it was uncanny.

'No, it's all right. She's attempting to distract me while we wait.' At least Uriel understood me.

My aunt gave a funny little snort. I tabbed her as a show pony tossing its mane in displeasure.

'I'll start. I always think I'd want to be a dolphin,' I con-fessed. 'Fabulous swimming ability combined with huge smile: what's not to like?'

A woman approached from behind Uriel, stethoscope stuffed into one pocket. Francie: it had to be. Petite, with a short brunette bob framing an elfin face, she struck me as appearing too young for the doctor's coat, reminding me of Peace and Felicity when I caught them tottering about in our mum's high heels. Opal's face lit up on Francie's arrival but Uriel had not yet noticed. Francie paused, not wanting to interrupt as Uriel had already started speaking.

'If I were an animal I'd be a . . . ' He rubbed his chest then leaned forward as an idea struck. 'Yeah, I'd be a condor. Imagine flying above the Andes. Amazing.' He stretched out his arms.

'Yes, that would be amazing,' said Francie.

Uriel leapt to his feet, the chair legs scraping on the floor with a horrid grating sound. If he had been a condor he would have squawked in surprise and shed a few feathers.

'Hello there. I'm Francie Coetzee.' She shook hands with Uriel in a matter-of-fact manner. 'I guess you must be Uriel. Nice to see you again, Opal. And this has to be your niece; Misty, isn't it?' She laughed. 'That sounds odd on a sunny day.'

'Yes, I get that a lot.'

'Sorry, I guess you do. Welcome to Cape Town.' She slid out of her white coat and folded it over the back of a chair. 'Can I get you anything?'

'We're good, thanks.' Uriel gestured to the round of barely touched drinks.

'I'll be back in a second.' She went over to the counter to order a coffee.

I had tried not to be nervous for Uriel's sake but I couldn't contain my excitement any longer. 'Well?'

Uriel's eyes followed Francie as she chatted with the barista. 'I don't know. I'm not sure what I'm supposed to be feeling.'

Opal did not look happy; she had really thought she had cracked the case. 'Please give it a chance. She's a perfect match in age, Uriel.'

'It's not that I'm not grateful, Opal, for all your work. She's pretty, and talented, but she doesn't seem to stand out from the crowd for me—and my brothers said that was the first thing they noticed about their partners.'

'Wait till she comes back and try telepathy.' I shifted in my seat, ill at ease with the tension and Uriel's disappointment. I

23

hadn't imagined the moment like this: I'd expected zap and we were getting zilch. Were we going to have to call in Crystal after all? I'd promised I'd sort it out for her. I was letting her down.

A man sitting across from us, who had been peacefully sharing a sandwich with a heavily pregnant woman, suddenly jumped up and thumped the table. The mum-to-be stared at him in shock. 'What do you mean: it's not my baby?'

'Did I say that?'

'Yes, you did!'

'I was going to tell you—eventually.'

The man slapped the car keys on the table and walked out. 'I'll catch a bus home.'

'Mason, Mason!' She scooped up the keys and hurried after him. 'I'm sorry!'

'I don't know how you can say that!' exclaimed a nurse who was passing with two friends. 'You always said you liked Benjamin. He is not a creep.'

I'd let go of the barrier I put around my gift.

Opal buried her head in her hands, knowing what was going on. I felt frantic. It is much easier to lose control than regain it after I've reached a certain point. Picture a game of spillikins: simple to drop them; next to impossible to pick them up without making others wobble. 'Do something,' she pleaded.

'I am, I am.' I tried to pull back the sticks of truth-telling that had escaped from me. My heart was pounding. I had to do this before Francie got back but she was already on her way.

'I hate my job,' growled the waiter to a surprised woman who had asked him to wipe the table. He wore a badge that declared him 'Happy to help'.

'Why are you working here then if it's too much trouble to please a customer?'

He opened his mouth fully intending to apologize for his

lapse in manners but out came: 'Customers like you are always complaining. I can't stand you moaners.'

Francie came back bearing a frothy latte. 'There: I deserve this after a day of pain-in-the-neck consultants.' She frowned. 'Did I just say that out loud?'

'I'm afraid so.' Uriel was now looking grimly amused. 'Misty here is having one of her moments.'

Francie turned her attention to me. If she could read minds she had to know mine was shouting 'Help!' and 'Sorry, everyone!'

'She has a truth gift?'

'Curse,' I muttered.

'And she lost control because she was . . . ' Francie's eyes flicked to Uriel, 'worried that you might not be my soulfinder after all? Opal, what have you been scheming behind my back?'

Opal couldn't duck this with a fib as she might under normal circumstances. 'I wanted Uriel to meet you as we think there's a possibility of a match. A strong likelihood. Your dates of birth are close and a soulseeker had a lead for him that mentioned a white building in Cape Town. I immediately thought of the hospital.'

Francie turned back to Uriel. 'I'm sorry. Not that you aren't a gorgeous man but there's no chance, even with a soulseeker tip-off.'

Uriel blinked at her strong rejection. 'Why? Shouldn't we at least check with telepathy?'

She patted his hand. 'Trust me, I know.'

'How do you know? Have you located your soulfinder?'

'No.'

'Then why?'

She took a sip of coffee, eyes sparkling over the rim of her tall glass. 'My soulfinder, when I meet her, is not likely to look like a GQ model.'

Oops: seems as if Opal's file missed out some essential facts about Francie.

I have never seen Uriel blush so red before.

'Awkward,' I whispered.

'I apologize for wasting your time,' he said stiffly.

'No worries. And I don't think you have wasted a second of my time. Thank you for thinking of me. I'm flattered.' She sipped her coffee, her gaze sweeping Uriel speculatively. 'You may not be my match but I'm thinking it might be a good idea to introduce you to my twin sister.'

'Twin?' Uriel looked like he had been on the receiving end of a second sucker punch. Good job he was sitting down.

'Yes, she's called Tarryn. I can assure you that you won't be wasted on her.'

I couldn't help myself: I started to giggle. The threads of control I had gathered scattered to the four winds again. Opal was going to be so embarrassed she had landed Uriel in this situation.

'You have a twin?' Opal looked horrified. 'How can I have missed that?'

'Because she keeps a low profile in savant circles—doesn't take part in the Net. She finds her gift . . . unpleasant and tries to keep it quiet.' Francie nudged me. 'As much as I like to hear you laugh, can you do us all a favour, Misty, and get a grip before you're responsible for the sacking of several employees round here?'

'I think I'd best leave. I'll see . . . ' I hiccupped. 'I'll see you at the car.'

I had myself back under control by the time Uriel, Opal, and Francie approached the Volvo.

'Everything OK?' I asked.

'Strangely, as soon as you left, things returned to normal,' Francie said dryly.

'Sorry about that.'

'Are you still ready to come meet my sister? When Opal asked me to introduce you to younger people, I planned to take you to a barbecue Tarryn is holding tonight for some of her pupils. They're your age, Misty, so I'd thought it would be more fun for you than hanging out with my doctor friends.'

I could hear that Francie was having doubts about launching me on her sister's social event, especially as Tarryn could be 'the one' (second attempt). I decided it had to be Uriel's call.

'Do you want me there?' *Don't be hurt if he sends you home*, I told myself. I would be, of course, but I'd try really hard not to show it.

He took a moment to reply, crafting the most diplomatic answer he could manage, knowing I'd sense if he were lying. 'I'm prepared to take the risk. But do you think, you could, you know, keep a grip on your gift, Misty?'

I drew a cross over my heart. 'I promise. I'll give it my best shot.'

'That's settled then. My car's just over there.' Francie waved to Opal. 'I'll bring them back to yours later. Say hi to Brand from me.'

I could tell my aunt would've liked to stay for the next stage in the hunt but she had promised to be back for the children's bedtime.

'Good luck!' Opal called as she got into her car.

'Tarryn's expecting us.' Francie led us over to a white BMW convertible. 'Most of the people at the party have nothing to do with us savants so if it happens,' she looked sideways at Uriel, 'can you find a private spot? I've not given her any warning.'

'I've no problem with that,' said Uriel, his lips curving in a smile that suggested he was giving plenty of thought to what use he might put privacy with a newly discovered soulfinder. After the dent to his confidence that meeting Francie must have made, this guy bounced back quickly.

'Feeling good about this one?' I asked softly.

'Strangely, yeah, though you'd think I'd learn from what happened earlier not to expect plain sailing. Tarryn. I love the name already.'

I patted his shoulder. 'Great.'

Tarryn lived in a house in the Rondebosch suburb of Cape Town, not far from the hospital. Set in the grounds of the school where Tarryn worked, it was a sweet little bungalow with a covered porch that ran the length of the building, surrounded by a garden that needed no attention from Uncle Milo to make it flourish. Beyond the fence, the lushness continued as there were acres of playing fields, white uprights of rugby posts, fluttering nets of football goals, a cricket pavilion. The whole school setup had the air of privilege and wealth.

As we drove through the gates, I could see that the party was already under way. The guests seemed to be predominantly boys dressed in white shirts and blue trousers or shorts. I noted the white school buildings further up the drive. Maybe Crystal had got that detail right after all?

'Let me guess: this is a private school for boys,' I said, my unease growing. I had imagined that when Francie said 'people my own age' she had meant girls. I never did well with boys. Never. I had the social grace of a giraffe on an ice rink.

'Yes, of course. They're lovely boys. So mature for their age.'

And I was the kind of girl who made Martian antennae and had fuzzball hair. I should've taken my chance and gone home with Opal. Francie smiled at me in the driver's mirror as if she heard my doubts.

'Can you see her?' Of course, Uriel's thoughts were travelling a totally different path from mine.

I was here for him, I reminded myself. This wasn't about me.

Francie parked in front of the bungalow, got out and waved at a woman hovering by the barbecue. An older man in a chef's hat was wielding a pair of tongs as he turned the burgers.

'Great, you made it!' Francie's sister left the grill to greet us properly.

'Oh my God,' said Uriel under his breath.

Tarryn certainly deserved such awe: she was so pretty. Long tanned legs well framed by her navy shorts, ballerina poise, swirls of brunette hair: I wondered how any boy in her class was ever able to concentrate. Perhaps her most striking feature, though, was her eyes: huge brown ones with long dark lashes. Something clicked inside me—and I guess Uriel was experiencing the same a hundredfold. I could tell she would be right with Uriel in a way that went beyond their surface good looks. For me, it was like the feeling I get when hearing someone speak the whole truth and nothing but the truth.

Tarryn's footsteps faltered. 'Francie, what's going on?'

Her sister looked wryly amused. 'Why don't you tell me?' She folded her arms and stood back so the next move could be theirs.

'Tarryn Coetzee, I'm Uriel Benedict, your soulfinder.' He held out a hand but I could see the sheen of tears in his eyes.

'Yes!' I punched the air.

Tarryn reached out her hand letting him enfold her palm in his. The poor woman looked as though she'd been hit over the head by a blunt instrument, such was her shock. He pulled her closer so he could hold her, offering comfort until she had a chance to find her balance. Their conversation was now going on telepathically. They looked so perfect, arms looped round each other's waists, bodies set slightly apart, heads together so their silhouette was naturally heart-shaped.

'Come on, Misty. We'd better leave them alone. Let me introduce you to some of the other people here.' Francie took my elbow.

'You knew, didn't you?'

'Let's just say I had a very good feeling about him as soon as I saw him. My twin and I aren't identical but I can sense her emotions from time to time and he had something like that about him.'

I glanced back. Uriel was now leading Tarryn further down the garden to where the shrubbery would hide them from the other guests.

'Fast worker,' I murmured.

'But you're not really surprised.' Francie must have picked that out of my thoughts.

'You should see the rest of his brothers. Runs in the family.' I just wished there would be someone like a Benedict for me when it came time to meet my soulfinder.

Chapter 3

Leaving Uriel and Tarryn to get better acquainted, Francie introduced me to the man at the barbecue.

'Jonas, this is Misty. She's visiting from England.'

'Pleased to meet you, Misty.' Jonas placed a meat patty in a bun and passed it over. It was only a little bit singed and smelt wonderful.

'Jonas teaches history with Tarryn up at the school.'

'Thanks.' I smiled and took the burger. That was so great: a history teacher matched with Uriel, who had a gift for seeing the past. Then I remembered Francie's earlier comment about her sister not liking her power. I wondered what Tarryn's 'unpleasant' gift could be; I could sympathize with someone who found her power more a jinx than a blessing.

'Why don't you go meet some of the pupils?' Francie gestured to the crowd of complete strangers as if expecting me to dive in with no qualms that I was totally unknown to them all. Had she forgotten what it was like to be sixteen? 'We're celebrating the senior school team winning the South African schools' debating competition.'

Oh crumbs. I could already tell her that this was not going

to go well. I am the opposite of a good debater as I can't defend a proposition in which I don't believe. My philosophy and ethics teacher gave up on me long ago for class discussions. She always entrusted me with timekeeping as it was the only thing I didn't mess up. The debate team and I were extremely unlikely to find any common ground for a conversation. 'Oh, er, well done them for winning.'

Jonas clearly had more experience than the doctor dealing with teenagers in social situations. 'Francie, if you take over here, I'll introduce Misty to a few of them.' Jonas put a warm hand between my shoulder blades, sensing my reluctance. 'Don't worry: they don't bite. They're nice lads.'

He steered me over to a group at the far end of the veranda. How picture-perfect they were, as if some cinematographer had purposely framed them standing bathed in the late sunshine as Table Mountain flushed pink above them. In the very centre was the most amazing guy I'd ever seen: dark brown hair, short at the sides but with what I called a negligent 'whoosh' on top that begged for you to run your fingers through it. It got even better on the way down: black brows, piercing light blue eyes circled by a navy ring that gave them added power, little lines on his jaw to emphasize his smile, strong tanned neck above his open collar, the muscle-tone of an Olympic rower, and height that I would put just shy of six feet.

Stop ogling the boy, I warned myself. If you don't want to embarrass yourself, act like an ordinary human, not a chocoholic on a visit to Cadbury World. And *do not* mention bums under any circumstances.

'Boys, I'd like to introduce you to Misty.' Jonas waved his hand to each of the debate team in turn, starting with 'Mr I'm-too-sexy-for-my-shirt'. 'Alex du Plessis, team captain.'

I nodded, not trusting what would pop out of my mouth if

I attempted to speak. I nailed down my gift, stuck it in a lead-lined coffin and buried it six feet deep so nothing leaked.

'Hello.' Alex glanced over at me, eyes resting for a moment on my hair, then he looked away. Was that a smile he was hiding?

'Michael Steyn, Hugo Smith, and Phil Cronje.'

I nodded again, tagging them the blond movie star, the African prince, and the ginger hunk, but the king of the jungle was undoubtedly Alex.

'Hi, Misty. Cool name,' said Michael, the blond one. He had kind, light blue eyes.

I could do this if I stuck to facts. 'Thanks. My parents like unusual names.'

'Bizarre,' muttered Alex, then frowned. I recognized that look: it meant he hadn't intended to say it. I checked my gift. Not my fault this time; I was in control.

'Maybe it sounds a little odd to a stranger,' I admitted, 'but we go for ones like that in my family. We were named in twos. My younger sister is called Gale; then come the twins, Peace and Felicity; my little brothers are Sunny and Tempest—though I just call the smallest Pest as he's three and always bugging me.' I really should stop talking now.

'That's not very nice of you.' Even though Alex was using it to criticize me, I had to admit he had a brandy-sauce voice that must have won him half his debates on tone alone. It poured over anything unpalatable and made it slide right down inside.

Still, I was driven to defend myself. 'I suppose it might sound that way, but it's meant affectionately. He likes it really—you know: a brother and sister thing?'

'No, I wouldn't know as I don't have any.'

That made sense as he had that heir-to-all-he-surveyed look to him that I found often went with being the sole focus of parent attention. 'Then perhaps you can try to imagine?'

'I'd really rather not.'

Phil, the ginger hunk, moved in to relieve the spiky atmosphere that had unexpectedly developed between us. 'I call my little sister worse things than that so I understand completely. How are you liking Cape Town, Misty?'

'Not seen it properly yet as we only arrived yesterday.'

'We?'

'I came with a sort of relative by marriage.' My gift makes me annoyingly literal. 'He's over there with your history teacher.'

The boys looked over to see Tarryn returning across the lawns with Uriel's arm around her shoulders.

'He knows Miss Coetzee?' asked Alex.

Uriel bent down and kissed her.

'He does now.'

'We thought she was holding out for someone special. That's what she always told us,' said blond-haired Michael.

'He is her someone special.'

'Whoa: major news.'

'Hearts will be breaking in the staff room,' said Hugo, his smile brilliant.

'I think my heart's breaking just a little,' admitted Alex, then he clenched his jaw, tick of a muscle giving away his annoyance at himself.

Of course, his friends wouldn't let him get away with it.

'Seriously? You have a crush on Miss Coetzee?' Michael crowed.

'Don't we all?' said Alex irritably.

Phil rubbed the spot over his heart. 'Ja, but you've never confessed while we've all put our reputations on the line about it.'

Michael began humming that old breakup classic, 'All By Myself'.

'Mike, you're so funny. I'm going to find someone with half a brain to talk to.' Alex strode off.

Hugo winked at me. 'He hates people laughing at him.'

'I kind of got that message.'

'He's not himself tonight; you notice that, bru?' Hugo turned to Phil, intrigued by this development.

'Ja, he was rude to Misty here. Does him good to be pushed out of his comfort zone; he so rarely is.'

Michael sighed with mock sorrow. 'Miss Coetzee out of the dating game—and I'd been hoping she'd wait for me.'

'In your dreams, partner.'

'Exactly.' Michael grinned.

This was venturing into boy-banter territory so I decided it was time to mingle with other guests. 'Nice meeting you and, er, congratulations on your win in the competition.'

'Thanks, Misty. See you around maybe?' Hugo was the only one paying attention as the other two were watching Uriel and Tarryn. The couple were making their way through the guests. It looked a little like a royal progress from here as Tarryn introduced her prince to her closest friends; a few of them had to be savants from their enthusiastic welcome. At least two women were wiping tears of joy discreetly from their eyes before their mascara gave the game away.

'Yes, see you.' I scooted off to the nearest clump of shrubbery to bolster myself for the next attempt at socializing. That hadn't gone too badly. That Alex guy had been a bit blunter than polite but I couldn't be to blame as I had all my spillikins tightly gripped. I was determined not to spoil Uriel's special night by releasing too much truth upon the party. Summer and Angel would be proud of me.

Then Jonas tapped his glass in the time-honoured signal to gain everyone's attention. The noise fell away, leaving only the hiss of leaves in the breeze and the distant hum of traffic.

'Ladies and gentlemen, thank you all for coming tonight to celebrate with us. I've asked Alex to say a few words on behalf of the team.'

Alex joined him at the top of the steps leading to the garden. He really was gorgeous even from this distance. I noticed that his stance was less stiff than when we had spoken, his relaxed poise restored. This was the Alex who had won every debate. He wasn't the first person to do better out of my radar range.

'Thank you, Mr Burns.' He ruffled his hair in a sweet just-gathering-my-thoughts-folks gesture. 'My team mates and I wanted to thank all of you who have supported us on our journey to the final. We wouldn't have made it so far without your generosity during the weeks spent with us on preparation.'

I closed my eyes, just enjoying his voice.

'Thanks must go to our friends and family for sponsoring our travel and putting up with hours of voice practice in the shower.' The crowd laughed. They were eating out of his hand and he'd only strung a few sentences together. As for me, I was busy trying not to think about Alex rehearsing with streams of hot water pouring over his seriously buff body. I held my ice-cold glass to my cheek. 'We would like to give two very special people a gift to express our gratitude.' I opened my eyes as Alex turned to Jonas. 'Mr Burns, we know you have a taste for the finest malts coming from the land of your ancestors so we'd like to present you with a bottle of Scotland's best whisky.'

Applause from the guests. Jonas held the bottle up like a Grand Prix winner, shaking it exuberantly.

'Careful, it's too good to waste on the front row,' joked Alex. His voice took on a deeper, even sexier tone. 'And Miss Coetzee, we cannot begin to say how helpful you have been to us, devoting so much of your free time to travelling with us around the country. It has been a pleasure to be in the company of such a lady, gracious under every circumstance.'

Gracious? That settled it: Tarryn was my female opposite.

'We dedicate this victory to you, Miss Coetzee—and we've prepared something special to say "thank you".' I felt a surge of power from Alex—something only another savant would pick up. He had just outed himself: Alex was one of us. He was spreading his gift to the audience like a fisherman casting a net. His team mates emerged from the edge of the crowd to stand at his shoulder. The audience seemed to be expecting something—I couldn't think what—then Michael tapped a beat, Hugo hummed the tone, and they began to sing unaccompanied. It was the kind of scene that worked in TV shows but I hadn't thought to see in real life. I recognized the song: 'Lucky Strike', a fast energetic track I happened to have on my 'Going for a run' playlist. *She's such a motivator . . . One in million, she's my lucky strike.* It could have been embarrassing, it could have been lame, but they came across as amazing. They had the crowd bopping along with them, the other boys from the school used to this impromptu break into song.

Why did this work? Closing my eyes to stretch out my savant senses, I realized that the performance was boosted to a sure success by the force of Alex's gift persuading us to love it. Under that influence, the boys aimed at cool and hit it in the bullseye. Was that cheating? Maybe, but great fun. I decided just to enjoy it.

Checking their reception with the chief audience, I saw that Tarryn was laughing along with Uriel as the group broke out some seriously good dance moves; I didn't need Francie's gift for thought-reading to know Tarryn was moved by their tribute. I was left thinking that, even with the help of a savant gift, you had to be super-confident to carry off what Alex and his friends were doing. I was the kind of person who struggled to join in a round of 'Happy Birthday' fearing I sounded a twit.

Whistles and cheers greeted the end of their performance. Alex produced a bouquet from behind his back like a magician pulling a dove from his sleeve. He bowed as he presented it to her. Letting go of Uriel, she kissed Alex on the cheek, then hugged the boys one by one.

'I didn't deserve that,' she said when the applause had died down. 'These boys create their own success, as I'm sure you've realized. This is the most amazing night of my life and your song has really put the icing on the cake.' She reached back for Uriel's hand. He squeezed it in support. 'For those of you who haven't had a chance to meet him yet, this is Uriel Benedict. My Uriel.' She brought him forward. 'You'll be seeing a lot more of him so do come and say hi before the party ends. For now, enjoy the barbecue and have a great time.'

The audience broke up now the formal part of the evening was over. The quartet was the first to take up the invitation to meet Uriel and he was quickly setting them at their ease. They challenged him to a game of table tennis and it was no hardship to watch such fine sportsmen engaged in a cut-throat competition. I guess they were testing if he was worthy of their favourite teacher.

I was so caught up in my spying from the shrubbery that I did not notice that Tarryn had found me.

'There you are, Misty. Uriel sent me to check on you. We didn't meet properly earlier but I hope you are enjoying yourself?'

I was embarrassed to be discovered lurking undercover when I should have been mingling. 'Um, yes, it's been very interesting. I'm so pleased for you and Uriel.'

'So you're a savant too?' She took my arm and propelled me gently back to the other guests.

'Truth power. And you?'

She grimaced. 'I see a person's fate.'

'You mean the future? Uriel's mother and youngest brother can do that.'

She shook her head. She struck me as having a deep seam of sadness running under the surface glamour; her eyes had seen too much even though she was only in her late twenties. 'I wish. I see their death and I'd really prefer not to know.'

No wonder she kept that quiet. It was far worse than my problem. 'I'm sorry you've been landed with that. Maybe, you know, with Uriel, you'll discover new sides to your gift? That's what has happened to other soulfinder couples I know.'

She bent her head towards me, trying to see if I was telling the truth—which of course I was. 'You're sweet.'

'I really mean it.'

'Then I hope you're right. It's always been hard for me, being around other gifted people like my sister, feeling such a grim ghost at the feast.' She frowned, wondering at her admission to a near stranger.

'Sorry, that's me. I make people leak the truth without meaning to.'

'I'll have to remember that.'

I wished she didn't have to. I had to do something about my control; it was getting worse. Now I didn't even know when I was letting it slip. 'I feel sure I'm right that you'll discover good things about your gift. I'm luckier than most savants; I'm surrounded by soulfinder couples back home and I've seen some amazing things.'

'Your parents?' She led me over to the tables set out with salads and bread.

'No, not them. They're the exception. Mum didn't marry a savant, deciding that by normal standards Dad was the one for her. They're happy together. I wouldn't have Dad be any other way: he's the best man I know. And the sanest compared to us savants at least.' She laughed at that. 'Makes me wonder sometimes if it's better to be outside the savant community than in.'

'I can imagine.'

'Mum's told Crystal—that's my aunt, the soulseeker who sent Uriel here—that she doesn't want to know who her soulfinder is.'

'Sensible woman. That is what I think about my having foreknowledge of someone's death: best not to know. I hate it when people ask me to tell them. It might change things—close down the escape routes from fate.'

I couldn't imagine asking for such a hard truth. It would radically alter how you lived the rest of your life, surely? 'Are there any other savants here?' I wanted to know if my guess about Alex was correct.

'Would you like a fruit salad?' Tarryn handed me a cup of exotic fruits. They looked like little jewels resting in honeyed water. 'Some of the older people belong to the community but I don't really mix with that crowd; they're more Francie's friends than mine. Of the younger ones, the only one I've identified at the school is Alex.'

So I was right. 'What year is he in?' A girl has to check, after all. Just in case.

'He was in the Junior Form—that's Lower Sixth here, but we've just advanced him a year: he's that good.'

So he had been in the year above me and now was at the top end of the school. Oh well. 'What's his gift?'

Tarryn patted my arm. 'Charm. You must've noticed. He can persuade a leopard to change his spots, talk the fish into leaving the sea, and make any girl fall for him.'

'Now that I did notice.' Not that he had been that charming to me, truth to be told. Which it always was around me.

'He doesn't use his power in debates—that would be unfair, like putting Superman in an arm-wrestling competition—but

I think the residual glow stays with him and makes him more riveting than any of the other speakers.'

I frowned at the back of the boy who was now battling Uriel over the ping-pong table. 'You mean his charm has like a radioactive half-life?'

'That's Alex: radioactive.' She chuckled, a rich, generous sound.

'I'm guessing that he is either the most annoying boy in the school or the most popular: which is it?'

She arched a brow. 'Most popular, of course.'

Something about the life-handed-to-him-on-a-plate Alex rubbed me up the wrong way. By contrast I was the life-sliding-off-the-plate-as-I-trip-over. 'I think I'll go challenge him to a game.'

'I'm glad to see you're brave enough to re-enter the party atmosphere,' she teased. 'When you splash down by them, maybe you could send Uriel back to me?'

'I don't think I could keep him away.' I put my empty fruit cup on the table and went over to the ping-pong with renewed enthusiasm. I poked Uriel in the side. 'Hi, there. Tarryn wants you.'

He passed me the bat with no argument. 'Be right back.'

'Don't hurry on my account. I'll take over here.' I turned to wave the bat at Alex and friends. 'Hi again. What's the score?'

'You want a turn?' asked Alex.

'That's why I'm here. Good singing, by the way. For a moment I thought it was going to be so embarrassing, like when I acted the Angel Gabriel at my primary school nativity play with my robe tucked into my knickers'—did I really have to blurt that out?—'but no, you really carried it off brilliantly.'

'Brilliantly?' Michael grinned at the other two. 'I told you it was the right song choice.'

Alex was still watching me with something like suspicion. Maybe my praise had been too gushing.

'You think I'm not telling the truth? I never lie.'

'Now that has to be a lie,' he said, throwing the ball and knocking it to me over the net—an easy shot to a beginner. 'Everyone lies.'

I smashed it past him. The white missile disappeared into a bush. 'No, I really don't.' I smiled innocently.

'Uh-oh, Alex, looks like your title as ping-pong champion might be at risk,' crowed Hugo as Alex fished among the thorns to retrieve the ball. 'A new game, Misty?' Hugo's hand hovered over the slate on which they had been keeping count. 'Uriel was a couple of points behind so it wouldn't be fair to let you inherit a handicap.'

'OK. If Alex agrees.'

'You're on. Are you sure you don't want a few points as a head start? The guys will tell you I'm pretty good and I don't want to be cruel to a visitor. I play to win.' He was taunting me, confident in his own ability.

'No need to cut me any slack, champ.' I have one useful skill in my repertoire and that is hand-eye coordination. If I had my way, Alex was about to have his perfect record ruined. 'Your serve.'

He threw the ball from an open palm and hit it so it bounced once on his side then over the net. I connected and sent it back with spin. He got to it but it flew off at an odd angle, missing my side of the table.

'Nil to one,' reported Hugo cheerfully.

'Played before?' Alex rolled the ball between his fingers.

'Some.' My hair was bobbing in my eyes. As I pushed it back he served. I couldn't get a bat to it in time.

'No fair!' challenged Phil, our ginger-haired referee.

'Weren't you ready? You should've said,' said Alex dryly.

Michael fetched the ball for me. I noticed he had a school baseball cap tucked in the belt of his trousers.

'Can I borrow that?'

'Sure.'

I balanced the ball on the table under the bat then bundled my hair into the cap, pulling the spare length out the back. Not an attractive look but this was war.

'I'm ready now,' I said, turning on extra sweetness to make Alex's teeth ache. 'Are you?'

'Always.'

I tossed the ball and snapped it over the net. He slammed it back. I returned the favour. Our rally pushed us further and further back from the table as we put more power behind the shots, shoes squeaking on the polished wood. Our little audience had to retreat to get out of the way. Then I saw my chance: I placed a nicely judged return that hit the very edge of the table just out of his reach.

'Two-one.' Hugo drew another line on my side of the tally.

Super-cool Alex was getting hot under the collar. I could see how it would appear to him: I didn't look much of a threat but I had taken an early lead. He glared at me across the expanse of dark green table. 'Good shot,' he said grudgingly.

'Yes, it was.' I can't do false modesty, which makes me sound a bighead most times but on this occasion I felt fully justified.

'Got any more like that in your locker?'

'Yes.' I served. The ball streaked by him. 'Oh, sorry, weren't you ready?'

Buckling down for a serious competition, he grabbed the ball and served. He wasn't going to catch me out again. I struck back, forcing him far to the left. He retaliated with a high shot that hit the veranda roof and came down at a weird angle. The gods of Ping-Pong were with him this time and it hit my side by the net, too far away for me to get a touch.

And so the game continued. We were closely matched when

we both played our best. His disloyal friends were totally on my side, cheering my sneaky shots, booing when he exploited the weakness of my shorter reach and placed the ball just out of my range. At nine all, I knew I had to produce my best game to reach eleven points first. I wafted my T-shirt to get some breeze to my heated skin. It was Alex's serve. He flipped it to my backhand. I returned. He smashed it past me but I jumped, twisted in the air and got a bat to it. I couldn't see where it was going but, from the satisfying 'pop', I knew that it had reached the table. Whether it had bounced on the right side of the net was another matter. I turned to see Alex on his knees, having failed to get to it in time.

'Did that hit your side?' I asked.

'Not sure.' But he was. He was lying.

'Come on, Alex, the ball just made it over the net,' said Phil.

'Ja, OK, if you say so,' he conceded.

'Only one more point to win,' said Hugo cheerfully. I grinned at him.

A white missile skimmed towards me as I stood with arms relaxed. Not again. I reacted quickly and got to it with a trick shot where I brought the bat up from behind my back. Hours of practice with Dad on my home table tennis set paid off and the ball arched sweetly over the net, hit the edge of the table to shoot at his stomach. He jumped back but couldn't get a bat to it in time and the ball bounced off his—well, let's just say it was a good job it wasn't cricket.

'And she wins!' shouted Hugo.

'With style!' Phil picked me up and spun me in a circle. He whisked off the hat and threw it into the air. 'Congratulations, Misty!'

Michael ruffled my already ruffled hair. 'Fantastic! You're the new champion.'

Slapping his bat down on the table, Alex approached. He held out a hand. 'Congratulations.' He looked as eager to take my fingers as I would be to pick up a wasps' nest. I quickly shook his hand, registering a little flick of static as we touched.

'Thanks. I always enjoy meeting someone who can give me a good game.'

'You're not what I expected.' His eyes narrowed. 'Who are you again?'

So glad I made such an impression on him first time round, I thought wryly. 'Misty Devon.'

'Are you at school near here?'

'No, on my summer holiday from England. I've just finished my GCSEs—they're a kind of exam you take when you're in Year Eleven.'

'I see.' He appeared satisfied by my answer, able to dismiss me now he had worked out we were a year apart. 'Well played.' He rubbed the back of his neck.

'Anyone else want a game?' I looked hopefully round at the other boys.

'No way, you're too good. I'm going to join in the football.' Hugo jumped over the edge of the veranda to the lawn. Jonas was organizing two teams for a quick five-a-side.

'Good idea.' Phil followed, then Michael.

Alex made to join them then paused. 'Do you play?'

I folded my arms. 'Not much.'

'Maybe that's a good thing. I don't think my ego could take more humiliation today.' He leapt down to the grass and jogged over to be absorbed into a team.

Bopping the ping-pong ball on my bat, I watched as the football game got under way. The only people at the party not joining in were the female guests. There were no other girls my age so I stuck out on my own. Perhaps I should have said I played a little with my baby brothers? I then saw Phil bring

Alex down in a messy tackle. Ouch. Perhaps not. With a sigh, I left my bat behind and wandered off to walk the perimeter of the garden. It felt a very male place even at Tarryn's cottage. Being a single-sex school, they clearly weren't used to factoring girls into the entertainment, especially ones that beat them. A smile bloomed from the inside, filling me up like the sip of a hot drink on a cold day. That had been one of my best-ever Misty moments. I'd have to tell Summer and Angel every detail of the match.

Chapter 4

It is funny how a good evening can quickly go pear-shaped and it wasn't even my fault. Not really. The plus column had been pretty stupendous: Uriel had found his soulfinder and I had emerged victor in a closely fought game of table tennis against someone who so needed to lose. On the minus column, the list was fairly short: not being a girl with bags of confidence, I couldn't summon the courage to mingle, and I felt shut out from the boys' club atmosphere of the school. Both minor faults but it did result in me moving from quiet spot to hidden place, trying to look as if I was enjoying myself. I was an old hand at the vague 'I'm fine' smile and the continual finding of things to do, plates to fetch, drinks to top up, anything to keep me from having to speak to a stranger. There was no way I would ask Francie to take me home yet as Uriel's situation was far more important than any little awkwardness I might experience. I was used to being isolated by my gift so being at the fringe of a party like this was not new. I found a spot on the veranda near the table tennis table where I had a good view of the lawn but was hidden from the other guests by the bushes in the flower bed below. Nearly everyone else had drifted down to the grass to take seats on the garden chairs in the late evening sunshine.

The football match ended. T-shirts were taken off so sweaty bodies could be cooled; drinks were guzzled; light-hearted teasing of mistakes mingled with praise of the skilful. I allowed myself a moment's awed silence as I admired the trim torsos on display. The quartet split off again, this time taking to some wicker sun-loungers just below my position on the veranda. They couldn't see me, thanks to the flourishing camellia bush but, hey, I was here first. If they didn't keep their voices down that was their lookout. I rubbed the condensation off the side of my lemonade wondering what boys like them talked about when they were alone. Call it a bit of harmless gender research.

'So what do you think of Miss Coetzee's guy?' asked Hugo. The chair creaked as he kicked back and took a swig of his drink.

'He's great. Did you hear him mention that he's a forensic scientist?' Michael sounded very impressed. Most people were when they paid attention to Uriel; he knew so much but wasn't in-your-face about his cleverness.

'That's awesome. I must talk to him about it.' That comment came from Phil. I could just see the tips of his spiky ginger hair over the top of the bush and a few glimpses of his face through the filigree of leaves.

'You still thinking of applying for medicine after Matric?' Alex now joined in, the violin soloist taking up the tune after the introduction.

'That's the plan but maybe I should keep my options open.' I saw a flick of colour through the camellias as Phil rubbed his face with a blue towel. Like many with his complexion, he had the kind of skin that went very red after exercise and he had left the match looking a bit 'boiled lobster'.

'And we all know how you love dissection in biology,' said

Hugo. 'What you did with those eyeballs last week was just gross.'

'I was thinking surgeon maybe but . . . '

'But maybe the world would be a safer place if you stuck to cutting up those already dead. Squish.'

Phil wasn't offended. 'You might be right. I was kinda clumsy.' He waved his plate-sized palms in acknowledgement. They did seem more adapted to swinging an axe rather than a scalpel. 'But not all forensic scientists do that stuff—autopsies. That's the job of a pathologist. There's more to it than that.'

'I think you'd be great at any of them—surgery, forensics.' Alex weighed in on Phil's side. 'Don't listen to Hugo: go for the one that really interests you.' Just listening to Alex turn on his persuasive power and I would've been signing up myself at the nearest medical school if I'd had the slightest ambition to wear a white coat and stethoscope.

'Thanks, bru. I'll have to talk to Uriel about the options. I don't think I have to pick for a few years if I choose the right undergrad course.'

'Cool.'

There were a few seconds of no chat as they downed their drinks.

Phil tapped his empty bottle. 'What about you, Alex? How are the scholarship applications going?'

'Not heard yet. Miss Coetzee thinks I've a good chance of getting a full one to do politics, philosophy and economics at Oxford or maybe law at Cambridge or Yale. She thinks I'll be ready this year with my grades.'

'That's big bucks you're talking. OK for some.' There was a rustle as Hugo chucked a crisp at Alex. 'So next year, while we're left behind in South Africa doing our last year at school, you'll be off to start your international career somewhere really exciting, with a whole new pool of American or European girls to date.'

'That's the plan.' Alex's smile, glimpsed between the branches, gave the impression he was ready to try a broad sample. My flimsy plastic cup split in my grip, spilling the dregs of my lemonade on my thigh.

'Girls like that cute little English girl?' Hugo continued, the group's troublemaker. 'What was her name? Misty Devon?' My heart missed a beat. I hadn't expected to find myself part of the conversation. 'You know, the one with the . . . ' He gestured to his head to indicate my curls. I could hear the glee in Hugo's question. I wanted to spit out at him that I was more than a bad hair day, but that would reveal my position. I wondered if I could retreat before they noticed I was there. But if I got up, they were sure to realize I had been listening and it would look, well, plain weird, if I crawled away on my hands and knees. Someone might come out of the house and see. I waited with a sick sense of anticipation for the answer.

To my eternal shame there was silence, then a snort of laughter from all of them.

'Maybe not,' said Alex coolly.

'She kicked your ass at table tennis,' Phil pointed out.

'But that doesn't make her the kind of girl I see myself dating. Far from it.'

'Aw, don't say you're holding it against her? I thought her stylish win over you proved it was a match made in heaven. You need someone who can keep you humble.'

'Maybe, but come on, guys: Misty?'

'She struck me as sweet.' Thank you, Michael, for that at least.

'She's way too young for me—and she looks like . . . ' Alex faltered.

'Looks like what?' asked Michael. I withdrew my thanks as he egged his friend on to say something unforgivable.

'Looks like she's been put through a spin cycle.'

They hooted with laughter.

'That's harsh, Alex. Not like you.' Hugo was enjoying his friend's sharp tongue. I wasn't: I was bleeding from the cuts.

'Harsh but true. No, if I date someone, I'd like it to be a girl who wouldn't make me feel embarrassed.'

Stuck-up feeble excuse of a charmer. I curled my knees to my chest, wishing I could vanish.

'Misty? Misty? Time to go!' Francie appeared in the kitchen doorway. 'Ah, there you are.'

The boys fell silent.

Francie could see me plainly from where she stood, as well as the debate team on the other side of the bush. Nothing else for it: I rose, pins and needles tingling from my cramped position.

'You ready to leave?'

'Yes.' No bribe on earth would make me look at Alex. I could feel his eyes on my back like sunrays.

'Not tearing you away too soon, am I? I have an early shift and Uriel's staying on to help Tarryn clear up.'

'No, I want to leave now.' Right now.

I'd forgotten Francie's power to hear thoughts. Her eyes shot to the boys then back to me. 'Oh.'

Yes, oh.

She scooped me up with a comforting arm around my hunched shoulders. 'Take no notice of them. Sticks and stones.'

'That proverb is so not true.' I folded my arms over my chest, feeling as though they had started an autopsy on me right there, not just talked about one.

She whisked me through the guests, not drawing out the farewells as she might otherwise have done. 'No, it's not. But eavesdroppers . . . '

'Yes, I know. I should've moved earlier.'

'But you felt shy.'

I had the first glimmer of humour about the situation. 'Francie, you are so easy to talk to. You know what I'm going to say before I do.'

'Ja, I often have long conversations with myself like that. Let's take you home. Have a relaxing bath, play with your little cousins, forget about those boys.'

'That's what the doctor orders?'

'Exactly. Distraction: best medicine there is.'

'When I break the news about Uriel, I think I'll have distraction enough for ten kinds of insults.' At least I hoped so. I feared that the overheard conversation had burrowed its way under my skin like chigoe flea, a parasite that got into feet in tropical climates. It would lay nasty side-effects unless I burned it out of my memory.

Chapter 5

As predicted, the next couple of days were filled with celebrations. Uriel and Tarryn had long Skype conversations with his family as he proudly introduced her to the Benedicts. Curled up on the sofa with a magazine, I enjoyed listening in on the one to Crystal and Xav, which they carried out on the family computer in Opal and Milo's sitting room. Xav was roaring with laughter as he heard about the twin confusion.

'Please, you're killing me, Uri.'

'It's true. And then Misty lost control of her gift. People were confessing left, right and centre.'

Xav held his stomach. 'No more.'

Crystal elbowed him. 'Forgive my idiot of a soulfinder here. I imagine it wasn't so funny for you at the time.'

Uriel's lips curved in a smile. 'It was ridiculous but I knew even then that I'd laugh later. Misty exiled herself to the parking lot so things settled down after that.' He kissed Tarryn on the ear, then took a cheeky little nip at her lobe. 'And then it got a whole lot better.'

'So what are your plans now?'

'We're trying to mesh our lives together. First, I have my investigation to complete.'

'Victor said it was going slowly.'

'Far too slowly. I had already arranged to work with Dr Surecross this September for a few months to see if we can get some new leads on the killer's identity. Have you heard of him, Xav?'

Xav had sobered now the conversation had turned serious. 'Surecross? He's based at Cambridge University, isn't he? What's his gift?'

'Deduction—connections. He might make sense of the puzzle pieces I've been trying to put together. At the moment it just seems like featureless sky.'

'And how about you, Tarryn?' asked Crystal.

'I'm going to carry on teaching here at least until the end of the academic year in December,' said Tarryn. 'I've got boys to see through their Matric and other school commitments. After that . . . ' She looked into Uriel's eyes and smiled.

I loved their total absorption in each other. Sure, they had a few issues to solve and needed time to get to know each other but their landing had been smooth after the minor turbulence on the way down. I couldn't help feeling envious of them being so natural in their new relationship. A little bit jealous, aware I was on the outside of the lovey-dovey stuff between soulfinder couples, I put down my magazine and got up from the sofa to see if Opal needed any help with dinner.

'There you are! How are you, Misty?' asked Crystal as she spotted me walking through the back of the frame.

'Good.'

'Really?'

I knew then that Francie had spilled the beans to her sister that I had had a miserable time at the party. Tarryn must have tipped off Uriel and he had said something to Crystal—that's how the jungle telegraph in our family works. I had to hope they didn't know the specifics.

'Yes, really. You know me: I carry embarrassing moments with me like a hippo does an oxpecker bird.' The comparison was truer than they knew: the bird, a semi-parasite, cleaned the hippo's wounds but also kept them open, just as the hurt reopened every time my mind circled back to Alex's remark. 'I wouldn't feel right if I didn't have something going wrong around me.'

Crystal smiled sadly. 'You have the oddest attachment to weird natural-world images. You and Brand must share the same family gene for that.'

I liked animals, was comfortable around them, because they couldn't lie. The thought of my little cousin cheered me up. 'He is the coolest two-year-old, Crystal. You'll have to visit soon. You would just love to hear him imitate a lion. I can't wait to see what he makes of the penguins.'

'Penguins?' asked Xav.

'We're going this afternoon to see them.'

'Isn't it a risk to take the animal magnet to a zoo? From what I've heard he's an out-of-control Dr Doolittle.'

'Not penguins in a zoo, Xav. Wild ones. This area is famous for them.'

'Penguins in Africa—that is so *Madagascar*.' Xav lounged back in his chair, ankle on knee. 'Loved that movie.'

'But these ones are native and don't talk—or dance.'

'They might if Brand is there,' laughed Crystal.

As we couldn't all fit in the Volvo, Uriel and Tarryn drove in her car to Simonstown, home of the Boulder Colony of penguins. A seaside resort south of Cape Town, Simonstown wasn't that far but Willow bagged the front seat with the age-old excuse that she got the worst travel sickness. That left me a place in the back row. I didn't mind as I was entertained by Brand's repertoire of animal noises. Just when it was getting annoying, he fell asleep with the suddenness only a toddler can manage.

'Did you take his batteries out?' I asked Opal.

'It's the car. Best sleep aid available.'

Willow was in charge of the music, selecting tracks off my phone. By chance she picked 'Lucky Strike', batting me right back into the evening at Tarryn's house. *Put it away*, I told myself. *You won't have to see any of the boys from the debate team again. They live in South Africa and you live in England so it's as if it never happened.*

Summer would be proud of me figuring that one out for myself.

We drove into Simonstown, taking a road that ran parallel to the railway track. Beyond that, just a stone's throw away, was the sea. The wind was strong, whipping white crests on the waves. The water's surface was streaked: glass green in the shallows where the sun hit, dark emerald when cloud shadows passed, navy blue over rocks and seaweed clumps.

As we approached the centre, I decided that the town looked a very unlikely place to have penguins. The shops, houses and restaurants were a run of ornate white wooden facades, elegant balconies and covered porches. The marina bristled with pleasure craft and beyond that lay the rather more serious blunt silhouettes of destroyers belonging to the South African navy. The town had that cheerful but overwrought holiday atmosphere that most seaside places can't shake off even in winter—a shade too many flags and promises of fun that aren't quite delivered.

'Where are the penguins?' I asked.

Opal spotted a rare parking spot and pounced. 'By the sea, of course. They're in a nature reserve.'

'You mean to protect them from the tourists?'

'Actually, it could well be the other way round. They might look cute but they bite.'

'Peck,' corrected Willow with all the authority of someone who had recently done a school project on the subject. 'They don't have teeth.'

'Cool.'

Eager to see the vicious birdlife of Simonstown, I got out and prepared the pushchair as Opal ladled a sleeping Brand from car seat to buggy. Willow fetched the changing bag and Hazel his drink, making it our record-breaker for parking to being ready to go, easily a match for a Formula One tyre change on a Grand Prix pit stop. I christened ours the Formula Milk race.

I propelled the pushchair along with thoughts of my favourite drivers whizzing round my brain circuitry. Brand slept through the rattling ride while Opal held her daughters' hands tightly for the walk along the seafront to the kiosk. There were far too many temptations for the girls to continue in a straight line. The windows in the parade were full of happy-looking penguin souvenirs, socks, hats, stickers and—my top choice—a 'Beware of the Penguin' sign. I'd have to get that for my little brother Sunny.

Finally we arrived at our destination to see Uriel waiting outside the sanctuary.

'I've already bought the tickets,' he said when we approached.

'Oh, you shouldn't have,' protested Opal.

'It's my pleasure after all you've done for me.' He gestured over his shoulder. 'Tarryn and Alex are in the shop.'

Tarryn and *Alex*. 'What's he doing here?' I blurted out.

Uriel gave me a warning look. 'Tarryn invited him, Misty. He's a boarder and she thought he'd like to escape the school for an afternoon.'

So she invited him and spoiled my day. 'Why did she think that a good idea? Is he a penguin enthusiast or something?' I couldn't imagine Mr Gorgeous-and-Sophisticated enjoying a kiddie expedition.

Uriel held me back as the others entered. He glanced into the building to check we weren't overheard. 'Be nice to him, please.'

I wanted to say something childish like 'I will if he will' but instead I settled for the more mature, 'I had no intention of being anything else.'

Uriel did not look convinced. 'I heard you didn't hit it off at the barbecue.'

'I was perfectly polite to him.' I crossed my arms. It was outside of enough to have to defend myself when I was the injured party.

'You beat him at table tennis.' So Francie hadn't mentioned the overheard comment—that was a relief.

'What was I supposed to do? Let him win?' I snorted.

'No, but you don't know how boys are—he's probably been teased non-stop since.'

'Do him good.'

Uriel reached for his patience. 'Just give him a break, OK? For my sake.'

'For you, yes.' For Alex, not likely.

We entered the kiosk that led out to the nature reserve. Alex stood a little to one side of my family.

'Hi!' I said, a shade too brightly considering we had last seen each other moments after the spin cycle comment. *See, Uriel,* I felt like saying, *I can be saintly too.* I hoped he was chalking the points up in my favour; I might need to cash them in later, knowing me.

'Hello.' Alex's eyes were filled with suspicion at my over-friendly tone.

'Alex, you remember Misty?' said Tarryn, trying to ease the way.

'Ja.' His gaze was now fixed on my hair, which had had the benefit of its usual taming treatment and looked completely normal for me, ripples rather than finger-in-a-socket crazy curls. 'You did something to it.'

That acted like a splash of cold water, waking me up out of my brief visit to my saintly side. And he was supposed to be charming? Around me he appeared to be my match for bluntness.

'Yes, I did.' I didn't want to test my 'be nice to Alex' attitude too much this early on; being sympathetic in theory was easier than in practice. He just wound me up by breathing and, to be fair to him, that was my problem rather than his.

But he did not know when to stop digging. 'Your hair looks . . . much better. Nice.'

Now wasn't that the word of the day? 'Why, thank you, kind sir.' I could feel my irritation levels rising. Who was he to pass judgement on my hair after all? I turned to the only male I could bear to face at the moment. 'Let's go see Pingu, Brand.' Nap over as swiftly as it had begun, the toddler's bright eyes were shiny with excitement. 'Buckle up, partner!' Pointing forwards, I pushed the buggy through the doors in a cavalry charge and took us onto the boardwalk.

Brand squawked.

Accompanied by the drum roll of chair wheels and the roar of the wind, Brand and I made our way down to the sea, not looking behind to check the others were following. I could hear distant calls, more like little donkeys than any bird I had ever heard. Brand jiggled in his seat in utter delight.

'Steady on, sweetpea. We're getting there.'

Then, among the grey rocks, we spotted them: hundreds of black and white ridiculous, wonderful penguins. Some lay on their stomachs, others stood tall, beaks up like they were volunteering for that night's waiter roster. A party of three emerged from the sea, waddling in synchronization. There was no way anyone could look at them and not laugh.

Brand clapped his hands and began mimicking the odd call they were making. The penguins went from relaxed chappies to mission-orientated commandos in a flap of a flipper.

Opal hurried up to us as the penguins began to converge. 'I'd better take over. I'm used to this.' She swivelled the push-chair round to find a position where Brand could watch without being mobbed. The little gentlemen birds were absolutely entranced by the new boy-shaped penguin. One end of the beach emptied as they formed an audience below his chair like the faithful listening to the Pope on Easter Sunday. He bobbed and brayed, hopefully offering some uplifting message and not 'Go forth and peck the humans!' There was no way the rest of us would be able to see any normal penguin behaviour without moving further off out of Brand's sphere of influence. Uriel and Tarryn wandered on, hand in hand. I doubt they were paying much attention to birdlife. Willow and Hazel sat cross-legged on the walkway and began to sketch the crowd. That left Alex to me. Big sigh but I had promised I would try.

'Great, aren't they?' See, Uriel; I can make polite conversation.

'Yes, they are.' This conversation was about as smooth going as pushing a shopping trolley with a dodgy wheel.

'So, er, have you been here before?' I heard echoes in my head of the cheesy line 'Do you come here often?' and blushed. Hand on heart, I was not chatting up this guy.

'With the school. When I was much younger.' He dug his hands in his pockets. 'Look, Misty, about the party.'

I started walking, getting out my camera. 'Let's not go there.'

'But I want to say something. I didn't mean my comment the way it came out.' His footsteps were keeping up with mine.

My teeth ached. 'Don't do that please.'

'Do what?'

'Lie to me. It hurts.' I meant it literally but he took it in the more ordinary sense of hurt feelings.

'I just—'

Then I did something few people dared do to Eloquent Alex: I interrupted him. 'You don't want to talk about it any more than I do, so, moving swiftly on . . . ' I swept my arm towards the seascape. 'Tourism.'

'But—'

'Buts are for nanny goats, or archery.' Do not mention what's on the tip of your tongue, Misty; do not! 'Or . . . um . . . smokers.' Phew—butt emergency avoided. 'Let's just enjoy the penguins, OK?' I tried to think up a peace offering as he still looked like he wanted a heart-to-heart about the party. 'Can you take my photo? I want to show my family what I've been doing today.'

'Sure.' Relieved to be given a task, he took my camera, our fingers touching briefly. I had that twitch of static shock, as at the party. What were the physics of that? He was the positive and I the negative charged object. That figured. We were poles apart in the way we came over to other people: me, the Screw-Up; him, the Boy Wonder.

'Smile,' said Alex, holding up the camera.

I wished his voice didn't make my stomach quiver in that first-night-nerves sensation. He probably wasn't even using his gift but something about his tone just rang all my bells. Not that I ever had a starring role in the school play. I couldn't speak lines I didn't mean. Being unable to escape the truth often stopped me in my tracks. Crystal teased me that I was like that old joke of one of the original Daleks facing a flight of stairs. Plans for world domination scuppered. Just like those *Dr Who* characters, I couldn't do ordinary stuff other people found dead simple.

'Misty? Are you listening?' Alex was getting testy.

'Um . . . ' No.

'Can you do it then?'

What had he asked? Oh yes: smile. I did my best, though it felt false, all teeth and no humour. He checked the image on the little screen, shading it from the sun.

'Another one. That one didn't come out well.' He held up the camera again.

'We'll be here all day if you're waiting for a good photo of me.'

He thought I was joking. 'That's much better. Your family will like that last shot.' He handed my camera back.

'Let me take one of you—to show the folks back home.'

'They won't be interested in me.'

'Wanna bet?'

Alex shrugged and scanned the walkway, looking for a good backdrop. 'Will this do?' He chose a spot where there was a break between the rocks showing the sea and a scattering of sunbathing birds. 'You get a sense of how close we are to the ocean here.'

'Perfect.' And he was. Again. The natural world loved him. If I didn't already know his gift was persuasion, I'd say he had the ability to arrange the world to show him off to advantage. Dark brown hair rippling in the breeze, glinting mahogany where the light touched the lighter strands, tanned skin, mesmerizing eyes, tight T-shirt that hinted at his muscle definition (I'd seen him strip off his top after his football game and the memory was etched on my visual cortex for all time). He might have the superior attitude of a boy who knew he was destined from birth to join the world's elite, leader-of-men material, but I couldn't help my gut reaction to him, a desire to press my face to his chest and just, sigh, *enjoy*.

Click. I had to face up to reality. He was in the year above me and so out of my reach that if we were planets, he would be mighty Mars or Jupiter and I one like Pluto, recently demoted to dwarf-planet status by astronomers. That was the natural hierarchy of things.

But this humble planetoid could have its moment in the sun. If I posted this on my Facebook page I could guarantee I'd increase the comments from my girlfriends exponentially. I took a couple more shots.

He had become suspicious of the time I was taking with my allowed ogling via a camera lens. 'Got enough now?'

Never. 'Um, thanks.'

He came closer and frowned.

'What?'

He gestured at my nose. 'You're burning. You have to be careful with fair skin like yours: the sun's really fierce by the sea. Not what you're used to in England.'

Of course, I would be burning. He looked like the sun merely kissed and caressed him before turning his skin a golden brown.

'Oh great.' I reached for my sunscreen, then remembered it was at Heathrow. 'I'll have to catch up with my aunt. She's bound to have some Factor Fifty for her children.'

I was surprised that Alex didn't take the chance to leave me behind as I turned back. He fell in step beside me, his stride loose and easy, hands swinging loose at his thighs almost close enough to hold mine.

Stop looking, Misty.

'I envy you,' said Alex, then frowned. 'Did I just say that aloud?'

'Yes.' Maybe I was leaking truth rays again? I wasn't going

to own up that it might be my fault he said such tactless things around me. We were battling enough personality clashes without adding that to the mix.

He dug his hands in his pockets. 'I didn't mean to mention it but it's true.'

'What can you possibly envy about me?' Stupidly, part of me was hoping for a personal compliment to make up for the party comment, something about my conversation skills or attractive sense of humour maybe?

'Your family. Your oddly named brothers and sisters. Aunts and uncles—masses of them from what I've heard. It's quite a tribe you've got there.'

Of course, he would envy what surrounded me rather than anything I could claim was down to my character. Still, points for trying to be friendly. 'I know. I'm very lucky. So you don't have many relatives then?'

'No.' He rolled his shoulders to ease tension in his neck. 'I don't think I know much about families.'

'They're all so different. No one really gets what goes on inside someone else's life.'

'You're probably right.'

We turned a corner to see Penguin Pope Brand was still holding the attention of his audience of the faithful. A warden had come out of the visitor's centre to check our party wasn't feeding the birds to make them behave like this. Finding nothing to complain about, she was standing with Opal, discussing the weird phenomenon. I could hear Opal explaining that it had to be that Brand had just eaten fish paste sandwiches before arriving and the smell must be attracting the penguins. I don't think the warden was convinced but that was the only rational answer to a bizarre situation so she had to accept it.

'See, I challenge you to figure out my family. Someone like you wouldn't understand but this is normal for us.' I grinned up at Alex conspiratorially, forgetting for a brief while that I didn't like him.

Instead of amused, blue eyes, my gaze met a stony expression. He looked almost angry with me. 'No, I wouldn't be able understand it, would I?'

What had just happened? He had been with me one moment and now he was miles away.

He turned on his heel. 'I'm going to catch up with Miss Coetzee.'

'OK, you do that then.' Puzzled, I watched him walk swiftly back the way we had just come.

'Is Alex all right?' called Opal.

I ran through our conversation and decided I could not be to blame for him getting the huff like that. 'I think so. Have you got any sunscreen?'

She fished around in the side of the changing bag and handed me the bottle.

'He strikes me as very . . . ' Opal searched for the right word, 'lonely. Don't you agree?' Occasionally, my aunt's insight into people was devastatingly on target.

I watched the upright figure walk swiftly round a large boulder like some demigod, a son of Poseidon, returning to sea. 'Yes, I think he is.'

Chapter 6

I didn't see Alex again for a few weeks after the penguin trip, though Summer and Angel had predictably drooled over the photo I had posted. His eyes matched the sea behind him and he managed to do the Hollywood idol smoulder to camera without even trying. By contrast, my photo revealed the full extent of my nose sunburn. If I could lie, I would've been tempted to claim Alex as a holiday romance and thus boost my ratings with my friends; but then, if I started down that path, I would have been forced to tell the truth, which was that he was my vacation personality clash. There: I had invented a new relationship category. Go me.

Even though I was busy enjoying my holiday, including a totally awesome safari in the Kruger National Park, I couldn't shake the memory of that glimpse of Alex striding out alone. I was beginning to question my assumptions about him: golden boy at school, but that didn't prevent him being a little lost like the rest of us.

The last day before I was scheduled to return home, Opal and Milo arranged to take me on the cable car to the top of Table Mountain. The plan was to eat at the restaurant, which boasted amazing views over the city bowl. Uriel and Tarryn were also invited.

Feeling generous as I was leaving the country, I texted Tarryn as we got ready for our day out. *Do you want to ask Alex?*

I half-hoped she'd say no but she replied almost immediately. *Great idea. I'll see if he's free. He's got Matric assessments soon so could do with a break from study.*

Braiding my hair in the mirror, I gave myself a pat on the back for thoughtfulness. Someone has to appreciate my saintliness as I can't seem to persuade my family to regard me in that light. To them, I am a slowly unfolding disaster that has to be managed.

When we got to the bottom of the mountain, I discovered that Tarryn had not only asked Alex to come, but also his partners in crime: Phil the redhead, Michael the blond movie star, and Hugo the prince. My halo slipped a little. I had mentally prepared myself for spending time with Alex, awkward though that could be, but I found the whole gang a bit much on what was supposed to be a treat for me. I braced myself for more jokes at my expense. They stood together waiting patiently for the kerfuffle of my family's arrival to subside. Tarryn introduced them to Milo and Opal. She was oozing pride—in a nice way.

'These are my boys, my debate team. I thought they deserved a reward; they've all been working so hard this term.'

'Hello, lads.' Milo shook hands. 'This is my team: my wife, Opal; our children, Willow, Hazel, and Brand. And our niece, Misty.'

Brand yipped and jiggled, spotting four new playmates. If he'd had a tail, it would have been wagging.

'Don't mind him,' Opal said quickly, 'it's just a stage he's going through.'

Hugo knelt beside the pushchair and solemnly shook hands with the toddler. Brand clapped.

'What stage is that?' he asked.

'Brand imitates animals.' I could hear Opal was keen that someone changed the subject. The less attention Brand attracted the better, otherwise he'd be starring on YouTube with his antics. Mind you, that wasn't such a bad idea. I could make a fortune from advertising revenue, outstripping even the giggling baby that had gone viral.

Focus, Misty. Help your aunt.

'Hi, guys,' I said brightly.

'Hey, Misty. Howzit?' Michael gave me a hug. I hadn't thought we'd quite reached that stage of friendliness but clearly they had other ideas as Hugo and Phil also gave me an embrace, lifting me off my feet each time. Maybe it was their form of an apology?

'Have you enjoyed your holiday?' asked Michael, his eyes telling me he was flirting just a little.

'I've had a blast. I'm sorry it's coming to an end. Hi, Alex.'

'Hi, Misty.' Alex hung back. He had dressed for mountain-top weather: chocolate-brown leather jacket over indigo-blue T-shirt and jeans.

Michael waggled his eyebrows at me. 'Don't tell me he's still sore that you beat him at table tennis? It's not like we teased him for more than a couple of weeks about that.'

I smiled.

'So, is it back to school straight away for you when you return?' asked Hugo while we waited for Uncle Milo to queue for tickets.

Whoa, what was this? Be nice to Misty week?

'Not quite. I've got a camp first. A week in Cornwall this time. I go every year.' The silver zips that closed the breast pockets on the front of Alex's jacket were distracting me. I had an urge to play with them. Resist, girl, resist.

Hugo was oblivious to my little mind-wander. 'I'm jealous

you're still off school. We're gearing up for our end-of-year assessments.'

'You have my sympathies.' I rather undercut this statement by beaming too broadly. I did pity them but I find it makes my time off even better when I know others are beavering away.

'Is your camp fun or under-canvas-dig-your-own-latrine survival torture like my old Scout ones?'

I laughed at the picture he painted. 'It's great fun. We usually stay under a roof with indoor bathrooms; we never quite know until we get there as the venue changes each year. My best friends go, Summer and Angel.'

'Pretty names.'

I was warming to Hugo. 'Thanks. I'll tell them you said so.' Alex wasn't the only charming one among the quartet.

'OK, team. All aboard!' Milo ushered us through the turnstiles.

'Have you done this before?' I asked Hugo.

'Ja, we all came at Christmas and abseiled down.' He pointed to what looked like a sheer rock face under the summit. 'That's our kind of fun, isn't it, Alex?'

As we filed into the car, the barriers forced Alex to come a little closer. 'Ja, it was great.'

Hugo frowned. 'You OK, Alex?'

'Sure. I'm fine.' Alex positioned himself on the far side of the pushchair and struck up a conversation with Uriel.

I broke into Hugo's puzzled thoughts. 'This abseiling thing: we're not all expected to do it, are we?'

Returning from his moody friend to happier thoughts, Hugo patted me on the back. 'I'd say for you, Misty, it's the only way down, if you want to experience the real Cape Town.'

'What a shame we came with a toddler in tow.' I gave an exaggerated sigh. 'Ah me, looks like I'll pass on abseiling this time.'

'Hey, Misty, come look.' Michael made a space for me by the window. He and Phil had given the girls a lift-up so they could see out.

The cable car is not for those who don't like heights. Starting near the base of the mountain, it climbs steeply, at one point the ground being hundreds of metres below. If you can tear your eyes from contemplating the chances of plummeting to your death, you can admire the spectacular sea, mountain and cityscape, and the expanse of sky. That's what I made myself do.

'Not got a good head for heights?' asked Hugo shrewdly as my knuckles whitened on the sill. On the other side of the car, I noticed that Alex was listening in to our conversation.

I gave Hugo my best brave smile. 'Let's just say my future does not hold me climbing Everest.'

'You're perfectly safe, as long as the car doesn't drop from its runner and the fail-safe chain is intact. Fatal accidents hardly ever happen, just in the weeks before its annual overhaul and—would you look at that notice!—that period starts tomorrow.' He grinned at me.

He was totally winding me up, something I didn't require the ache in my back teeth to know. I was about to tell him he was rumbled when Alex butted in.

'Hugo, cut it out. If she's scared, she doesn't need you making it worse.' He sounded quite angry on my behalf.

Hugo looked chastened. 'Sorry, Misty. I was just joking. The cable car has an excellent safety record.'

'I guessed, but thanks.' I risked a glance at Alex but he had backed away again. I couldn't fault him for caring when it counted.

When we got out of the cable car, I was pleased I'd brought a hoodie. The clear cold conditions made for a fantastic view, even if it was a few degrees cooler than I expected from being in the valley. We made our way round to the viewing platform that jutted out over the city.

'What's that pimple of a mountain?' I asked Michael, who happened to be standing next to me, fair hair whipping about in the stiff breeze. There appeared to be a mini-mountain right in the middle of Cape Town, bare rock summit on green swelling.

He slapped his hand to his chest in an 'I'm having a heart attack here' gesture. 'Pimple? Come on, Misty, where's your cultural sensitivity?'

'I left that at home with my tact,' I admitted.

'That's the Lion's Head. Don't tell any Cape Towner you called it a pimple or you may not make it to the plane in one piece.'

'Or they may frogmarch her there and put her on an earlier flight.' That was Alex. So he had decided to break his self-imposed avoidance rule, had he?

'Be pleased to see the back of me, will you?' I asked Alex.

He looked as if he regretted being drawn into the conversation. 'I didn't say that.'

Wrong: the right answer was *No, Misty, we loved having you!*

'You didn't need to. I get the message that I'm not your favourite visitor. You do realize that this outing is supposed to be my goodbye present, don't you?'

Michael thumped his friend in the stomach. 'Ja, quit spoiling the girl's last day.'

Alex held up his hands. 'I didn't say anything.'

'Sometimes it's what you don't say that matters.' I turned back to the view from the annoying one behind me. 'Don't worry: you won't have to see me again after today.'

Uriel and Tarryn joined us, sunshine glinting on their heads, golden and chestnut, hand in hand. *Why not just carry around a big arrow saying 'Perfect Couple'?* I thought wryly. Some guys get all the breaks. Was I the only person nature didn't like to frame to make me more attractive? If I stood like them, I'd probably get bird droppings on me, or the wind would blow my skirt up the wrong way.

'What was that about today?' asked Uriel, having caught the tail end of my remarks.

'I said that they wouldn't be seeing me as I'm heading home.' That was the truth—I'd just left out the argumentative subtext.

'I wouldn't bet on that, Misty.' Uriel rubbed the back of Tarryn's hand with his thumb. Whenever I saw him now, he was always giving her these little touches in a sweet I-can't-believe-my-luck way. 'Seems like fate has been generous and has put the international debate final in Cambridge, England, this year.'

Tarryn smiled wryly. 'And I suppose that had nothing to do with the phone calls you made offering to sort out a venue?' She looked over to the debate-team boys. 'Cairo had to pull out of hosting last week due to security issues.'

Uriel's kind eyes twinkled with humour. 'Maybe I could've pulled in favours in Denver too but, well, I decided that I might as well please myself on this one. If I'm to be in Cambridge, then why not bring you there?'

'You've arranged for the debate final to be in my city?' I asked. This could not be happening.

'Cool!' Hugo was delighted. 'I'm sorry to miss Cairo but I've never been to England. What should I pack, Misty?'

'When are you coming?' I half-hoped it would be over and done with before I went back to school in September.

'Towards the end of November,' said Tarryn. 'As it's after your assessments, boys, and Alex's Matric, you should ask your parents if you can stay on a week or two. We could extend the tour to other places. Shame to go all the way to Europe and not sightsee.'

Various choice words hip-hopped through my brain. There would be no escape for me as that was slap in the middle of term. 'You should pack raincoats and warm clothes then.'

'You go to school in Cambridge, don't you, Misty?'

Thanks for pointing that out, Tarryn.

'Yes, I do. But the chances are you'll be on the other side of town.'

'Oh no,' said Uriel, winking at me, 'you'll be pleased to know we'll be right on your doorstep. Your school is one of the venues as its team are the English champions. I'm surprised you didn't know.'

'Right. I must've missed that.' Not surprising actually as the debate team and I moved in completely different circles and add the fact that I had been hiding for the last few days of term due to the Sean incident. So that was what Uriel had been doing when I hadn't seen him during the last few weeks. I'd assumed he was spending quality time with Tarryn, but no. He had devoted himself to messing up my autumn.

'You can show us round town.' Hugo was getting really into the idea of a European trip.

'I'd be . . . ' I couldn't say *happy*, 'OK with doing that.'

'Cool.' Hugo swept his arms to the view before us. 'Can Cambridge beat this?'

'It has its pretty bits,' I said loyally. As Cambridge was in an area of England that was as flat as a pancake, Table Mountain was going to be an impossible act to follow but I wasn't going to admit that. 'The colleges are spectacular. You can't move without tripping over a famous dead person. Newton, Darwin, those DNA guys, Crick and Watson.'

'Strictly speaking, not all of those are dead,' said Alex dryly.

'Alex, you're applying to Trinity, aren't you?' Hugo asked.

'Yes, it's on my list.' No surprise: Alex didn't seem as pleased by the news that he was heading my way as the others.

Tarryn squeezed his arm. 'I thought we could arrange for you to have your interview while you're there, Alex. The dates work out well.'

'Sounds like a plan. So, is it time to eat?' Alex broke up the discussion by heading for the restaurant.

Our party was seated at the long table by the picture window, so Alex and I were able to choose chairs at opposite ends. Both of us could breathe a sigh of relief and eat in peace. I ordered a garden burger—juicy, thick mushroom pretending to be meat and tasting just as good. I was perfectly happy with my dining companions: I had Uriel on one side and Michael on the other. Hugo and Phil sat opposite. That made Alex's choice to sit down by the girls more glaring, but that was his lookout. He gave every sign of being entertained by Willow and Hazel's sketches with the kids' crayons the waitress provided so maybe he was enjoying himself.

Hugo, Phil, and Michael cross-examined me on Cambridge. I didn't know a huge amount about the town as I had only lived there since I changed schools. I was a boarder because my home was the other side of London. We had exhausted the schools in my local area so my parents had to look further afield after my last close encounter with too much truth. The head teacher at the Fen School was a savant, so sympathetic to my situation. On hearing about the bullying that resulted from my out-of-control mouth, he had let me enter Year 11 despite my far-from-stellar GCSE exam predictions. I couldn't explain all that to the boys so I left the reason for my being there vague. I did, however, admit that I wasn't an expert. Uriel made up for the gaps in my knowledge as he had often visited the university.

The conversation turned to cricket and I tuned out. Uriel nudged me.

'Misty, can I ask something?'

I squeezed the ketchup on my mushroom and squidged down the bun lid. 'Fire away.'

'What's with you and Alex? Is there something more going on between you than Tarryn and I know about? His awkwardness with you seems a bit extreme for a lost table tennis match.'

'You're right there.' I took a bite and thought about how to frame my answer. 'I think it's me. Or rather him-plus-me. He doesn't like the person he becomes when he's in my company.' I hadn't realized it until I spoke the words but I thought I now understood what had been going on.

'Your gifts clash?' Uriel got my point at once.

'Think about it: he's always charming but in my zone I make him rude and a bit harsh. He hates it. I think he feels out of control.'

Uriel rubbed his chin, making that brittle sound that only guys can do as fingers meet emerging bristles. 'I can see how that might shake him up. I'll let Tarryn know. She's been worrying about him. She's told me that he has been really down the last few weeks.'

Since he met me.

'She's worried she made the wrong choice advancing him a year, but he really is outstandingly intelligent.'

'Have you told Alex what my gift is?'

Uriel wrinkled his brow, remembering. 'No, I don't think it came up.'

'He might feel better about himself if you explain it's my fault.' Second thoughts: I didn't like offering myself up to shoulder the blame. 'But maybe it's good for him to be exposed to me. Remind him he's fallible like the rest of us.'

Uriel did not share my glee at the thought of cutting Alex down to size. 'I don't think he needs anyone attacking his confidence.' He glanced down the table to where Alex was making

Willow a crown out of serviettes, charming the socks off the under tens. So adorable. I had no trouble liking Alex from a distance; it was the close-up thing that caused the problems.

Uriel pushed his empty plate aside, voice low. 'It might help you to understand where he's coming from when you know that he's got no one to care for him other than Tarryn and the staff at the school.'

I put down my wilting garden burger. 'What do you mean by that? Is he an orphan?'

Uriel shook his head. 'That might've been easier. He was abandoned by his parents when his gift came through. They aren't savants and have some really strong prejudices against us. They think it must be witchcraft or black magic. Having a son able to juggle toys with his mind sent them crazy. They tried to beat it out of him, then threw him out when that failed.'

'But surely you can't just kick out your child for being different? There have to be laws to prevent that.'

'You'd think so but the rest of his family left the country, last heard of in Argentina. They're on the run. They told Alex—he was three at the time—that they were running from a demon. They meant him.'

'Geez.' I rubbed my chest, feeling the echo of that harsh truth as Uriel's words sank in. 'Only three. Yeah, sure, I'll be nicer to him now I know that.'

'Thanks. Maybe I shouldn't have told you but as he's coming to Cambridge I thought it better to set you straight on a few things. Tarryn wants to build up his confidence, not undermine it. Try not to let him know you know.'

'Uriel, I can't lie.'

'Right. I forgot.' He ran his hand through his hair, annoyed at his oversight. 'Just don't raise the subject. He's sensitive about it as you can imagine.'

'Yeah, I can imagine.' Alex put the finished crown on Willow's head and turned to making one for Hazel. He claimed he knew nothing about families and I could now understand why he said that, but he was doing a grand job entertaining the girls. He had more skills than he knew. If the time seemed right, I'd tell him.

Uriel's phone beeped.

'Apologies. I should've turned it off.' Uriel checked the message.

Tarryn, sitting with Milo and Opal, looked up, alert to anything that disturbed her soulfinder. 'Uri, what's happened?'

Uriel's mood darkened considerably.

'Bad news?' I asked, mind dashing to all my family and friends.

'Yes.' Uriel got up. 'But it's a work matter.' He brushed my shoulder. 'Nothing you need worry about. Enjoy your party. I'll just take this outside.'

Uriel headed out to the viewpoint. Tarryn made her excuses and hurried to join him.

'Work?' asked Hugo. 'I thought he was an academic.'

'Academics do work, bru,' Phil drawled, eating his last chip.

'Uriel does forensic investigations for the American authorities,' I explained, recalling the conversation on the plane and the murders that he was looking into for the FBI. I thought I could say that much without breaking any confidences.

'So does that mean someone has died?' asked Phil, sounding keen rather than upset at the idea. He would make a good pathologist with that ghoulish enthusiasm.

'Probably, but I don't think he likes talking about it,' I warned.

'Now who wants dessert?' called Uncle Milo, changing the mood from sombre to happy. Several hands went up among the younger members of our party.

'Great idea. What've they got?' I took the menu from the waitress. My choice was obvious. 'Chocolate Penguin Surprise, please.'

Down the other end of the table, Brand made his impressive penguin call which sounded like a car with a flat battery trying to start. He banged a spoon on his high chair table. The restaurant fell silent.

'Oops,' I murmured. 'Note to self: don't mention penguins.'

Alex leapt up and put a bottle in Brand's mouth to stop the noise. 'Something caught in his throat,' he lied quickly.

Right on cue, Brand made a sound like a cat with a fur ball. Opal hurried over to pat his back but from the gleam in the toddler's eye it was just another act. She murmured thanks to Alex, who smiled charmingly in reply.

I gave him a point for a good save even though his fib made my throat ache.

No doubt about it: Alex and I were better off living on different continents.

As if hearing my thoughts, Alex's eyes met mine down the length of the table, a thrilling jolt of blue fire. My bones tingled in the aftermath of my lie. It appeared there was more doubt in my mind than I liked to admit.

Chapter 7

Cornwall, England

I got off the minibus outside the Smugglers Cove Lodge to find Angel and Summer were waiting for me. Bag thrown on the ground, I disappeared into a group hug.

'Hey, you guys, it's so great to see you!' I checked them over to see if they'd changed since Easter when we last met up. 'Summer, you look fabulous!'

She did. Were those some sneaky long layers in her black hair? The bits at the front now curled round onto her chest rather than falling down the back with the rest.

Summer wiped the back of her hand across her brow with exaggerated relief. 'Phew! I wasn't sure what you were going to say. You reduced my confidence to dust over those white jeans last time.'

'And what about me?' asked Angel, prodding my ribs. 'Don't I look gorgeous too?'

I grinned. 'Angel, you look just the same as ever.'

'Bah. I'm taking that as a compliment.'

'It is.' I always envied Angel for her straight hair, the colour of wild honey; she told me she was jealous of my curls. Both of us spent a fortune on hair products trying to be like the other. The only party happy with that outcome were the makers of the lotions and potions. Moral of that story: I should quit worrying about my hair and invest in the cosmetics industry.

'Earth to Misty?' Summer was used to my little mind-wanders.

'Oh, sorry. Just planning how I'm going to make my first million.' I picked up my bag. The other savants who had come in my busload had already gone inside the lodge to reception. The campsite at Smugglers Cove looked more like a wooded dell than a sea inlet. I could see cabins scattered among the silver birch trees. 'Verdict?'

'Not bad,' said Angel, leading me inside. 'We're sharing a cabin. There was supposed to be a fourth girl but they said something about her being a no-show.'

'That's a shame but then it's fun to be just the three of us.' I put my bag down by the desk and signed in, my name a big looping scrawl compared to the neat ones above mine.

'Having a fourth would've made it even more Famous Five,' said Summer. 'Do you think they thought about that when they chose the name for this place?'

Angel shook her head. 'No, it really is what the cove is called. I checked a map.'

'Awesome. So we're near the sea?' I asked.

'You can't see it from here but it's not far. Just through the trees and then down a steep path.'

The sun was shining; the first event wasn't until four; I had my two best friends with me and my swimming costume in my bag . . .

'Let me just dump my stuff in the cabin, then are you up for a swim?'

'Need you ask?' said Angel.

The cove was everything you could hope for in a little

Cornish beach: a half-moon of pale sand, plenty of interesting rocks to climb or jump from, a chilly but blue stretch of sheltered water. The tide was coming in so we had to leave our towels and shoes further up the beach. Holding hands we readied ourselves for our annual ritual.

'On the count of three. No hesitations. No deviations. No turning back,' said Angel.

'One. Two. Three!' counted Summer.

Screaming as we ran down the beach, we went straight into the water, wincing at the cold. The penalty for not going in first time was to have the others throw you in so there was a big incentive not to chicken out.

'I can't feel my legs!' squawked Angel.

'You're lucky. I can and they're begging me to get out.' Summer strode on further. 'Now for the waist. Ooo-ow!'

'Shoulders under and then it gets better!' I shouted as I always did. I struck out, going for a vigorous crawl to get the blood circulating. My friends were only a stroke behind. We swam around a half-submerged rock. By the time we faced the shore again we were all acclimatized to the temperature. I hung weightless, enjoying the rocking sensation of the waves.

'Beats swimming in a pool,' sighed Angel.

'Certainly does.' I smiled as Angel played with the droplets running off her fingers, making them spin in the sunshine. 'I haven't been in the sea since last year.'

'But I thought you went on the beach in South Africa. We saw the photographs.' She giggled.

'I don't know if you've noticed, Angel, but it's winter at the other end of the world. Far too cold. I went in my aunt and uncle's pool but that's heated by solar power.'

'And did Hunk-of-the-Month go in with you?'

Both my friends had been quick to 'like' my postings of Alex.

'It wasn't that way between us.' I floated on my back, enjoying the tickle of my hair drifting around me. Alex: blue eyes, charming smile, swirl of chestnut hair, deep voice that got inside you . . .

A girl-made wave splashed me. 'Why ever not?' said Angel. 'Here was I hoping you'd come back with tales of romance to while away the campfire evenings.'

I trod water and shook the droplets from my face. 'I'll pay you back for that.'

'Of course.' Angel would expect no less from me. 'But first tell me how you could possibly turn down a guy like that. He was looking at you taking the photo with such, ooo, *hunger*.' She shivered.

'Sadly, he manages to project that rip-off-my-shirt sex-appeal to everyone. It's as natural to him as breathing. He and I didn't hit it off. Our gifts clashed.' I frowned. 'Or more accurately, mine cancelled his out. Not a good combo.'

'Really?' This piqued Summer's interest. 'He's a savant? Did you check his date of birth?'

I started swimming for shore. If I was going to be interrogated on my awkward relationship with Alex, I preferred to do so with sand under my feet. 'Why? Are you saying that clashing with each other is a promising sign? I don't think so. Besides, he's a year ahead so must be too old for me. My birthday's the thirtieth of December. He must be well outside the two weeks either side normally allowed for potential hits.'

I waded out and wrapped myself in a towel. Grains of sand coated my feet like slippers. Angel and Summer joined me on the shore. Summer had a butterfly-print cotton robe to put on so wasn't freezing like Angel and I were. She's good at forward planning.

Summer squeezed her hair. 'I'm just saying you shouldn't discount it. As you pointed out, it's winter down there. Their school years run differently from ours. He might not be as old as you think.'

Oh my goodness. 'You're right. I'm as dumb as a brick sometimes.' It suddenly seemed of immense importance to text Tarryn and ask. 'Shall we go back and shower?' I dragged my sandals nearer with a tug of telekinesis.

'Sure. First one to the cabin gets the bathroom!' Angel was already running as she shouted this.

Summer and I walked back, knowing we'd lost that race.

'Now remind me: why did her parents pick that name for her?' asked Summer.

'I don't think either of them had a gift of foresight,' I replied.

When we arrived for the camp briefing in the lodge games room, we discovered that many old friends had pitched up during the afternoon. The English savant youth camp had a core member-ship of teens from thirteen to eighteen; most of us were regulars and we had already checked out the birthday thing so knew that, unless a new person joined us, we were all destined just to be friends rather than soulfinders. The outcome was that we could all relax in each other's company. It was great to be with the other people of our age who understood the trials of living with a gift. We could rehash our triumphs and failures over the year and expect a sympathetic audience. I was usually much in demand for an account of my last twelve months as I was some-thing of a long-running joke for most of them. I was sort of OK with that but under my bluff laugh-it-off demeanour, I didn't find it so amusing. It worried me that I couldn't control my gift. If my experience in South Africa was anything to judge by, I was getting worse at it, not better. I tried to console myself with the thought that at least I didn't start fires like Yves Benedict, Xav's younger brother, when I let it slip.

I scanned the room, revelling in the knowledge that I had a whole week with old friends. A couple of guys appeared to be missing and there were some new faces too. Funny to think my sister Gale would be joining us next year; this was the last year of being the only Devon at camp.

Paul Hampton, organizer of Youth Savant activities in England, came into the meeting room.

'Hello again, guys. Great to see you back for another dose of camp. As well as the usual fun and games, I've got some new ideas for us to try out this week, following the feedback forms from last year.' Paul perched on the edge of the snooker table, waiting for us to settle on the chairs, tables, and floor around him. He was in his late twenties, not classically handsome but he had this twinkle to his eye that made you look twice. 'I've got Lara with me this year to help with you girls so give her an easy time of it, won't you?' He waved to a young woman whom I recognized as an old camp student from some years back. With a halo of Afro black hair, gorgeous dark complexion, and huge brown eyes, Lara packed quite a punch in the looks department. 'I don't want you scaring her away like you did my last helper.'

We laughed at the suggestion that we frightened off his old assistant. Elise had been a terrifying Danish lady who had kept us all on our toes with unannounced room inspections. Fortunately she had found her soulfinder in India and was now, according to Summer, terrorizing the youth of Goa at their camp.

Paul and Lara passed round the camp brochures. I flicked through mine, recognizing most of the outdoor activity choices from previous years. I made a mental note to go for body boarding. The morning slots, however, were all blocked out for something called Personal Development.

Finn, a savant from Manchester, put the question for everyone.

'Hey, Paul, what's with the morning slots?'

'That's the big change this year. Some of you expressed an interest at the end of last camp in learning related to your gifts. Traditionally, we let you figure it out on your own but there have been a number of incidents over recent months that have forced a rethink. We believe you could benefit from some guidance from more experienced savants.'

I could feel my blush creeping up my cheeks. I had written on the form last year that I would like more help controlling my gift (I had been feeling particularly sore after being bullied out of my last school). I must have foreseen that I would make zero progress over the year that had just gone. But as I didn't want to be blamed for spoiling the fun factor of camp with work, I kept quiet.

Finn wrinkled his nose. 'You mean you're putting us through exercises or something? Won't that be like school?'

Paul grinned. 'I promise you, it'll be great fun. Your tutors know you're on holiday and have been asked to think of ways of teaching that'll appeal to you.'

'Aw, man.'

'Finn.' Paul's smile dimmed. 'Give it a chance, please. And now, while we are on more serious subjects, there's something you need to know. We have two special guests for the evening to explain. A few of you have already met them but they are here for a tragic reason so please listen carefully to what they have to say. Lara, can you invite them in?'

Lara popped her head round the door and then Uriel entered, followed by his younger brother Victor. Passing my seat, Uriel stopped and gave me a quick hug.

'Sorry, Misty, I couldn't text you to tell you I was coming. You'll understand in a moment why.' He then joined his brother at the front as Paul continued speaking.

'Our two visitors are Uriel and Victor Benedict. You all know Misty.' A buzz of agreement went round the room. 'Well, two of Misty's aunts are soulfinders to their brothers—how many of you are there?' Paul said, trying to keep the tone light, though I knew with Victor, the FBI agent, in the room we were headed for dark territory.

'Seven,' said Victor. His features had a sharper edge than Uriel's, the hawk among the Benedicts. His eyes were particularly intense—a grey iris rimmed by a darker ring. He wore his dark brown hair quite long but it was slicked back from his face in a manner that suited his air of ruthless control. I found him fascinating but made a point of trying to pass under his notice at family gatherings. Working on my quick-to-assume-guilt conscience, he made me feel I were about to commit a crime or had already done so and he was about to arrest me. If he had my gift, I'm sure he would never let go of a single spillikin.

He held the room with his intense gaze; I could sense even the most rebellious of us settling down to be on our best behaviour. 'Sorry to interrupt your vacation. We are here to give you a safety briefing.'

Safety briefing? This was new. I exchanged a glance with Angel and Summer. They seemed to expect me to know something. *I'm clueless*, I admitted telepathically.

'You may have already noticed that a number of your colleagues aren't joining us this week,' said Paul.

I ran a quick roll call in my head: no Joey Marston; Ellie Fisher was missing; and Callum MacDonald wasn't sitting with Finn as he normally would.

'They've stayed away because there is alarm in the savant community for the safety of younger members,' Paul explained. 'Some parents have elected to keep their children at home.'

The image of the map Uriel had showed me popped up in my mind. On the flight out, none of the murders had been in the UK and I had not felt particularly at risk.

'Two weeks ago Mia Gordon, a newly identified savant from London, was abducted,' said Victor, confirming my worst fear. 'She should have been listening to this briefing with you—she was only sixteen and about to attend her first camp.'

That's the name of the girl who should've been in our cabin, Summer told Angel and me.

'Her gift was treasure seeking.' Victor flexed his fingers, the only sign that he was upset by what he was saying as he kept his expression impassive.

Was? Oh God.

'She turned up dead, body dumped in the Thames last week. We've concluded that she is the latest victim of a killer who moves round the world picking exclusively on young savants. The murderer has claimed thirteen victims that we know about: one here; five in America; two in Australia; two in New Zealand, three on mainland Europe in Germany, Denmark, and France. That's why we're here. I'm briefing every youth camp around the world to warn you to be on your guard. This person will kill again unless we find them first.'

Horrified silence followed these words. How should we react when one of the people who should've sat among us had been murdered? Death had always seemed remote—a problem for the future—but now it had terrifyingly walked into the room.

'We're very sorry to bring you this bad news but it's also why we are including the morning sessions this year.' Paul picked up from where Victor had stopped. 'We want to keep you safe. The killer targets those who have not mastered their gift. The FBI profiler who dealt with the homicides in the US thinks that this is because it makes them easier to subdue and the killer is basically a coward. If you can fight back, he'll leave you alone.'

Victor raised a hand, finger pointing for emphasis. 'That's not to suggest the victims are in any way to be blamed for what happened to them. Our intention is to reduce the likelihood you'll be targeted. Unfortunately a person of this nature will always find someone he or she can overpower. Are there any questions?'

Zillions. I put my hand up, arm trembling.

'Misty?'

'Do you know anything about the killer—what he looks like?'

'He or she,' Victor corrected me. 'We know very little. The profiler puts him—and she thinks it is more likely to be a him—at around thirty to fifty so not someone in this room. Uriel, can you explain what else we do know?'

Uriel stood up from leaning against the snooker table. 'Some of you are aware that my speciality is forensics. I also have a gift for taking people and things back to the past. It works best with living subjects but I can draw some impressions from bodies. The strangest aspect of these murders is that there is no trace of the killer, or indeed how he or she kills. The last victim was dead before the body was dumped but the results read as if she spontaneously stopped living.'

'So you don't know anything?' asked Finn, sounding aggressive because he, like the rest of us, was scared.

'I didn't say that. The absence of evidence *is* a trail. We can conclude that the killer is one of us, a savant, and their gift is for just this: wiping out any physical or savant-detectable signs of his or her presence. We can also conclude that the means of murder is part of that gift—a cancelling, if you like, of life.'

'Geez,' murmured Angel, rubbing her arms. 'That's really creepy.'

'It is,' agreed Uriel. 'There's a team working hard on tracking down this killer but we are determined to prevent another death. In addition to learning how to handle your gifts, you'll also be taught some basic personal security measures and how to raise the alarm if you are in a situation where you have reason to suspect the person.'

'I want to emphasize,' said Victor, 'that none of the victims were able to send a distress call before they were killed. This means that either the murderer is able to block telepathy or the victims went to their death without suspecting him or her.'

Paul took the floor again. 'I'm sorry that we had to cast this cloud over the start of camp but you can understand, I'm sure, that the stakes couldn't be any higher. Please learn as much as you can this week and make sure you practise it when you go back to your usual routines.'

'I'll be here for the first two days to see small groups of you for mental defence training,' said Victor. 'Other volunteers from the Savant Net will be arriving tomorrow to help you with your gifts.'

Summer raised her hand.

'Yes?' Victor's expression brightened with interest as his gaze fell on my friend. 'Summer, isn't it?'

She gave a flustered smile. 'How did you know?'

'You've got a gift similar to mine so I'll be working with you one-to-one.'

'Oh, um, cool.' I could tell Summer was alarmed at that news. I wish I could tell her Victor was all bark and no bite but I couldn't lie. He was more all bite and no bark if his reputation was anything to go by. There were hundreds of criminals behind bars who had not seen him coming until he seized them: think swimmer in water and *Jaws*.

'You had a question?'

'Yes.' Recalled to herself, Summer regained some of her usual poise. 'You said that the killer was one of us.'

'Correct.'

'How do we know then that we can trust the people we are training with this week?'

Victor smiled approvingly. 'Good question. You can't absolutely.' Victor was never one to offer false comfort. 'I've called in people I know I can trust so if you can extend your faith to me then I'll vouch for them.'

'So, are you sure?' Summer pressed.

'I'd stake my life on it as I'm related to half of them. Four of my brothers and three of their soulfinders will be spending the week here. Misty knows them too if you've questions about them. They've just finished at the summer camp in California so will arrive tomorrow morning.'

'Oh wow, the fabulous Benedict brothers are coming our way,' whispered Angel to me, patting her heart. I had told her about my aunts' new relations and shown her the wedding photos from Venice.

'Who's coming?' I asked.

Uriel took over the briefing. 'Your aunt, Diamond, and Trace are leading the team.' He turned to address the whole room. 'Misty's aunt is an expert in conflict resolution; my eldest brother, Trace, is a police officer but also a tracker. Also with them is Will—he senses danger and will be running the personal safety briefings with Vick. The younger team members are Yves, Phoenix, Sky, and Zed.'

You'll love Phoenix and Sky, I told my friends. *They're such fun.*

'They all have very different gifts but both Sky and Phoenix have experience of being trapped by a stronger savant so will be able to give you survival tips. Our hope, of course, is that you'll never have to use them. However, as our killer often strikes more than once in the same country within weeks of taking the previous victim, Mia's murder means the UK is now our priority.'

A chill ran down my spine: a strange sense of foreboding that someone in this room would be the next to die.

'Everyone clear on what's happening?' asked Paul. 'Now for the moment of truth! Lara, please hand round the sheets giving details of who is working with whom.'

Angel shrieked when she got hers. 'Oh double wow, I've got Yves.'

'Don't let Phoenix hear you say it in quite that tone,' I joked weakly, struggling to shake off my premonition.

'I know they're devoted to each other, but, oh my!' She pretended to swoon.

'I suppose they think your ability to manipulate water is close to his gift to control energy.'

'I don't care what they think; I just like the result.' She gave me a cheeky grin.

I opened my paper. Zed. I couldn't think how my truth gift was like his skills: as seventh son of a seventh child, Zed had a little of all his brothers' gifts as well as his own one for foreknowledge. Putting it bluntly, he was the whole circus whereas I was a one-trick pony.

Why Zed for me? I asked Uriel, using telepathy so I didn't set off a whole round of demands for explanations from each student.

Because he has to control input from all of us when we combine our gifts. Victor thinks that's a little like your grip on truth—so much sensory information that it gets away from you.

I nodded, pleased. Zed was a bit scary but I knew the way to neutralize him was to get Sky on my side and fortunately she and I were mates. *Thanks.*

'OK, if you've all got your packs,' said Paul, 'I suggest you dump them in the cabins and come back for dinner. We are not going to give this evil individual the victory of spoiling your holiday, so put it away for now. We'll start on the protection agenda tomorrow.'

Grumble though we did about being given 'work', it was more just for show as we were all behind the new regime. We had caught the chill of fear. In fact, the morning exercises proved to be the best part of camp. Will, the middle-in-age of the Benedict brothers, in his early twenties, had the square-shaped face and broad shoulders that read as dependable in my book. He also had a sweet sense of humour and came across as gentler than his intimidating brothers. We were all a little surprised to find that he ran the personal security sessions with Victor taking a back seat. Victor only came to the front when asked to act out the baddie in the scenarios Will created. That was an astute strategy because it meant that Victor remained aloof from us, making his pretend attacks almost as scary as the real thing, or so I imagined.

'Come on, Misty, build a wall against him,' urged Will as for the fifth time my attempt to rebuff Victor's mind probe crumbled like a flaky chocolate bar.

I ran my hands through my hair in frustration and squeezed the roots. Angel and Summer looked on patiently. They had both mastered this particular skill on the first attempt. 'OK, Victor, sock it to me.' I screwed my eyes shut and threw everything against his mind-grab. I thought for a moment I had succeeded, but he then projected an image of himself eating said chocolate bar while lying on a sun lounger.

I opened my eyes and looked down at my feet. At least my toenails looked pretty in their shell-pink varnish; it was the rest of me that was a disaster.

'How did she do?' asked Will.

Victor shook his head.

'I offer about as much resistance as a wet tissue,' I admitted.

'It's odd.' Victor patted me briefly on the shoulder as he went back to stand with Will at the front of our little classroom in one of the cabins. I think he meant it as a comfort but I'm never quite sure with him. It could also have been an 'arrest this one' gesture. 'I've not met a mind like hers before. She's completely unguarded. That made me wonder if we're asking her to do something that her gift won't allow.'

My gaze lifted. 'You mean, it might not be my fault?'

'I never said it was your fault.' Victor rubbed the side of his jaw, reviewing what he knew about my gift. He was looking at me as if I were a problem to solve. 'We can all see you're trying but I guess that putting up a wall feels like a lie to your subconscious—it's a trick, a diversion, not a real wall.'

'Great. So my nothing-but-the-truth brain won't even relax the rules to protect itself?'

'That's how I read the situation.'

'So I'm screwed if anyone picks on me?'

'Now that I don't know. Nothing about being a savant is one-size-fits-all. It's just a question of adapting your strengths to find a new way of defending your boundaries.'

'My strength being . . . ?'

'You tell me.'

'I'm good at table tennis,' I offered.

Will laughed. 'I don't think that's what my brother had in mind, Misty. He means your gift.'

That's a very short list. 'I know a liar, I suppose. And people can't lie around me if I let my control slip.'

'Then your best defence is to expose anyone with bad intentions before they get to you—build the barrier further out in the truth zone where you are queen.' Will's dark eyes sparkled with amusement. He projected a playful little telepathic image of me wearing a tiara walking over villains in a Lady Gaga-style dance routine.

'Thanks, I like that—me being queen.' Yet the problems were obvious. 'But if I go around with my truth force field active, won't I just annoy a lot of innocent people?'

'That's a judgement call and one you'll have to make on your own,' said Victor. He never softened the truth, or thought we were too young for the full facts; I admired him for it even if it was unsettling. 'If you're suspicious of someone, do your own version of a mind probe and expose their motives. A few bruised feelings are a price worth paying to stop becoming this killer's target.'

Summer laced her fingers with mine. 'But how is Misty to know who to test?'

'Instinct.' Will folded his arms across his chest, biceps attractively displayed by the short sleeves of his black T-shirt. 'My gift is sensing danger but really that's just a souped up version of the gut instincts we all have for survival. Listen to what your intuition is telling you. It's there for a very good reason.'

Pay attention, Misty. Stop looking at muscles.

'Yeah, the poor schmucks who didn't have that instinct dropped off the evolutionary tree,' said Angel.

Will flashed her a grin. 'You're right. I'm sure you all know what we're talking about—it's one of the primal senses we all share. Go with that and you'll be OK.'

But every generation produces a few schmucks, I thought gloomily. I always considered myself a candidate for that title with my numerous Misty moments. I just hoped I could hang on to my twig.

Chapter 8

On arrival back at our cabin, I found an answer to my text to Tarryn.

Should have checked earlier. Sorry—didn't think.

Couldn't blame her for not thinking: we were as unlikely a match as a capybara and a leopard: we might live in the same jungle but that was it.

Alex's DOB? 12 December, same year of birth. Puts him just outside your range. Possible match?

Hardly, but it was worth asking. The bad news was, now I knew his date of birth, I could also work out that he was a closer potential match for at least five other girls I knew in the Savant Net, one of whom was Summer. Oh boy. I didn't want to tell her but I had to. I could see them fitting really well together: organized, brilliant Summer and charming, sophisticated Alex. My jealousy made me a very mean dog-in-the-manger Misty.

OK, Misty: whistle up better self and confess.

'Hey, Summer?'

My friend was sitting in the sun chairs outside our cabin reading a novel.

'Yes?' She looked up, lifting her sunglasses on to the top of her head so they held back her hair in movie-star-on-Rivera style.

'That Alex guy . . . '

Angel stuck her head out of the bedroom window. She was halfway through applying a face pack gorgeous Lara had recommended and it was cracking into a thousand bits. 'You're a possible match—I just knew it!'

'That's not a good look, Angel. As I was saying, Summer, before I was rudely interrupted by Swamp Monster here, on the date of birth, he's an outside chance. His birthday is twelfth December. So unless I was late and he was a little early . . . '

'Or maybe he was born premature. We don't take enough notice of that kind of thing in the Savant Net and loads of babies are preemies these days.' Angel was more eager about this than I was, having decided he was too stunning to let pass. 'Get him to ask his parents.'

'That's not possible.'

'Why?' Angel gave up on the face pack and started to wipe it off her cheeks.

'Complicated.'

Meanwhile, Summer had been doing her maths. 'My birthday is first December.'

'Yes. He's closer to you in age than me.'

'You should ask your aunt Crystal,' said Angel.

'*No soulfinders before you're eighteen,*' Summer and I chanted, having heard Crystal on the subject numerous times.

'But, come on, this is an emergency!'

Summer raised a brow. 'In what way is it an emergency, Angel?'

'I'm dying of curiosity.'

'You'll have to limp along on life support until November. Alex is coming to Cambridge. Summer, if you come over to visit one weekend you can meet him—see if you get the vibe.'

'What about you? Didn't you get the vibe?' Angel solved the problem of being half out of the building by climbing onto the sill and dropping down beside us.

There were vibes all right but they had felt oddly like hitting a raw nerve. 'I don't know. I got something but it was messed up by the incompatibility between our gifts. I didn't even think to try telepathy.'

'It does seem too personal with someone you don't know well.' Summer understood me without me having to explain. 'I'm like that too.'

'Let's be honest, soulfinders are supposed to build up each other's powers, not undermine them.' I dug deep. 'And Summer, you and he are the same kind.'

'What do you mean?' Summer put her novel on her lap.

I pointed to her copy of *The Woman in White*. 'You read intellectual books—old ones with a million pages.'

'Wilkie Collins does run on a bit,' she admitted with a smile. 'Great page-turner though.'

'I think Alex would really like that about you.'

'Don't run yourself down: you read poetry and novels.'

'Yeah, but not your sort of novels. Mine are YA romances and chick lit.'

'Don't diss chick lit. They are relationship novels that publishers belittle with cutesy covers. Did you know that women make up well over half the book-buying public and there are more female published authors? And what do they do? Makes us into a minority—a subset!' Summer stroked the cover of her paperback as if soothing it.

Summer is very even tempered about most things but this was her red-rag-to-a-bull subject. I could tell she found it easier to talk about than the delicate issue of Alex. She must have guessed I had a softer spot for him than I had admitted and was trying to build up my confidence that I was good enough to be a match.

'O-kay. I read *relationship* novels. Thanks, Summer.'

'I think we should bring in a new term for guys' stories. How about bloke books, testosterone tripe, or macho-mush?' Angel looked to us to vote.

Summer gave her a nod of approval. 'Any of them will do—make as much sense as chick lit. Anyway, go on, Misty. Why do you think he and I might be soulfinders and not him and you?'

I hesitated, remembering how Alex moved among other people as if he was touched by something special. 'You know that bit at the end of *Peter Pan?*'

'When Tinker Bell sprinkles the ship with fairy dust?' asked Angel. 'Love that film.'

'Yes. Alex is like that ship—sprinkled with, I don't know, let's call it Gorgeous Dust.'

'Hot Dust?' suggested Angel.

'That sounds like something emerging from a malfunctioning hoover. No, let's stick with Gorgeous Dust.'

'What's that got to do with me?' asked Summer, her brow furrowed.

I glanced at Angel. *She doesn't know.*

That makes her bearable, replied Angel.

'I have to break it to you, Summer, but you are the female equivalent.'

'Yep, you are shiny with GD,' agreed Angel.

Summer blushed and put her sunglasses back down on her nose, hiding her pale jade eyes. 'Don't be silly.'

'It's true.' My saying that ended the discussion because they both knew I meant it. I didn't do flattery.

Summer looked sweetly flustered. 'So you think that . . . maybe . . . he and I?'

I shrugged, trying to appear neutral on the subject. 'It's worth finding out.'

Angel cocked her head sideways. 'Which weekend in November is he in Cambridge, Misty?'

I told her the dates.

'OK. I'll be there.'

Summer bit her thumbnail. 'You're inviting yourself, Angel?'

'Of course! There's a chance that one of you might, you know, score big time. I'm not going to miss that.'

'You do get that the chances are still very slight?' said Summer, but I could see I had started a very pleasant chain of thoughts in her mind. I predicted that the first thing she would do post-conversation was revisit my photos on Facebook.

'Slight-schmight.' Angel snapped her fingers. 'This is epic! Summer and Alex: I like the sound of that already.'

I didn't. Part of me was howling that he was my find, my possible.

'He could still be Misty's,' Summer pointed out reasonably.

I love Summer.

'But she's met him and *nada*.'

Angel, on the other hand . . .

'You, Summer, are still in with a very strong chance.' Angel did a little hip wiggle dance to finish that sentence.

'It wasn't exactly *nada*,' I muttered, but Angel was off on one of her flights of enthusiasm. We expected at least two of these a day so we were due.

'Misty can introduce you, then oh-so-subtly leave you to . . . you know . . . get friendly.'

'Anyone else thinking "eggs before hatched"?' asked Summer.

'I'm thinking "counting eggs before even buying the hens to lay them",' I agreed swiftly.

'Oh, come on, guys! It's like Christmas: the anticipation is way better than the day itself.'

Summer smiled ruefully at me and checked her watch. 'Well, go anticipate somewhere on your own. I've got a lesson with Victor.'

Angel grabbed Summer's wrist to find out the time. She never bothered with her own watch. 'Geez, I'm late for Yves.' She cackled at her own half-rhyme. 'Later.'

I caught her by the back of her summer dress. 'Face pack.'

'I missed a bit?' Angel made an unsuccessful attempt to see her own nose.

'Lots of bits. You look as though you've caught some dreaded lurgy.'

'Overeager-itis, maybe?' quipped Summer.

Angel hurried back inside to wash, not having time to think up a clever response and still get to her lesson.

'Wish me luck,' Summer said, heading to the cabin Victor was sharing with Paul. I fell into step.

'You'll be fine.' I knew Victor would look after Summer even if he scared the bejeezus out of her.

'What about you, Misty?'

'I've got my session with Zed.'

'The intimidating but hot?'

'That's like a title?'

Summer laughed. 'I think it is now.'

Zed the Intimidating but Hot was at the pool table in the games room. He was passing the time waiting for me by playing a game with Sky. I paused in the door to watch them together. Sky was cheating outrageously, bending the balls with her telekinetic powers when they went off track. He was blocking her from doing the same to his shots so he was still winning.

'You just sunk the white in the pocket after that yellow,' he told her.

'Did not.' Sky made the ball jump out again.

He backed her up against the table, his six-feet-plus frame dwarfing her slight stature. They were a study in contrast: Sky was all wavy blonde hair and forget-me-not blue eyes, whereas Zed was dark and dangerous with a moody blue-green gaze. Seeing them together reminded me that the not-so-obvious couple could make a really great match. Sometimes a soul-finder pair only makes sense after you see the two people come together. Maybe I had a chance.

'Cheating like that incurs a penalty,' he said in a deep, spine-tingling voice.

'A severe penalty?' Sky asked hopefully.

'Very.' He took the pool cue from her hand and placed it on the table. 'Pay up, Miss Bright.'

She gave an unconvincing put-upon sigh. 'If I must, Mr Benedict.'

Sky lifted her face and he bent down for a kiss. Wow. I should so not be here. They were making out like they'd only just found each other, not the behaviour expected of a couple who had been dating for nearly two years. I turned to leave them their privacy but my flip-flop squeaked on the floorboard. Awkward.

Zed looked round. He was not pleased.

'Sorry. I'll just . . . um . . . go.' I waved vaguely in the direction of anywhere-but-here.

Sky batted him in the chest, her cheeks understandably pink. 'Stop that, Zed. Hi, Misty. Zed was expecting you. We got a little sidetracked.' She slid from the side of the pool table where he had lifted her during the kiss. 'How are you?'

'I'm . . . ' *fine* would just not come out, 'really embarrassed right now.'

'We'll catch up later, OK?' She gave Zed another 'behave' look then left us alone.

'Sorry.' I edged inside the room. 'Timing was never my strong point.'

Zed held out the cue Sky had left behind. 'You play?'

'Yes, but aren't we having a lesson? I should tell you right up front, I really need some help. I'm rubbish at control.'

'So I've heard. Uri mentioned something about a hospital.' Seeing I wasn't making any progress into the room, he took my hand and led me to the table. 'Here.'

I took the cue. You don't refuse Zed.

He set up the rack of balls. 'You know the rules?'

'I think so.'

'OK. You break.'

Along with table tennis, pool was another of my accomplishments. You can see where I spent the time I should have been studying. I made a good start, one red potted, and the balls in a nice range of positions.

'So, your gift is for truth?'

'Yes.' I potted a second red and lined up for another.

Zed leaned against the wall, his cue resting in front of him as he watched the game. 'All kinds?'

A third red disappeared. 'What do you mean?'

'Do you sense if it is the truth no matter what the person telling you thinks?'

'I'm not sure.'

'OK, for example, say you've got someone who really believes in way-out conspiracy theories; if you listen to them, do you hear it as a lie or as a truth as far as they are concerned?'

'Oh, I hadn't thought about that.' Distracted, I just missed my fourth red.

'Unlucky.' Zed moved in and started potting yellows like he had a plane to catch—thump, thump, thump in the pockets.

Normally that would annoy me but just then I was caught up in reviewing my experience.

'I think it must be to do with what the person believes. I'm thinking about beliefs rather than facts now. I mean, I can say "I believe in God" knowing I'm not a hundred per cent sure, just more a believer than not. If my gift gave me the power to know if it were true then I'd be, well, doing something centuries of theologians have not been able to settle.'

Zed missed a tricky yellow and stood back to let me take over. 'OK, let's assume then that we are working with a gift that functions by tuning you in to the intentions of the other person.'

'Uh-huh.' I sank a red and was back in the game. 'Victor thinks that for me I don't have to be totally conscious of it to still work. I couldn't build a defensive wall as it read as fake to my brain. I can't even tell a truth knowing I mean the opposite—I struggle with irony. It registers as a lie.'

'Interesting. I'd like to get Phoenix to watch you later, see what your mind is doing. It seems to be undermining you.' Phoenix, his brother Yves' soulfinder, has the power of seeing our mental landscapes; it is the first step in her ability to make time seem to stop. 'My guess is that you're taking in a huge spectrum of information, both conscious and instinctive. It's why it's so hard for you to control it. You're only aware of seeing a small part of the spread, like visible light in the wave spectrum, which is only a tiny part of the whole.'

'I'm glad you've got an excuse for me.' I was down to my last two reds.

He approached the table. 'You think you're going to win this frame?'

'Why, yes!' I was too far ahead to lose now.

As my next red zipped to the corner pocket, Zed used his power to bend it away. Taking over he pocketed all the remaining yellows and the black.

'And now?'

'Still yes: it's a moral victory.' I thumped my cue down on the table.

He laughed, seeing how I was really riled with him. 'That establishes the facts then. You don't give objective truth, as I won by cheating, just what is felt to be true, even for yourself.'

My anger fizzled out. 'You were testing me?'

'Yep.' He called all the balls back into position. 'Now, Misty, let's start working on those strands of truth you feel. Think of each pool ball as something you need to control— yellow are the conscious truths, red the flying-under-the-radar truths . . .'

My brain felt like ice cream left out in the sun by the time I'd finished with Zed. I walked zombie-fashion back to our cabin, too tired to take much notice of the lovely sunshine through mint-green birch leaves and the swish-hush of the waves breaking on the beach. Sky and Phoenix were sitting on deck chairs with Angel and Summer. They had a cold drink just poured for me. Zed must have sent word ahead.

'How was it?' asked Sky.

'Really good.' I dropped my notebook beside her. 'I don't think I made great strides in control but I learned a lot about why I suck at it.'

'Zed said you did well—and that you are miles better at pool than me.'

'He might've mentioned something about you not being that good at it,' I admitted.

'No, no, it's much more than that: I'm incredibly gifted at pool . . .'

Strange: her comment wasn't registering as a lie.

'I raise making a hash of it to an art form. Then I have to

cheat and that winds him up to . . . well, you saw the conse-
quences.'

Hadn't I just.

'It's kind of you guys to give up the time,' I said, dodging
commenting on what I walked in on to spare our blushes.

'It's our pleasure—really it is. Fortunately, we had a gap.
I start at the Juilliard on the music programme this autumn;
Zed's going to Columbia to study biochem, though, between
you and me, he's really more interested in getting a band
together. We had a few weeks free before beginning life in
New York.'

'So you'll be in the same city as Crystal and Xav—awesome!'

'I wanted them in California with us but we lost,' said
Phoenix, a pixyish brunette with multiple ear piercings.

'I'm afraid the time zone argument won. My parents are
back here now so I wanted to be able to get to the UK.' Sky
smiled apologetically at Phee.

'And the Juilliard is like only one of the best music colleges.
Congratulations for getting in! So how was Victor?' I asked
Summer.

She smiled mysteriously. 'Intriguing.'

'Oooh, do tell!' begged Angel.

Summer shrugged. 'I'm still thinking about it. My lips
are . . . ' She drew a finger across her mouth.

'And Yves?' I asked Angel before she had another curiosity
meltdown.

Angel put her hands over Phee's ears. 'So yummy. He has
this cute little serious frown when he tries to make me pay
attention.'

Phee pushed her palms away, eyes narrowing in mock-
anger. 'Do I have to defend my man here?' And she would if
called on—Phee had grown up streetwise.

'Totally,' agreed Angel. 'I'm so jealous that I'm in danger of turning into a Yves groupie. You'd better slap me sensible.' She offered a cheek that Phee obligingly patted. 'Thanks, that's better. Yves was great. I learned more in an hour with him than I have for a year trying things out on my own.'

'That's the idea,' said Sky.

'So what are you guys going to teach us?' I asked.

Phee and Sky exchanged a look.

'What to do when the worst happens,' said Phee. 'The things no one had a chance to tell Mia.'

I sat on the cabin steps and looped my arms round my knees. Paul had gone to Mia's funeral that morning and returned looking devastated. I cleared the lump in my throat. 'And . . . and what's that?'

She counted them off on her fingers. 'Use every weapon you have—even things you've never thought were weapons. Resist, but don't give them a reason to bump you off immediately. Never give up hope.'

'It also helps if you have a soulfinder backing you up,' added Sky. 'Zed made all the difference to me.'

'As Yves did for me.'

'Oh, don't you hate these "I've-found-my-guy" savants,' teased Angel, lightening the mood. 'You are reading way high on my Smugometer.'

We all smiled.

'Sorry, we'll dial it down for the rest of the week,' promised Phee.

'If I had a Benedict, I wouldn't,' I told her. 'If you've got it, flaunt it. Angel will survive the ordeal.'

'Only just,' she said darkly, prompting our laughter.

Chapter 9

I left camp at the end of August with a suntan and plenty of homework on how to build up my controls. In the excitement of body boarding and learning to windsurf in the afternoons, I tried to forget that the morning training sessions were made necessary by a serial killer preying on savants of our age—one who might strike again at any moment. Returning to our cabin and seeing the empty fourth bed provided a constant reminder of what really lay outside the cocoon of the camp. We left the bed clear of belongings and put a spray of wild flowers in a vase on the bedside, our tribute to Mia, who would have been a friend by the end of the week. We all hugged just that little bit tighter when we went our separate ways, urging each other to be careful.

Back for a brief few days at Devon Central—also known as my chaotic family home—I caught up with my sisters and brothers. I was touched to find that Gale, in particular, had missed me while I had been away from the family for most of the last year and much of the summer. I realized that she had become quite grown up now she was about to start her second year at secondary school and become someone with interesting views of her own. We promised to do a better job of keeping in contact. Junior school terrors Felicity and Peace were proving to be the opposite of their names, plotting mischief every moment our parents' backs were turned. Their latest triumph had been giving Tempest a Mohawk with his full delighted consent but, as he was only three, Mum had not been impressed. Sonny, five, was now noisily demanding one to match.

Leaving this dispute behind for the day, Mum and Dad drove me back to school. It was lovely to have them to myself for a few hours. Grandma was babysitting so if the little ones got too much of a handful, Tempest and Sunny would spend the day sleeping. The threat was usually enough to make them behave.

The atmosphere in the car was not as relaxed as it had been on other journeys. Fear had reached everyone in the savant community. As far as we knew, there had been no more abductions, but there was a pattern, according to Uriel: several victims in quick succession, then nothing. Waiting for a second strike in the UK was like waiting for a volcano to blow: you knew it was going to happen but no one could say when. Mum gave me a serious 'no talking to strangers' lecture in the car, repeating it as we unpacked my stuff. Dad stood by my little window in my study bedroom, toying with the bamboo-print curtains, bemused by the savant business but putting up with it as usual. When she had finished, I agreed with everything she said, promised to be on my guard, then walked into Dad's hug.

'Love you.' I buried my head against his sweater.

'Love you too.' He brushed his thumbs over my brows. His own were a rusty brown; Mum was the one who had given me my fair colouring. If my parents were shoes, he would be the comfy slipper, Mum the Italian sandal. 'I worry about you, all the way over here and this killer hunting young savants. Do what Mum says, OK?' His eyes lit up at a new thought. 'Or you could just keep away from other savants for a few years. Give the authorities time to catch him.'

'Keep away like you did with Mum, you mean?'

He cleared his throat, gaze going to my mother. 'Ah yes. I see what you're getting at. Some savants are irresistible.'

With a sweet smile, Mum joined in the hug.

'We'd best get back, Topaz, before the girls give your mother a Mohawk too,' said Dad, giving us both a final squeeze.

My mum laughed. 'Oh you!'

He jingled the car keys. 'She just might let them; you know how devoted she is to her grandchildren. Aren't I right, Misty?'

I grinned. 'You absolutely are.'

Mum's smile faded, hearing the truth from me. 'Quickly, Mark.'

My dad winked at me. 'Let's hope we don't run into traffic.'

School trundled back into its normal routines. I had chosen my AS levels after doing better than expected in my GCSE exams. The Fens careers adviser was big on preparing us all for the future and was busy dispatching us to visit most of the major universities before the summer. When I had had my interview with him last June, even he had been stumped what career to suggest. His best line had been, 'No, not diplomacy; not for you.'

Thanks, Mr Graves; I'd worked that out for myself.

After taking Summer and Angel's advice, I'd gone for geography, maths, chemistry and biology as there was less scope for me to make a spectacle of myself in those subjects than, say, an arts one. I wouldn't call myself a gifted scientist but it was better than writing essays where I had to express myself truthfully about books or plays that I really disliked or didn't get. For some reason that annoyed the examiners.

An interruption to business-as-usual came as November arrived. My school, co-hosting the final with the Cambridge University Debating Society, prepared to welcome the international teams. The plan was to hold a welcome reception for students and their teachers on Friday night in the Union building, which was like a mini-parliament—the perfect venue for trainee politicians, many of whom dreamed of making it into the real thing in their home countries. The debates would follow during the week at different locations around the city, with the final on the last Saturday. It turned out to be quite a big deal with the international education press interested in the outcome. I was surprised how many countries had sent finalists, including those where English was not the first language.

My school friends Hafsa, Tony, and Annalise had signed up to help at the reception; with a little arm twisting, they got me to join them. I was torn. I wanted to see Alex and his friends again despite the mixed feelings I had towards him, but I also didn't want to seem too eager. If he turned out to be the soulfinder of someone I knew—Summer sprang immediately to mind—I'd look pathetic. Yet there was still the slight chance he and I . . .

Dream on, Misty.

I put my name down, deciding I was used to pathetic. I was going to see the South Africans one way or another so at the very least I could arrange for Alex to meet Summer at the reception. That would settle the question and I could stop torturing myself with the thought that maybe they were destined for each other.

On Friday afternoon, Summer and Angel arrived on the train from London, a burst of familiar energy and anticipation like a shot of espresso on a dull morning. I corralled them in my room after herding Angel away from the stalls in the marketplace in the city centre. She has an irresistible attraction to anyone selling tie dye, beads and dingle-dangle sun-catchers. As one of the waitresses, I had been instructed to wear a black shirt and skirt to the reception. As I'd put their names down as guests, Summer and Angel got to dress up, using my bedroom to get ready.

'How's it been?' asked Summer, flicking the mascara wand over her lashes.

I wriggled into my skirt. 'Fine. Quiet, really.'

'No major Misty moments?'

'No, I've done well. No one is going to notice the ladder in my tights are they?' I pivoted to show the run high up on my thigh.

Summer made no answer.

'Oh well. I don't have another pair.' I slipped my feet into black pumps. 'The exercises Zed taught me have helped and I'm learning not to put myself in situations where I usually mess up.' Except for tonight. 'You?'

Summer didn't have a happy home life. She smiled bravely. 'Oh, same old, you know.'

We did know, and we also understood that she didn't want to talk about it now and spoil her evening. She only told us the tip of the iceberg of what went on and that was bad enough.

'Angel?'

Our friend was outlining her exotically slanted eyes with kohl. 'Nothing much to report. Total boy wasteland. I've had a few gigs locally. There's a band that likes bringing me in as female vocalist.' She grinned. 'They even pay me.'

'That's great. What are they called?'

'You wouldn't have heard of them. Seventh Edition.'

'Why that name?'

'Because their lead singer is a walking ego-in-jeans and falls out with so many of his band mates that they are now on their seventh line-up.' She paused to apply lipgloss. 'I doubt they'll make it before they reach their century.' She zipped up her cosmetics bag. 'How do I look?' She was wearing a silk swing dress in mint that went well with her honey blonde hair. The just-above-knee hemline flirted with her legs as she walked in her heels, doing the hand-on-hip catwalk slouch.

'That really works,' said Summer.

Angel raised a brow at me.

'I agree.'

'And what about me?' Summer stood up to show her jacquard fabric dress in white with blue flowers.

'Perfect.' I stood between my two friends, feeling very plain in my black on black ensemble. Summer met my gaze in the mirror. Both of us were nervous. It always was an outside chance, meeting a savant in the right age band, but the bubbles in the stomach, slight shiver came anyway.

Thank you, she said privately. *I know you wanted to keep him to yourself.*

How did you know that? I'd suspected that she had rumbled me, so I wasn't surprised.

Misty, I've been your friend now for years; I know when my friend is interested in a guy. You get this—sorry, but it's true—dreamy look in your eyes.

I already had reason to know that I did not have a poker face but it was distressing to find I was broadcasting my feelings so loudly. *Summer, if he's yours . . .*

He could be yours.

He could be no one's—in the room, I mean. If he's yours, I'll be really pleased for you both. At least, I'd try hard to make that true so I wasn't lying.

Same here. Summer picked up her clutch bag. 'Ready?'

The debate organizers had me handing around drinks on a tray, not the world's most glamorous assignment but at least it allowed me to mingle. The delegation from India had just arrived, looking amazing in their colourful saris and tunics. I chatted for a moment with one of them, finding out that they were from Amritsar. A couple of Cambridge Union students came over to welcome them so I moved on. Out of the corner of my eye I saw Angel in the middle of the American debate team, an all-male affair from Dallas. The Texans appeared thoroughly enchanted with their pocket-sized English girl with her swinging hair and expansive hand movements. Like a humming bird at a sugar feeder, Angel couldn't keep still. The Danish champions—four stunning girls—were being chatted up by my school team. Not a chance, boys. As yet, no South Africans.

Uriel entered, Tarryn on his arm. Wouldn't be long now.

I put down my tray to give them both a hug. 'Hi. How was the journey?'

'Great, thanks.' Tarryn squeezed my hand, telling me subtly that she hadn't forgotten my text. 'How've you been?'

'Quite good. Not done anything too embarrassing yet this term.' For honesty's sake I felt I had to add the 'yet'. This was exactly the kind of situation—lots of people making small talk stuffed full of insincerity—that I could ruin. 'Any progress on catching the killer, Uri?'

He took a drink from my tray. 'Some, but not enough. We've narrowed down the kind of gifts that attract our suspect. I'll tell you more about it when this is over. This isn't the place.'

'No, and I'm supposed to be serving. See you later then.' I whirled off with my tray, eyes sliding to the door every other second.

Angel and Summer found me restocking my drinks at the bar and offloading the empties.

'Aren't they here yet?' asked Angel.

There was a flurry of activity by the entrance as a new team signed in with Tony on reception. Tony, bless him, was a little chubby guy so they dwarfed him. 'They are now.'

Alex. My heart did a strange tumble-turn fall in my chest.

Three months had passed since I'd last seen him, but it felt longer. He was a stranger again, no smile in his expression. In contrast, his friends looked really pleased to be there: pinning on their name badges, joking with Tony, and glancing into the big room where the reception was being held. Michael saw me and waved.

'They're coming our way.' I felt a twit standing there with a tray so I rested it on the bar and turned to greet him. 'Hi, Michael. Lovely to see you again.'

He kissed my cheek. 'Howzit, Misty?'

'I'm good.'

'You're looking great as ever.'

Odd. That didn't register as a lie.

Hugo and Phil followed, though they both went for a hug that lifted my feet off the ground. They enjoyed my squeak of surprise. Alex glowered at his friends and sidetracked to Uriel.

'What's up with him?' I asked Hugo.

'Jealous.' Hugo grinned.

'Of what?'

Hugo just shrugged. 'Work it out.'

'I don't . . .' Angel nudged me, reminding me I didn't have time to ponder Alex's behaviour. 'Sorry, Hugo, these are my friends, Angel and Summer.'

'I think you mentioned them before when we went for the cable-car ride,' said Hugo, treating them both to his million-dollar smile. Or maybe that should be rand? 'I'm Hugo.'

'Full marks for memory,' said Summer.

My school friend Hafsa came over with her empty tray, her merry, round face alive with curiosity. She had changed her usually colourful hijab for a black one so at least she joined me in looking like a ninja warrior in our dark outfits.

'And this is Hafsa.' If I stood here any longer the entire waitressing staff would be clustered in our corner. Yep, I was right. Hot on Hafsa's heels was Annalise, her ginger bob a shade or two darker than Phil's colouring. 'And, what do you know, here comes Annalise.'

Hugo, Phil, and Michael smiled round at the cluster of English girls. I beckoned to Summer to get out from their midst, leaving the others to complete the introductions.

'Shall I take you to Alex?' I whispered, the glasses on my tray clanking as I pushed our way through the crowds.

She gulped. 'OK. Let's do it.'

As we approached, Tarryn looked up. *You want to try this now?* she asked doubtfully. Alex had his back to us and couldn't see us coming.

Summer here is the right age too, closer than me, and she's only here this weekend. I thought I should, you know . . .

OK, I'll remove Uri from the mix. She gave her soulfinder a single glance and he quickly finished what he was saying to Alex and made an excuse to move on. Alex stood alone for a second then swivelled round to locate his friends. Instead he found us.

'Hi.' My voice sounded rubbish, weedy and the opposite of sultry. 'Alex, how are you?'

'Nervous.' He took a Coke off my tray.

'Really?' Did he know the reason we had approached him? 'Why are you nervous?'

He gave me an odd look. 'The competition starts tomorrow.'

'Right. Yes. Of course it does.' Summer stepped on my toe. 'Alex, I'd like you to meet my friend, Summer.' How to broach the subject? 'I know her from youth camp.' He should be able to guess she was a savant from that.

He found a smile for her that had been lacking for me. 'Pleased to meet you, Summer.'

'And you.' Summer repositioned her clutch bag across her stomach, fingers playing with the clasp. 'Misty's told me a lot about you.'

He looked surprised. 'She has? What does she know about me?' My 'let's-be-blunt' zone must have affected him again as he clearly hadn't meant to include that last sentence.

This was too painful. I wasn't one to tiptoe around a subject; I went for the blurting-out-the-truth approach that was Misty standard.

'Alex, we didn't get to discuss this in Cape Town, but you know I'm a savant. Summer is too. Like you.'

He glanced around. Savants weren't supposed to go around announcing this in public places; our presence among the ordinary population was kept on a need-to-know basis. 'Misty, maybe we should . . . '

I had to get it off my chest or I would chicken out. 'There's more. I found out that your birthday is mid-December. That puts you in the possible range for both Summer and me.'

'You mean, you're the same age as me, not a year younger?'

'School years are different here. They run from September, not January.'

'I didn't think of that.' And from the look on his face the news was not welcome.

'So we thought, Summer and I, that we should just check that we aren't . . . ' My voice trailed away as a deep sense of unhappiness took over. I was going about this all wrong. The glasses on my tray began to shudder.

Summer sensed I was close to meltdown and took over. ' . . . Check that we aren't soulfinders. Obviously, we know it is a huge outside chance but there aren't so many opportunities to meet other savants our age from your country so, why not?'

Alex shrugged. 'Why not? Yes, let's try.' He took Summer's hand. 'Telepathy?'

She laughed, clearly feeling awkward that he had ignored me even though I was the one who had introduced us. Then again, I was carrying a tray. I looked for somewhere to leave it but a guest came over and dumped his empty on it; I had to juggle to keep hold. I looked down at the ice cubes left at the bottom of the drained glass. They had slumped into hard pellets marooned with a chewed lemon slice.

Silence—then laughter.

Summer patted her chest. I imagined her heart was pounding—mine certainly was. 'Oh well, it's nice meeting you, Alex, even so. Sorry to hurry you into it. Misty and I have had months to wind each other up after we found out so forgive us for dumping it on you the moment you arrived.'

'I don't blame you for trying.' His voice was warm now, maybe even relieved. 'It's like Prince Charming going round with the slipper.'

That made Summer laugh even louder. 'Not a flattering comparison but I know what you mean.'

He shook his head. 'I didn't intend to suggest you were . . . well, you know. The story is that he tries all the ladies in the land, not just Cinderella's family. In this case we're both the prince with our savant slipper waiting for the one that fits.' His eyes took on the same deep blue as her dress; it was a crime against perfection that they hadn't matched.

'So will you try with Misty now?' asked Summer, turning to smile encouragingly at me.

Her back was to him but I saw the run of emotions passing over his face. One of them definitely included distaste before he masked it with his company smile. 'I'd be happy to.'

Lie.

Tears rushed to my eyes. 'I think we should leave it for

now.' For ever, I was thinking. 'I've got a job to do and I'm a little outside his range in any case. Summer, you were always the better candidate.' I quickly took my tray over to a group of new arrivals, offloading the last of the soft drinks.

Misty, what happened? Summer asked softly as she excused my abrupt departure to Alex.

He doesn't want to try. You know he can't pretend around me. I nodded to a man who asked me to fetch him a beer, attempting to hide the fact I was having a telepathic conversation with someone else at the same time. 'Of course, sir.'

I dumped my empty tray on the bar and grabbed Annalise. 'Take a beer to that man with the red shirt, will you? I need a break.' I couldn't stay in the room. Summer or—worse—Angel would hunt me down. I'd have to tell them the truth—that I was really hurt—and then I'd probably cry and throw something at Alex. I had learned the hard way to avoid potential Misty moments and here was a big one brewing.

I retreated to the Ladies' and immediately caused an argument as one girl, who was reapplying lipgloss in the mirror, candidly confessed to her best friend that she had stolen ten pounds from her purse earlier that evening. I had to get out but I couldn't run far enough to escape myself. Yanking my coat off the peg in the cloakroom, I walked swiftly outside and took huddled refuge on a bench in the yard of the Round Church, a medieval building next door to the Union. It was a huge relief to get away from other savants. The green patch smelt of damp earth, yew leaves, and discarded fast food wrappers. Knees up, I rested my head, imagining myself a tombstone—cold and hard enough not to feel anything. It didn't work. What was so wrong with me that Alex didn't even want to try? I wasn't perfect like Summer, or confident and talented like Angel, but I wasn't totally awful, was I?

Someone sat down beside me. I peeked, half expecting to see one of the local winos with his cider bottle swinging like a club. It was Alex. I thought that, of the two, I'd prefer the drunk.

'Why did you run?' he asked.

I wiped my eyes hurriedly on my knees and looked up. His face was thrown into shadow by the headlights passing on the road just the other side of the churchyard wall. A few tiny flakes of snow began to fall, landing on the shoulders of his jacket and not melting. 'Do you know what my gift is?'

'Tarryn said you make people tell the truth.'

'That's not the whole story. I know when someone lies.'

'You do?' He rubbed his hands together and blew on them. His breath came in white puffs. I couldn't tell if he really was more interested in the fact that he was freezing, or that he wanted to disguise the fact that he was nervous.

'And I can't lie even if I want to. So I'll tell you that I saw what you felt about testing the link with me.'

He folded his arms, chin disappearing into the collar of his jacket.

'I get that I'm not the girl of your dreams, but what's so wrong about me that you don't even want to ask the question?' There: I'd said it.

'Wrong with *you*?' He turned so that one knee was half on the bench and he was facing me. 'You think this is about you? No, Misty. I'm sorry if you thought that.'

'Don't tell me: *it's not you, it's me.*'

He smiled wryly. 'It does sound a cliché but yes, it's my problem.'

He was telling the truth as he knew it. I wasn't sure that it helped. 'I think I know the rest: you're swimming along, being your usual charming self, and come near me, you sink. I'm the equivalent of cramp.'

He reached out and brushed a fingertip over the back of my hand, leaving a trail of sparks. 'I wish you weren't.' Truth.

'So it would be a disaster if we were soulfinders?'

'Ja . . . nee . . . maybe.' The guy looked away, confused enough to lapse into his native Afrikaans.

I had to laugh. 'Well, that answer covers all possibilities.'

His gaze came back to my face. 'I'm not used to being lost for words—and you make me stumble repeatedly. But it wouldn't change the fundamental truth, would it?'

'No, it wouldn't. Either we are, or we aren't.'

He took a firmer grip on my hand. 'So do you want to find out?'

Did I? 'My aunt says no soulfinders until you're eighteen. I kinda see the sense in that.'

'So do you want to find out?' His voice went a little deeper.

It was torture—but not knowing was worse. 'Yes.'

'Close your eyes then.'

I let my lids drift down—then quickly opened them again just in case he was having me on. He had shut his too. I could trust him. I closed mine and waited. There was someone at the door to my mind.

Hello, Misty.

Chapter 10

Alex.

I was flying. Sprinkled with fairy dust, I was no longer held down by gravity. If I opened my eyes, surely I'd be floating above the bench, soaring over the ancient round nave of the church and the brightly lit stained-glass windows. Traffic noise ebbed. There was only the rush of the wind and the needle-sharp constellations in the night sky ducking in and out of patchy clouds. But I wasn't alone. My hand was held tightly by my companion on this flight. Second star on the right and straight on till morning. The grip pulled me closer and became a hug: two strong arms around me, eliminating thoughts of being cold, of falling.

I opened my eyes. I was still on the bench, but now had my head against Alex's chest as we absorbed the truth.

My soulfinder. His voice was full of wonder. *I can't believe it.*

Yes. Linked by telepathy I was glimpsing what he wanted to show me of his private thoughts, part of the amazing new intimacy. His mind whirled like mine. He had taken the test with no expectation that this would be the outcome; he had done it to be kind to me—to heal my hurt. Yet the reason he had not anticipated this moment was nothing to do with me not being good enough.

It was because I have no one close to me, no one who is mine. Superman Alex was an act to protect himself. Rejected by his family, he had assumed from very young that would be the pattern of all his relationships. *I don't hope for this kind of luck.* His fingers skated over my leg which was half on his lap as I had somehow turned into his embrace while my eyes were closed. He found the ladder in my tights and tickled the gap that had grown huge during the evening. So much for nobody noticing. I could feel him smiling even if I hadn't yet worked up the courage to look at his face. I guess that hole gave him fair warning of the kind of imperfect person I was.

It was too much to take in.

Then don't. He had caught the beginning of my panic attack.

What are we going to do? I asked. I meant in the future, bringing our two very different lives together, overcoming my negative effect on his gift, but he chose to misunderstand me.

'I think the best plan,' he had reverted to speaking aloud, 'is to kiss you. That way you won't have time to panic.'

That made me look up. His eyes were bright with exhilaration at our discovery. He was also teasing me.

I had to check. 'You *want* to kiss me?'

He rolled his eyes, showing a humorous side I hadn't yet glimpsed, appealing to the heavens to help him with his idiotic soulfinder. 'Give me strength. Misty, don't you know when a guy has been dying to kiss you for months?'

Clearly not. 'You mean you wanted to kiss me in Cape Town?'

'Yes, in Cape Town, and with those ridiculous penguins, and on the top of Table Mountain. Don't you know how kissable you are?'

I quickly licked my lips, worrying that they might be too

dry and cold. 'But I thought you wanted to dump a bucket of ice over my head when I beat you at table tennis.'

His mouth quirked charmingly. 'That too. I never claimed I was consistent. You infuriate and attract me in equal parts.' He leaned forward and kissed the end of my nose. 'By the way, I demand a rematch.'

'Only if you're ready for me to thrash you again.'

'I'm ready for you this time; I won't be so easy to beat.'

I was still thinking through the 'kissable' comment. He was telling the truth but it didn't chime with my impressions of our encounters in South Africa. 'But at the beach, you walked away from me.'

He sighed, knowing that the kiss had been put back a while so we could sort this out. 'I walked away from the family I didn't have. You told me I didn't have it in me understand yours.'

I replayed the conversation, seeing how he might have thought that if he was particularly sensitive. 'I didn't mean it as an insult! I meant we are a bunch of loonies, beyond anyone normal's comprehension. I was putting you in normal camp, not mocking you.'

His palm had settled on my hip, warmth seeping through the layers of coat and skirt. 'I've always wanted to be part of that kind of crazy gang, more than anything. All the savants I've met have that; I felt a freak of nature being alone.'

I may be incompatible software as far as his gift went, but I could at least give him his heart's desire because I came from the box fully charged with family: Mum, Dad, sisters and brothers, grandparents, uncles and aunts galore. 'Welcome to mine then. They will be embarrassingly delighted to have you.'

Alex moved his hands to frame my face, thumbs brushing stray curls off my cheeks. Kiss back on the agenda.

'My stupid hair; it's always in the way.' I hurried to bundle it back but he stopped me.

'Leave it. I love your wayward hair. Gorgeous colour—streaks of sunshine. It's like you.' He twisted a curl round a finger, fascinated by how it clung.

'I'm not sure I believe you because you told your friends . . . '

'I know what I told my friends. I could hardly admit to them that I wanted to bury my hands in your hair.' His actions matched his words.

'So, what, you were like the little boy who flings frogspawn at a girl to show he likes her?'

He laughed at the picture. 'Not entirely. See, I didn't know my girl was listening. I was playing down my attraction to you—and you did look wilder than normal that evening. Super cute. It was very funny.'

'And my presence forced you into speaking a truth but you slanted it for your audience.'

He nodded. 'You blow me off course; you can't help it. I meant to be cool and it came out cruel.'

Was I going to let him off? 'But what about all that "she's the last girl I'd date" stuff?'

'Ah.' I'd caught him out. 'You can't expect me to say in front of my big-mouth friends that you're *lekker*.'

'*Lekker*?'

'Beautiful.'

From the slant of his smile I guessed that wasn't quite the right translation but I decided to look it up later.

'They've been trying to get me to admit that I had a thing for you with me acting so different around you. But you saw how they were when you made me confess that I'd had a crush on Miss Coetzee; they would've been really annoying for weeks if I'd even hinted I liked you.'

A little alarm bell rang that he had felt forced. 'That's the only reason?'

'You're not letting me duck this one?'

'What you said about me embarrassing you haunted me for months.'

He took my right hand to his mouth and kissed the fingers. 'I'm sorry. I can't get away with half-truths around you, can I? It's going to take some getting used to. I guess the real reason was because you seemed too young and sweet for me and I became a fool around you. As I'm waiting for my soulfinder, I only date girls who don't turn me into an idiot.'

'Only *dated* girls. Past tense.'

'Yes, past tense.' He brushed a snowflake from my cheek. 'And I'm well past tense waiting to kiss you. Am I done explaining myself?'

I nodded. Oh lord, it was more difficult now he had announced his intention. I'd never kissed a boy, not properly. Until now it had always been short-lived experiments in dark corners of parties, which I hadn't really liked. Something had always gone a bit wrong, usually me laughing nervously and annoying my partner. No boy had said he had had his socks blown off kissing me so I considered myself a failure at it.

'What do I do?' I asked.

'I was hoping you'd just enjoy it.' He smiled self-deprecatingly. 'It's not a test.' He closed the gap and put his lips to mine. This was no clumsy mashing of mouths and teeth; no desire to laugh; it was a sweet exploration of soft textures and warmth. He shifted our positions so that I was leaning back, his face above mine. One firm hand supported me between the shoulder blades while the other caressed my hair, neck, even my ear. I hadn't realized how sensitive these places could be; it was as though he was switching them all on to hyperawareness with every pass of his fingers. It was a hello of a kiss, a this-is-what-we-can-be-together promise. His embrace felt so strong, so right, as he guided me through the moves without hesitation or awkwardness. I wanted it to go on for ever; it made so much more sense than talking; but finally he broke away. We held each other's gaze as gently as we had kissed.

'Did I do it right?' I whispered. Stupid! What did I expect him to say if I were a disappointment to him?

'You did it right,' he confirmed. Then endearingly he added, 'Did I?'

'Oh yes.'

'I'm pleased. I've never kissed my soulfinder before.'

Fine flakes of snow fell steadily. I could no longer ignore that my holed tights were doing an inadequate job of keeping me warm and that Alex had to be freezing having come from a South African summer. 'Shall we go in?'

He pulled me to his side, sharing body heat. 'You've just found your soulfinder and you want to go back in there so you can stand with a tray all evening?'

'No—I really don't.'

'Not to mention answering all the questions your friends will have for you—and Uriel—and Miss Coetzee.'

'Oh no.' I shivered. They would go crazy when they heard and it would be so cringeworthy.

'Good. I vote we leave a message that we're not returning to the party and go for a walk together.'

'In the snow?' I looked down at my shallow-heeled pumps.

'Yes, in the snow.'

'That's insane.'

'Yes, it is.'

'Let's do it.' Standing up, I stamped my feet to get the blood flowing. *Hey, Summer, can you and Angel cover for me. I'm going for a walk with Alex.*

She was onto me like a shot. *Going for a walk with Alex!*

What are you now: a parrot?

So is he . . . ?

Yes.

A telepathic shriek is even more deafening than the audible version. *I knew it!*

No, you didn't.

Well, I hoped. I can't wait to tell Angel.

That was a good plan. The two of them could get over the initial most flustering phase of celebration before they met us. *Can you tell Alex's team mates he'll see them later?*

Will do. Oh Misty, it's just so right. I can't tell you how much it means to me!

Thanks, Summer. Just as she had promised, she was thrilled for us both. I can't say I would have been so noble if fate had been the other way round, even with my best efforts, but then it had been my soulfinder with whom I had been trying to set her up. Maybe I had known . . . ?

Nah. I was just not such a nice person. I would have been green with envy. *See you later then, Summer.*

Don't hurry back; I've got it covered this end. Summer ended the link.

'All done. We are free to go.'

Alex brushed the snow off my shoulders. 'Show me your city, Misty.' I loved the way my name rolled off his tongue in his accent, giving the 't' a little kick.

Cambridge is a beautiful place: quaint streets, old colleges built like castles or cathedrals. The city was full of students, the roads busy with other young people like us out for the night; we were hardly noticed as we moved among them. A busker played a violin under the cover of a cafe awning. A hen party in riotous white and pink clipped past on the scent of some free drinks. Cyclists wound through the throng, ringing their bells with little reaction from the slow walkers in the middle of the carriageway.

'Is there somewhere quieter?' asked Alex. Neither of us wanted a party atmosphere.

'Yes, if the gates are still open. The paths through the colleges onto the Backs—that's the riverbank—are usually locked at night.'

Alex steered me out of the path of a cyclist with no lights. 'That won't be a problem.'

He wasn't lying. 'You sure?'

'Yes. You don't know everything about me, Misty.'

'Actually, I know next to nothing: it's pretty scary.'

'Same for me about you.' He took a woollen hat out of his jacket pocket and pulled it down over my cold ears. 'You know my gift works—present company excluded—as a kind of charm?'

'Yes, Tarryn explained.' Again, there was that issue which we hadn't yet faced; it clearly worried him as he kept mentioning it. Should I say something? Bring it out into the open? Alex, however, took the conversation off in another direction.

'It's not just people. I can charm locks too—and many other things.'

That news distracted me from my worries. I'd never heard of a gift like this before. 'How does that connect?'

He linked his hand with mine. I had gloves in my pocket but much preferred to feel his touch on my skin. 'I think I persuade them into the state I want them to be. If it's a person, I convince them my argument is right; if it's a locked door, I persuade it that it really wants to be open.'

'That's . . . amazing and a recipe for you to be a master criminal.'

'I admit there've been times when I've been tempted.' A new thought struck him. 'Just as well I'm linked to someone who would make me confess—no itch to try my hand at a heist if I know I'll just spill all to the police later when questioned.'

'At least I'm good for something.'

'I expect you, Misty, are good for everything.'

That wasn't quite a truth but neither did it register as a lie. Sometimes I wished I could switch off my gift and just allow myself to enjoy flattery without dissecting it. 'It's sweet of you to say so.'

We reached the gates of Clare College. Kings and Trinity may be more famous, but I always thought Clare was the real gem of the colleges on the Backs. Blending with a party of students, we got past the porters at the main entrance, crossed the quad of pale stone buildings and approached the wrought iron gates guarding the bridge over the Cam to the gardens. This had a key code.

I stood at Alex's shoulder trying to see what he was going to do.

'Maybe you'd better stand back,' he warned.

'Oh yes. Sorry.' We hadn't tested how close I needed to be to him to cancel his gift. I walked about twenty metres away. When I turned, he had the gate open.

'Wow, that was quick! Ocean's Eleven could do with you on the team.'

He gave me a mischievous little smile that even George Clooney could not beat. 'Those guys? Misty, I wouldn't need ten partners to break into a casino. I could do it myself.' And I could just see it. He could take the manager aside and persuade him that it was a really great idea to hand over the cash and then forget all about him.

Linking arms with my Ocean's One, we slipped through the gate and walked onto the bridge.

'This is breathtaking.' Alex stood in the centre, taking in the beauty of the gardens and colleges of Cambridge neatly outlined in snow. 'I love how old everything is here.'

'We've got plenty of old, it's true.' I looked over the broad stone parapet, thinking of the generations of students who had stood here in their black robes and mortar board caps. The river was a bolt of inky silk constantly unrolling. On either side, the low banks were luminous with their fresh covering of white. I could even make out the reeds and grasses sagging under the weight of the snow, bowed like thousands of tailors sewing away at the seams of the water. The pinnacles of King's College chapel razored the sky with their blades. Each tree and bush was an impossibly intricate lacework of twigs. The bridge we stood on, a hinged ruler over the river, had pale grey stone balls marking the angles of the arch. The snow had settled on the spheres like very silly toupees on display in the window of some eighteenth-century wigmaker.

'Pretty, isn't it?' I didn't add that I also thought it intensely romantic. It was inspired of Alex to suggest we stayed away from the party.

He leaned beside me, small finger on his right hand touching my left. I wished I could take a photo to keep the memory: his square-nailed strong fingers and my small oval-shaped ones resting lightly on newly fallen snow. His and hers.

'Very pretty.' He was so close I could feel the warmth of his breath on my cheek. 'But I like the view this way even better.' His head was turned towards me.

I moved to face him. 'You know, I was thinking just the same thing.' Though I was trying to sound as confident of my moves as he was, there was a tight knot in my chest—excitement but so much fear that I was going to mess up. 'Sorry, but it's so much to take in, Alex. You—me—soulfinders. I think I'm having a little trouble just breathing.'

'Let me help you with that.' He brought his forehead to mine, cool hand cupping my neck. 'Breathe with me.' We took a couple of breaths together. 'Better?'

I nodded.

'Part two of your relaxation therapy.' He pulled me into another kiss. We were both smiling at each other. I went on tiptoes to meet his lips; he leaned down to me. My hands fluttered then rested on his shoulders, his settled on my hips. This time was even better as I was less anxious. Very quickly I would be addicted to his taste and scent. I was determined to keep hold of the details, learn him as I knew myself. His aftershave had traces of spice and sandalwood, but there was also something under that which was purely him. It spoke to my body, waking me up, tuning me into my soulfinder on a level much deeper than conscious thought. Slowly we were working our way to harmony.

His mouth was impossibly soft. It was not just charming words that came from it; every kiss cast its spell. There was no gift being exerted persuading me he was good at this—he didn't dare risk it near me. I was thankful because that would have felt fake. It had to be just innate talent.

We broke apart.

I laughed, a little nervously. 'Wow. I am one lucky girl.'

'And I am one happy guy.' He brushed the back of his fingers against my cheek.

We walked slowly back to the party through the silent snowy gardens along the river. That night, it was hard to believe that anything could upset the bond we had so quickly established.

Chapter 11

'So, Alex, what do you think makes a good debater?'

That question came from a man on the front row. I sat at the back of the Cambridge Union debating chamber as far away from Alex as possible as the South African team fielded the questions from the small group of specialist journalists gathered to interview them. This year's competition had attracted more interest than usual because three countries had coincidentally elected presidents or prime ministers who had been former winners of the International Debate Team Cup.

'The first thing you need is an understanding of the subject.' Alex leaned a little closer to the microphone, fingers touching lightly in front of him as if dancing through the words. 'By that I mean you have to know the different opinions people hold so you can argue effectively and win them round, like a cook selecting the right spices to appeal to a diner's taste buds.'

Alex was so gorgeous when he was earnest. Had anyone else noticed? I thought the thirty-something reporter from the *Times Educational Supplement* had, because she was doing that coy flick-of-the-hair-with-a-pencil thing. Hands off, I thought grumpily, catching a glimpse of my future of predatory females driving me nuts.

'Picking up on my colleague's question,' she said in a sultry tone worthy of a late-night radio announcer, 'I think there's more to it than that. Winners aren't just about intellect. What do your team mates think?'

'Obviously, charisma wins half the battle—just look at us,' Hugo said, spreading his arms as if to say 'what's not to like?' about his own personal appeal.

She gave an annoying little laugh. 'I get your point.'

The shifty-looking man who had asked the original question spoke up again, pencil making a rapid tapping on his pad. 'Apart from the usual charisma, I was interested to find out if Alex here thought any special powers were necessary?'

Tarryn, who was sitting quietly at the side of the news conference, turned her head sharply in the direction of the questioner. She had also caught the peculiar emphasis the guy had placed on 'special powers'.

Is he a savant? I asked her.

Not to my knowledge.

I tried to make out his face but I was sitting in the wrong place. All I could glimpse was his short black hair liberally sprinkled with grey, a large right ear, a ship's prow of a nose. He was wearing a creased linen blazer and had a spiral bound notebook resting on his raised knee.

Alex paused before answering, probably double-checking my truth influence wasn't poised to warp what he said into a confession of his gift. 'I guess that all of us who have got as far as the international final must have something special.' He looked to his team mates for support.

'Ja, I met the Danish team last night at the reception and I tell you they make for one powerful combination,' joked Phil, sweetly blushing a little as he said it.

Who is that guy? I asked Tarryn. The man hadn't taken his eyes off Alex even though others were speaking.

I think he's with the Los Angeles Courier. *I can't remember his name though he did tell me last night. He made a point of introducing himself and asked where Alex was as he'd met the other boys and noticed he was missing.*

Because Alex was out with me. The best night of my life.

I didn't think anything of it but now . . .

Yeah, he feels creepy.

And far too interested in Alex.

Our mutual resolution to protect him did not need mentioning: it just was.

At the end, you go to Alex, get him away; I'll distract the reporter, said Tarryn.

My pleasure.

I could feel her smile. Tarryn and Uriel had been great when we broke the news. They had shown their heartfelt delight but not the mortifying explosion of oh-my-god-I'm-so-excited Angel when she saw us come back in from our walk together. She had acted like a match had been dropped in her, the box of firecrackers. Fortunately, the reception was so packed and noisy by then that only about half the room had heard her. Angel doesn't do discretion.

The conference broke up after two more questions. Journalists headed off to enjoy the buffet lunch laid out in the Union library; only creepy guy and foxy lady lingered. I suppose I should thank the woman because she stopped the Los Angeles reporter cornering Alex by getting in there first.

'So, Alex,' I heard her saying as I approached, 'I was hoping to persuade you to let me do a profile piece on you. My colleagues in the Johannesburg office heard you in the final there and said you were amazingly talented—quite the one to watch. What do you think? Can I tempt you?'

Alex raised his gaze over her shoulder to meet my glower. 'It is very kind of you to think of me, but I'm a team player. I don't want to be interviewed separately from my friends.'

I had to hand it to her: she got A for persistence. 'That's very sweet of you, Alex, but I'm sure they won't mind. After all, they must also admire you, knowing how you have succeeded against the odds.'

Alex's expression gave away his unease that she knew something of his story. He probably wished me to Jericho so he could persuade her out of this idea.

'You see, like any good journalist, I've been doing some digging before I approached you and I've got to say, being advanced a year and still coming out top of your peer group at one of your country's best schools, and all that after such a rough start, is a brilliant testimony to your intelligence and other personal qualities.'

Past time I rescued him.

'Hi, Alex!' I said breezily, pushing past her and snagging his arm. 'Sorry, I kept you waiting but I'm ready now to show you round Cambridge.' Subtext: back off, cougar woman, with your double agenda of sweet-talking *and* using my guy to fill your newspaper column.

Alex bent down to kiss me in greeting. 'Hey, Misty. Sure. Let's go.' *Thanks for the rescue.* Then, over his shoulder: 'I appreciate you thinking of me, but that's really not my kind of thing.'

We escaped, walking quickly past Tarryn, who had collared the man from Los Angeles. He tried to break away but she kept on talking animatedly about South Africa's education policies. His eyes followed Alex as we passed; they were filled with an expression that read to me as equal parts frustration and cunning.

'Did you notice the creepy reporter?' I asked Alex.

'Hard to miss him. He came up to me at the beginning. Says

his name is Eli Davis. He's doing an article on the American president's education and has an agenda about these competitions training privileged young kids to manipulate others, and ultimately the American voter. Not sure why a South African should be of any interest to him.'

We joined the queue at the buffet.

'Is that his only interest? I thought his last question was really pointing at . . . well . . . your gift.'

'I got that too.' Alex took a quick glance round the library, its acres of shelves stocked with matching bound volumes. Small knots of debaters, teachers, and press were deep in conversation. 'I'd like to see what Miss Coetzee and Uriel think but now's not the time. And we've got our first debate this afternoon.'

'I'm looking forward to it.' I'd already memorized his schedule. It was a knockout competition with only the winners going through to the next round. His team was up against the Texans on the motion 'This house believes that the public is safer with strict gun controls'. That should make for a lively debate considering the gun culture in both home countries; the Texans had been given the task of speaking for the motion.

Alex cleared his throat. 'Er, Misty, would you mind sitting this one out?'

'Out?'

'I mean outside the room.'

'Oh.'

'You know you're like kryptonite to my gift and I'm going to have to lie convincingly to defeat the motion. You might shoot me down mid-argument by mistake. Miss Coetzee suggested that we play safe.'

'But it's taking place at my school.'

He looked away over my head. 'Uriel says you're welcome to visit him in his college rooms.'

I understood. Of course I did. 'I see. OK.'

'Thanks.'

I pushed aside my disappointment and changed subject. 'I really don't like that journalist so don't, you know, get trapped on your own with him or something if I'm not there.'

I could hear Alex thinking 'What am I? Five?' but he bore with it because it was me worrying. 'I won't. Miss Coetzee has me on a strict "no meeting strangers" regime.'

'She sounds like my mum.' I decorated my plate with sandwiches and fresh fruit slices. Little curls of melon sat with arcs of pineapple and knobbly hills of grapes so I built a smiley face of food as I transferred my choices. 'She's freaking out about this savant killer.'

He stole a grape-nose from my work of art. 'So you'll take care too?'

'Yes, but I'm not in the public eye like you. I'm not so noticeable.'

He replaced the nose he had nabbed with a huge triangle of watermelon. 'I don't know about that. I can't stop noticing you.'

'That's because you are doomed by fate to find me fascinating. Believe me, you're in a minority.'

'Finished your fruit sculpture?

'Yes. Shall we sit over there?' I pointed to a sunny spot that a party had just vacated.

Angel and Summer joined our table by the bay window between bookshelves.

'Hi Misty, hi Alex,' said Angel gleefully.

'Oh lord, here we go,' I groaned. 'Are you going to behave? We're surrounded by normal people here.'

'Not a chance.' She picked up a crisp. 'Look at that: heart-shaped. You guys can have it.' She put it on my plate. It was typical of her to assume we'd fallen instantly in love but I would have to take her aside and explain that deep, bottom-of-the-soul attachment didn't feel quite the same as love, not at this stage when we'd hardly had a chance to get to know each other. My emotions were churning away, and I guess Alex's were too, but I did not recognize the shapes into which they were separating.

I wondered what it was like for other girls when they first met their soulfinder. Crystal had told me she hadn't recognized Xav for a long time, and then a crisis had struck, forcing them to discover their link. When the dust settled, they saw that they'd worked through many of their issues on the fly. It was almost worse having time to think. I had ten days to make a start before Alex went home, and most of those I had to be at school. Not the most romantic of venues.

I don't know: I kinda like the idea of sitting behind you in class and passing notes. I hadn't shut him out and Alex had caught the tail end of my thoughts.

You don't need to pass notes; we've got telepathy, I reminded him.

That's not the same. It's the 'will the teacher catch us out?' jeopardy that adds to the experience. He projected a cartoon picture of him passing me a folded piece of paper under the desk as the teacher walked past; in the next frame was the single word 'Busted!'

Don't worry, I'd wait for you if the teacher kept you behind.

And here was I was hoping you'd do detention with me.

Our school didn't do detention for sixth formers—we were supposed to be beyond that—but it was a tempting thought. *Any time.*

I left Summer and Angel with strict instructions to tweet the debate telepathically to me while I made myself scarce in Uriel's rooms in Trinity College. As I arrived he was just finishing a meeting with his Cambridge research partner, Dr Surecross. We had met a couple of times recently. The doctor was a harried-looking man in his late fifties, short and stout like a bag of flour put next to the spaghetti packet of Uriel. I had the impression that if I tapped Dr Surecross a puff of white dust would billow from his collar and sleeves. He nodded to me in passing and scurried off to his laboratory.

'Hey, Misty, come in.' Uriel stood back to let me enter.

'Nice digs.' He had been given a set of rooms overlooking the Great Court with its ornate fountain surrounded by four green mini-lawns. The expanse was intersected by paths and edged by pale stone buildings, pierced with many windows. Students moved at tangents across the square, never setting foot on the grass, each keeping to their own trajectory like comets passing across our patch of sky.

'What can I get you? Tea?'

'Coffee, thanks.'

He picked up a jar of the dried stuff. 'This is all I've got. You OK with that?'

'Fine.' I slumped down in a saggy armchair. The kettle rumbled to the boil.

'So how does it feel, Miss Soulfinder?' he asked, handing me a mug. A couple of undissolved grains swirled on the top like moles on mocha-coloured skin.

'Terrifying.'

He took the chair opposite. 'I can relate to that.'

I knew I could talk to him; he was the most approachable of the Benedict brothers, at least as far as I was concerned. I'd been present at the most memorable night of his life so that had made us close; he felt like the older brother I didn't have. 'Is it OK, Uri, that I keep thinking I'm going to mess up?'

'So do I. All the time.' He sipped his drink. 'But you have to remember your soulfinder is probably thinking the same thing.'

'But yours is Tarryn; she already told me she feels she has a flaw—you know, her gift?'

Uriel frowned slightly, thoughts turned inward. 'Yeah, that is an issue for her. We're working on it.'

'But I'm linked to Mr Perfect-and-Charming. You can't possibly call what Alex does a flaw: it's awesome and really useful.'

'It could be annoying,' suggested Uriel, leaning back, balancing the mug on the broad, worn arm of the chair.

'But it isn't, is it, because he mixes in this self-deprecatory thing. Haven't you noticed?'

Uriel made that half-laughing 'humph!' sound of recognition. 'I must have because I still like the guy.'

I put my cup on a pile of papers then rested my head back on the chair, eyes closed. Some things are easier to say without meeting another person's gaze. 'It's my gift that's the problem. Remember I told you when we were at Table Mountain that I figured out that I take Alex to a bad place, preventing him using his gift? That hasn't stopped—you know that's why I'm here and not at the debate.' I swallowed against the lump in my throat. 'Have you ever heard of a soulfinder making things worse for their partner? You see, I thought we were supposed to build each other up?'

'That's the theory—and I've seen it work that way in practice in my family.' I could hear him fumbling with a packet. 'Here, have a cookie.'

I opened my eyes to find a packet of chocolate chip biscuits under my nose. 'Thanks. I hope the application of chocolate to the problem isn't a sign that you think me beyond saving?'

'I need no excuse to offer cookies.' He helped himself to one. 'You mustn't panic, Misty. How long have you had to sort this out? Not even a full day. You really don't know very much about each other so can't possibly know how to mesh your gifts. You like Alex, don't you?'

'Yes, very much. He just scares me, being so . . . so Alex about everything. I thought my first proper relationship would be like taking a driving test—you know, a chance to have another go if I messed up—but I seem to have gone straight to the starting grid of the Grand Prix, no room for driver error.'

He laughed at my image. 'Just give it time. You might not like to hear this but from my perspective you are so young, Misty, just finding your way, so don't expect your relationships to be fixed any more than your own character is.'

'I don't mind hearing that at all; it's terrifying having to make all these big decisions now when I haven't even left school. I mean, what do I know about anything?'

'More than you think. I've never met anyone who puts herself down so consistently. You think you don't match Alex: that he's talented, cool, good-looking—the top-of-its-class racing car.'

'Well, he is!'

'And he will think the same about you, I'm sure of it.'

I laughed at that. 'Uriel, I am not cool. Compared to him, I'm the entrant for the demolition derby.'

He grinned, conceding the point. 'OK, quirky. You have a quirky charm of your own.'

His phone rang and he got up to take the call at his desk. Encouraged by the kind things he had said, I got out my homework and began to work on the maths problems I'd been set. As I chewed the end of my pencil, I listened into the 'tweet' updates Angel was sending me. It was almost as good as being there as she was very vivid in her description of the participants. One guy she described as having a habit of moving his head like a nodding-donkey oil well—fitting as he came from Texas.

How is Alex doing?

Your guy is amazing. Every time he gets up, it's like a special charge runs through the crowd. You sure he's not cheating and using his gift?

No. Tarryn explained it like a kind of lingering effect. An afterglow.

Or the guy is just naturally talented so his gift is overkill.

There is that possibility. I sent her the impression of a smile but the full truth was that I felt sad being excluded, like the only kid in the class left off a birthday invitation list. *Let me know if he wins.*

When he wins, you mean.

Uriel finished his call. 'That was Victor. He says congratulations, by the way.'

'Oh.' I'd not anticipated how the news would spread so fast, how many such messages I could expect from friends and family. I hadn't even yet changed my Facebook status.

Uriel returned to his chair and drained his coffee. 'Misty, if you've got a moment, I wanted to talk to you about this killer we're hunting.'

I put maths aside. 'Go ahead.'

'Victor has been looking into the similarities between victims and put more detail on the profile we'd already outlined. Our perp goes for isolated savants, usually those with no family or new to our world. He likes gifts that influence others, maybe with a chance to generate wealth for himself. Three of the five American savants he killed had predictive abilities; we think he used them to buy stocks and shares. The Australian victim, Jody Gaspard, could find natural resources by scanning geological maps. I could give you more examples.'

I had a horrid feeling where he was going with this.

'Gender doesn't seem to matter but his target age is fourteen to eighteen. Victor has come up with something new: he thinks the killer chooses that age range so he can take them to places where adults go—pubs, clubs, casinos. He is gathering assets—money, stocks, land. All of his victims have looked mature for their age. He is following a plan that makes sense to him.'

'You think Alex fits the profile.'

'Yes. So does Summer—and I guess you could think of a few others in your circle. Can you spread the word—tip them off that they have to be particularly alert? It's been a while since the last abduction and I'm thinking our guy will be getting twitchy, ready for his next fix.'

'Fix?'

'With repeat offenders like this, it isn't impulse, it's a carefully planned feeding of his habit of taking life. The whole process gives him a rush and he won't stop until we stop him. I'd be very surprised if he doesn't strike very soon either here or somewhere close—mainland Europe or Ireland. That's his pattern.'

I put my feet up on the seat, hugging my knees. The split in my jeans had progressed to the point where there was more skin than denim showing on my left kneecap, a few frail white threads left behind which I plucked nervously. 'I really hope you catch him soon. I hate this feeling of having to keep looking over my shoulder.'

'I know.'

'Did Tarryn tell you about the slimy guy at the news conference?'

'Yes. Victor's checking his background.'

'Good. Will told me to listen to my instinct about strangers and mine is screaming that the reporter is not here for the debate competition.'

'Interesting. I'll see if I can put someone on him.' He fired off a quick text. 'Thanks, Misty, that's really helpful.'

Chapter 12

Alex's team won. Of course. They went out immediately after-wards with the Texans to commiserate with the losers so I didn't see Alex again until evening. By then my mum and dad, to whom I had broken the news about my soulfinder the night before, had arrived in a flurry of concerned parenting. It wasn't exactly a relaxing night off for us both in prospect.

Dad booked a table for our get-together where they were staying. I had managed to persuade them to meet us there so at least I could have the walk over the river to the Old Mill Hotel in which to prepare Alex for the grilling that was in store. It felt a little like the walk into an examination hall for a paper that I hadn't revised. I didn't know how they would react. Dad was usually laid back but Mum could be unpredictable.

Alex scooped me up when he saw me waiting for him on the low wall outside King's College, hugging me tight. 'Hi! How was your afternoon?' His face was still reflecting his astonish-ment that we'd found each other, a soft glow in his expression as he looked at me. We didn't quite have our moves sorted. Should we kiss? By silent agreement, we went for playful.

'It was no fun without you,' I admitted.

He spun me round once and put me back down. I added effortless strength to the things I liked about Alex. 'Ready to face the lions?'

'You feel it too?'

'I'm not stupid, Misty. I'd be running for the hills if I could avoid it.'

'Hate to break it to you but you're in the wrong city for hills.'

'Do you think they'll like me?'

I started walking and he fell in step. 'How can they not? I just hope you like them. You've met my Auntie Opal. Mum is her big sister. They're pretty alike in that they both can be intense.'

Alex was taking in all this family dynamic stuff with a bemused smile. 'What's her gift?'

'Seeing through things.'

'Like?'

This was the embarrassing bit. 'Walls and so on.'

Alex was quick to grasp the connotations. 'It's the "so on" I'm worried about.' He peered down the front of his jacket. 'Phew, clean on this morning. She sounds scary.'

'Tell me about it. But she has her gift under strict control. You don't have to worry about her peeking.' Not unless she employed the motherly trump card of 'but I was so worried about you!' which she occasionally applied to breaches of my privacy. He didn't need to know that.

'And your dad, the non-savant?' Alex threaded his fingers through mine, letting our arms swing loosely between us. We were following a parallel path to the one we had taken the night before, crossing the river by the punts near the Fen Causeway road bridge. With few tourists up for a chilly river excursion, the empty, flat-bottomed boats huddled together at their moorings like a huge wooden piano keyboard. If you jumped from one to another, would they play a tune? I mused.

'You've gone very quiet,' said Alex. 'What are you thinking about?'

'Sorry. I got distracted.' I wasn't quite ready to share my oddness with him, not when I was still in the trying-to-impress phase.

'You were going to tell me about your non-savant dad.'

'I'm not sure he'd like you to call him that. After all, most people out there aren't savants.' I gestured to the crowds crossing the bridge, the cars whizzing by as they avoided the city centre—life in full flood on a Saturday evening.

He squeezed my knuckles lightly with his fingers, a gesture of understanding. 'You're right. What about the *normal* one in your family?'

I smiled at that. 'He works for a telecommunications firm in London. He's patient with the rest of us but we have to remember not to let him feel left out. I think he often does.'

'OK. I see. So he might be easily offended on that subject. Does he mind about soulfinders? It could be intimidating for him realizing that your mum, you know . . .'

'Luckily he's very secure about who he is and Mum is very level-headed. She won't go dashing off on a whim to find her match when she knows the value of the one she has at home.' At least I hoped so. No child could control what happened in their parents' marriage. I think Dad just didn't realize the strength of the bond my mum had given up for him; if he did, he might be more concerned. What's that old saying? Ignorance is bliss? In this case it was true. I would have to be careful what I said about my own feelings tonight in case it put pressure on Mum and him.

'Nerves are getting worse.' Alex rolled his shoulders as we approached the bright lights of the hotel. He was wearing his chocolate leather jacket tightly fastened against the cold. I paused at the door of the restaurant to fulfil a dream.

'What are you doing?' Alex looked down at my fingers.

'Do you know how tempting these zips are?' I did up the breast pockets, then slid them open again.

'You crazy girl? They're just zips.'

I tapped his chest. 'On this jacket, worn by this boy, they are pure temptation and I couldn't resist. I've been thinking of doing that since I first saw you in it.'

His smile broadened and he moved a step closer. 'Have you now?' His voice had dropped into dangerous, can't-wait-to-get-you-alone territory. He put his mouth to my earlobe and nuzzled. 'Do you want to hear some of my thoughts about what I'd like to do to you?'

I couldn't get away with a lie. 'Yes.'

He touched my ear lightly with the tip of his tongue. 'I start by—'

Misty, there are two things you should know. My mother's voice reached me telepathically. *First we are waiting for you, and second our table is by a window with a good view of the entrance.*

'Alex, my parents can see us.'

Alex froze, lips having reached the corner of my jaw. 'That's not good.'

'No.' I gave a nervous giggle.

'So what now?'

'We go in and pretend they didn't notice us.' I took his hand. 'Ready?'

My parents stood up when we arrived at their table. They had already opened a bottle of wine; it was half gone and I noticed Dad's glass was almost empty. He didn't usually drink very much at all so I guessed we weren't the only ones feeling anxious.

Mum gave me a tight hug. 'Stunning, Misty, he's absolutely stunning,' she whispered in my ear. 'And Uriel promises that he's a really nice young man, which is all I'm worried about.'

'Thanks, Mum.'

Dad was regarding Alex suspiciously. He held out a hand. 'Alex.'

'Mr Devon.' I gave Alex points for keeping eye contact as they shook hands. 'It's a pleasure to meet you.'

'We'll see.'

'Dad!' I gave him a reproving kiss on the cheek. 'Don't be like that, please.' My plan for Alex to fall in love with my family as part of my package deal looked wildly over-optimistic.

Dad refused to let me sit down with just a kiss. 'Come here, darling.' He hugged me, pulling my head to his shoulder. 'You don't have to do it this way, Misty. You know that, don't you?' He meant that I didn't have to follow the savant script and accept my soulfinder as my destiny.

'I realize that, Dad. Please, just give Alex a chance.' We took our places, Dad sitting opposite me. We were allowed a reprieve as we placed our orders but I knew the questions would start soon. There were a few exchanges on the menu choices but then my father got down to business.

'So, tell us about yourself, Alex. What's your family like?' Dad asked, more in a cross-examination tone than the light chit-chat suited to what was supposed to be a getting-to-know-you meal. 'Savants, I suppose?'

The waiter returned and put my salmon starter in front of me. *Sorry about this*, I told Alex. *Dad's taken it worse than I expected.*

'I don't know much about my family, sir.' Alex leaned back to make room for the waiter to deliver his soup. 'Thanks.' The waiter retreated, probably sensing that it was a good idea to take cover. 'They left the country when I was about three. I was taken in by social services and lived in a series of placements in foster families until I went to my current school.'

'I'm sorry to hear that,' said my mum. 'So your parents didn't keep in touch?'

'No. They didn't like the way I turned out.' Alex stirred the soup, not making much progress on eating.

I rearranged the food on my plate. It was unfortunate that my presence put a damper on Alex's gift for charm as he was making little headway persuading my father to think him a good thing in my life. The problem for Alex was that he had to carry the burden of my dad's misgivings about the whole savant world. To my father, I was first and foremost his little girl; he could tolerate savants while they remained amusing extensions of my mother with minimal effect on his immediate family, but now I looked set to live my life according to a weird genetic pairing he didn't understand, he was worried and a little angry. How could I counter this? I tried to play up the achievements in ordinary life that Dad would understand.

'You know, Dad, Alex has been really successful at the school he attends,' I said brightly, 'put up a year and still coming out number one. He's going to get a full scholarship to . . . well, I'm not sure which university but one of the top colleges in the world.' We hadn't got so far as discussing all this.

How do you know about the scholarship? Alex asked.

Part of the conversation at the barbecue I shouldn't have overheard, I explained.

'I imagine that must've been very lonely for you,' my mum continued, casting 'be nice' looks at my father. 'I've always been grateful to belong to a large family. I can hardly imagine what it was like being alone.'

This was turning out the exact opposite to how I had imagined this meal: my mum the ally, my dad the obstacle.

Alex gave her a grateful smile. 'I guess I learned early on to rely on myself.'

My dad wasn't eating a thing. 'And now you think you can

undo years of habit and bring Misty into your life?' He ripped a bread roll apart. 'She's a very tender-hearted girl; she can't flourish with someone who won't let her lean on them and vice versa. A relationship is about mutual support, not standing apart.'

I sensed Alex's temper was rising. He didn't deserve this from my dad.

'Please, Dad, don't do this.' I couldn't bear seeing my father disapproving of the first major choice I had made in my life.

Alex shot me a look, warning me to keep out of this battle. 'I didn't say I had no experience of caring about others, sir. I have people around me whom I think of as family. I can certainly learn to look after someone else. I promise you that Misty's happiness will come before my own.'

'Fine words. No doubt you are sincere as Misty is here and we all know what that means.' Dad topped up his wine. 'But you are so young, both trapped by this thing between you. It's not healthy.'

'Mark,' pleaded my mum.

'No, Topaz, I'm going to have my say.'

'But with Misty at the table, you know you won't say it delicately. It will sound like you are attacking Alex, and none of this is his fault.'

That's me: the baseball bat of tact. 'Shall I go outside for a moment?'

'No, Misty, stay and hear what I've got to say. It concerns you and your future.' Dad took a mouthful of Sauvignon and swallowed. 'I'm not attacking you personally, Alex. I've had my doubts about some of the ways you savants behave for a long time and now there's this murderer among you, my misgivings have got more severe. Your community encourages unhealthy fixations. It's not good how you have this power and no accountability. I believe you'll find this criminal is warped by the fact he has this ability that sets him apart. You'd do better rejoining the mainstream, forgetting this soulfinder business and living ordinary lives that don't breed this kind of perversion.'

My mum's mouth had fallen open. 'Mark, I didn't know you felt this way.'

'Well, Misty hasn't been at home to make me as frank about my thoughts, has she? And that's another thing: as I see it, your gift has only brought you misery, Misty. You've moved from school to school, never being able to outrun its problems, being bullied for being different.'

I hadn't wanted to tell Alex about the bullying: it made me sound so pathetic.

My dad wasn't finished. 'I thought you might grow out of it but it's getting worse as you grow older. I wish you could just switch it off.'

Inside, I was reeling. I understood that Dad's worry for me and my brothers and sisters was boiling over. It was also partly defensive because, with Crystal identified as a soulseeker, he had to be more concerned about his own marriage than he had let on. Yet, it sounded very much to my ears that he didn't like me—not the way I was. I hadn't realized. He had always treated the bad sides of my gift as a joke, waving away my numerous embarrassments.

He hadn't finished. 'Now you turn up, not even seventeen yet, and say your genes or whatever have put you together with this stranger. He seems a nice enough boy, but I don't believe in arranging your future like that. He needs to earn the right to be with you, not have you handed to him on a plate. You deserve more than that.'

'Have you finished your starters?' asked the waiter, seeing none of us were eating.

'No, not yet. Please, give us a moment,' my mum said, a definite edge to her voice.

The hapless waiter quickly retreated behind the serving screen.

I didn't know what I was feeling. Yesterday had been the best day of my life; today was coming out close to the worst.

Mum took my hand. 'Have you quite finished, Mark?'

Dad gave a curt nod and took a bite of his meal.

'Then let me have my say. Alex, I am delighted to meet you. Please, forgive my husband if he sounds like he has no wish to welcome you to our family. It's hard for him.'

'You can't go around apologizing for me,' grumbled my dad.

'When you don't realize how rude you are being, I will damn well make your apology for you.' Even such mild swearing was unheard of from my mother; my dad's eyebrows winged up. 'Give him time, please, Alex.'

'But he's right that I don't deserve to be allowed into Misty's life without earning my place,' said Alex quietly. 'Misty is a gift, not an award I've won.'

'It's sweet of you to put it like that, but no one earns places in our family; they are given one because we want to make them feel at home. It might mean we all need to shift up and make adjustments, but that is what we do. I'm sure Mark will remember that when he thinks about it.' She turned to me, hand gently cupping my cheek. 'And Misty, your gift is part of you. We know it sometimes causes you grief but one day my hope is that you will find it a strength. I wouldn't change it; it makes you you: a refreshingly honest girl. Your dad loves you too, just as you are.'

'Of course I love her!' spluttered my father. 'I just want to spare her the pain of being a misfit.'

'Don't use that word about our daughter! Mark, you see it as an add-on; I'm trying to tell you it is integral to who our daughter is. You can't love one and dislike the other.' My mum pointed at his heart. 'It's important you understand this, or what are you going to do when the others reach Misty's stage in life?'

My brothers and sisters were still too young to worry Dad, though Gale with her gift for anticipating the contents of examinations was likely to soon cause headaches as she was earning an undeserved record for cheating. I really thought this was a conversation that they shouldn't be having in front of my new soulfinder, but Alex showed no signs of wanting to bail. At least the target had moved from him to my father.

'But wouldn't Misty be better off just being . . . ' Dad searched for a word and chose the wrong one, 'normal?'

'Your daughter can't be normal, Mark. You've had sixteen years to get to grips with that fact.'

'But now it makes her a target for this killer. If she didn't have this savant label hung round her neck, she'd be safe.'

'Don't fool yourself. No life is completely safe.'

'But a savant's life has more risks attached.'

'So does a fighter pilot's but you wouldn't argue that an air-force recruit shouldn't aspire to defend us.'

'I might, if the recruit was my own child.'

'Then you'll never let them be fully adult. Parenting is about knowing when and how to let go.'

'But I bloody well don't want to let go and see her fall into the wrong hands.'

I rubbed my sweating palms on my knees. *Sorry, Alex.*

Don't be. I get where your dad is coming from. It must be terrifying for him.

You're kinder about him than I can be at the moment. 'Dad?' I broke into their argument.

'Yes, darling?'

'Do you really think I'd be better without my gift—not just the truth thing but the telepathy and the telekinesis and so on?'

153

He looked uncomfortable, reducing his seeded roll to crumbs. 'I suppose if I could pick and choose then I'd be happy for you to have those other aspects, but I know it hurts you when the truth-telling makes things go wrong.'

'But it hurts more to be told I'm not the daughter you want.' I could feel tears gathering at the back of my throat.

Sweetheart, he loves you, said Alex.

Dad swallowed. 'I don't mean it like that.'

'Don't you?'

'If you saw your child heading into danger, wouldn't you try to stop her?'

'I don't know. In this case, I think if I knew she had to take that path, I might ask to go along with her and see if I can help.'

Dad subsided into a dark silence.

Predictably, the rest of the meal was horrible. I was hurt; Alex was probably wishing he'd never met me and my family; my mum was embarrassed; and Dad was alone in Fort Normal Person thinking the rest of us needed to come on inside. Our goodbyes in the foyer didn't solve anything. Dad gave me a longer than usual hug, but he couldn't take back what he'd said. That's the problem with my gift: there's no defence like you hear politicians use: *I was misunderstood, I misspoke*, or *my remarks were taken out of context*. I megaphone the truth, leaving no one in any doubt of what was said and what they heard.

Exiling myself to the North Pole, like Frankenstein's monster did when he found his effect on others too much of a burden, seemed a very attractive idea.

In answer to this stray notion, Alex projected a picture of him and me sitting in an igloo side by side.

I'm sorry.

Don't be.

He was awful.

He was worried sick. Believe me, an excessively concerned parent is better than the kind I've got.

We had reached the punts again.

Let's sit in one of them, suggested Alex.

They're locked up.

And that's a problem?

Alex went first, then beckoned me to follow once he'd done his thing. He handed me into the punt with a sweet little bow. There were no cushions and it was a bit damp under the seat, but it felt good just to sit for a moment, bobbing gently on the Cam. The lights of a pub spilled onto the water, early Christmas decorations sparkling in the window. The clamour of people shouting to make themselves heard at the bar reached us like the roar of a distant battle. Down where we were in the shadows, it was quiet. I could hear the trickle of a stream joining the main channel, the slap and slop of water hitting the side of the punt. Rocking the boat, Alex sat down next to me and put his arm around my shoulders, his strength offered for my support.

'Better?'

I rested my head on him. 'Yes.'

'Maybe next time I should see him alone—use my gift to straighten things out.'

'He wouldn't ever trust you if he realized what you were doing.'

'I guess not.' Alex tapped his free hand on his knee in irritation. 'The one guy in the world I care most about impressing and I can't do what I'm good at doing.'

'You don't need that—you shouldn't need to use your gift. He'll have to accept you for what you are, not what you make him think you are.'

'And what's that? A boy with no background and a skill he hates? Yeah, sure he'll like me.'

His irony hurt. 'Please, don't. It feels like you're drilling my teeth when you say something meaning the opposite.'

'Sorry. I forgot for a moment.' He puffed out a breath of pure frustration. 'This isn't easy, is it?'

'Did you think it would be?'

'I didn't think at all. I didn't expect you in my life.'

I was feeling exhausted and ready to weep but I hated that he might think he was matched with an emotional wreck. 'Could we just drop the subject, Alex? Think about something else?'

'Sorry. I didn't mean for us to sit here going over what happened. I wanted to spend a few moments at peace. Just you and me.'

Things felt right when we stopped struggling. Our togetherness needed no excusing or questioning; it just was. I was beginning to see that this was the heart of a soulfinder bond.

After five minutes of calm had flowed past like the water in the river, I was ready to be optimistic.

'You'll win him over,' I said. 'You're amazing, and kind, and caring—when he sees what I see, he'll be happy for me.'

Alex dropped a kiss on the top of my head. 'I hope so, Misty. I've never wanted anything so much as you in my life and he is a big part of your world.'

I pulled away so I could look him in the eyes. 'Yes, he's important, but Alex, you are too. It won't come to this but if I had to choose between you, you'd win.'

He looked a little confused. 'No one has ever put me first. Never.'

'Well, now they do. I do. So get used to it.' I leaned in for a kiss.

'Oh, I could very quickly get used to that.' He smiled and brushed a thumb over my lips, coaxing them apart. He then put his mouth to mine.

Chapter 13

Even though my life was right in the middle of its biggest ever Misty moment, Summer and Angel had to return to their homes on Sunday. Angel had thought up some pretty inventive excuses, hoping to be allowed to stay, but her mum wasn't buying it and Angel was given her marching orders. Summer knew better than to ask at her home for a favour and had already texted that she was on her way. Alex and I accompanied them to see them catch their train. This wasn't something I usually did when they visited—I just waved them off on the bus to the station—so Angel claimed we were behaving like the sheriffs running her out of town. Alex agreed, teasing her that this town wasn't big enough for the both of them, then he pretended to twirl his imaginary pistols. I fell just a little more in love with him for that; Angel adored someone making fun of her.

Ticket purchased, Summer gave me a hug, promising that my dad would come round.

'You don't know that,' I whispered so Alex wouldn't hear. Fortunately he was busy putting a make-believe Stetson on Angel's head.

'No, but it stands to reason. Look on the bright side: you've caught yourself a good one in Alex and you've plenty of time to convince your dad you're serious about each other.'

'Thanks, Summer. You're always so sensible. I wish you ran the world.'

Angel broke away from Alex and tweaked the end of my scarf. 'I'm so jealous. I think I'm going to have to learn to hate you.'

'Don't envy me. It's not all sweetness and light in Devon Central.'

'Yeah, your dad. But come on, girl, you've got Alex as your soulfinder! I bet mine is going to turn out some geeky bloke with pimples who spends all his life in his bedroom hacking into the Pentagon.'

I gave her a hug. 'Fate would not be so cruel.'

'You sure?'

'Even if he were ultra geeky you'd learn to love him as he is.'

'Oh brother,' groaned Angel, 'is that how this soulfinder thing works? Chemistry overrules good sense? Come on, Summer, let's go before I get too depressed to move.'

Alex put his arm around me while we waved them through the ticket barrier, a little comforting touch that said far more than words.

'I like your friends,' he said as we turned to leave.

'That's a good start. I like yours too.'

Alex's phone pinged. He checked the message. 'Tarryn wants me back immediately.'

I flinched as a pigeon crossing the station concourse flew too close. 'But I thought your next debate wasn't until this evening?'

'It is—and we've got a practice after lunch—but I thought I'd have a few free hours before then. I'm not ready to leave you yet. Do you want to come with me to see what she wants?'

My parents had asked to see me for lunch *on my own*—Dad's request—but I had some time before then. 'OK. She probably just wants to keep an eye on you with that weirdo journalist on the prowl. And none of us should be wandering about alone.' I remembered Uriel's warning. I'd passed it on to Summer and Angel but hadn't had a moment to tell Alex with all the upset the night before. 'Uriel said the serial killer goes for savants with certain skills, and that you fit the profile.'

Alex rolled his shoulders, betraying how tense he really felt. 'Tarryn took me aside and told me the same thing.'

'So, you're taking care?'

He stopped in front of me. 'Misty, when will there be time for a serial killer to lure me away? I've got my soulfinder to worry about now.' He ran the back of his fingers over my cheek.

Tarryn had asked Alex to meet her at a teashop on King's Parade. Cambridge's knot of narrow streets open out here to a marketplace and green verge in front of King's and the Senate House. It's a traditional meeting place and great for people-watching. I liked just wandering around, guessing who everyone was and their story for being here. Tarryn had secured a table at the window of the tea room where she could observe the ebbs and flows of tourists, but as the sky was a threatening steel grey behind the clotted-cream pinnacles of King's College Chapel, people weren't lingering.

'Sorry to interrupt your morning,' she said, making room for us by shifting her seat along to the one by the glass. 'I know how special these early days are.'

Uriel arrived hot on our heels, summoned by telepathy from his room in the college just down the road.

'Hi, guys, how was last night?' he asked.

'Horrible,' I said, taking the seat Tarryn had just vacated. I pushed her coffee along in front of her.

That tripped him up. 'I'm sorry to hear that.'

'My dad is feeling his distance from all things savant at the moment.'

'I guess it's not unreasonable for him to take it that way. We're quite a lot to handle.'

'Is that why you wanted to see me?' asked Alex.

Tarryn rubbed her index finger on the leather cover of her phone. 'It's not about Misty's family, no.'

Uriel met her eyes. Some rapid communication passed between them. 'I'll get the drinks. Coffee?'

'I'll have a tea, please,' I said.

'Americano for me.' Alex took off his jacket and hung it on the back of the chair at the head of the table next to me. 'OK, Miss Coetzee, what's this about?'

Tarryn folded her hands together, briefly stilling her nervous fidgeting. 'I got an email this morning from someone who claims to know you.'

Alex's puzzlement grew. 'Who?'

'That's the odd thing. He says he knows you from when you were little and only found out recently where you were living. He's in England on business, saw the reports in a magazine feature that you were part of the debate team in the final, so dropped me a line asking if he could meet you.'

I was instantly suspicious. 'You can't just let strangers get in to see Alex. What if he's the guy stalking savants and killing them?'

Tarryn rearranged the spoon on her saucer. 'I know that, Misty, which is why I suggested meeting here—in a neutral zone with Uriel and me present. And you're a nice bonus too. You'll be able to tell us if he is what he claims to be.'

'But still, we don't know him! Now's not the time to take risks!'

'No. But if he's speaking the truth, he's very far from a stranger. He's family. Alex, that's what I'm trying to tell you: he says he's your uncle.'

Alex took a moment to absorb that bombshell. With perfect timing, Uriel came back with our drinks.

'Here you are.' He put a black coffee in front of Alex and a dinky white teapot by my place. 'I took the gamble of getting some cakes.'

Alex hadn't really heard Uriel's remarks; he was still stuck on Tarryn's announcement. 'How can I have an uncle?'

'The usual way.' Tarryn smiled wryly. 'He says he is your father's brother. His name is Johan du Plessis.'

Alex scratched his fingers up and down his forearm, a kind of anxious clutching movement. I reached out to still his hand but he moved out of the way, nerves raw. 'Why hasn't he contacted me until today?'

Tarryn glanced over Alex's shoulder.

'Is he coming here?' I asked. I wanted to be with Alex in this but things were moving too quickly and I had to meet my parents.

'Yes. I said he should be here at eleven.' It was five-to now. 'He doesn't have long before he goes on to his next meeting in another city so I thought it best to make an arrangement rather than lose this chance. Did I do the right thing, Alex? I had to think fast.'

Alex cradled his drink in his palms. 'Yes, thanks. I wouldn't want to miss a chance of meeting him.'

You OK? I asked.

Alex had gone silent, not reaching out to me with telepathy as he had been doing since Friday. I wondered what was going on in his head, feeling a new distance yawn between us. At the back of my mind, I remembered how I had let him support me over my dad; it seemed this wasn't a two-way street when it came to his uncle.

Don't be unreasonable, Misty. Give the guy a break, my sensible side whispered.

'I don't know much apart from what he said in his email,' continued Tarryn, 'but you should know, Alex, that he's a savant. He said that was why he didn't know where you were. His brother had cut him off, much as he did you, and Johan had no idea they had not taken you with them when they went to Argentina. They've moved around since then. It was quite by chance, through a business contact in America who knows them, that he learned that his brother's family had no boy of your age at home. He then started looking for you separately.'

'I . . . this is quite a lot to take in,' Alex admitted.

'I know: first you find Misty and now it looks like you've got family set to walk back into your life. We'll forgive you for being confused.'

The bell over the shop door rang. Sensing something momentous was about to happen, we all looked round. Johan du Plessis; it had to be. He even looked a little like Alex: tall and square-jawed, same hairline and eyebrows; he carried with him that air of family resemblance that's definitely there but hard to put a finger on, something to do with expression and the way he held himself. However, there were clear differences: his skin was very closely shaved, reminding me of the slightly waxy surface of soapstone. He gave the impression of length—long neck, arms, tapering fingers; even his nose was thin and long—how Alex might be if put through a stretching machine. His brown eyes swept the tea room and fixed on our table. His face broke into a delighted smile.

'Miss Coetzee?' He offered Tarryn his hand, which she shook. He put down his briefcase and held out both arms to Alex in a 'would you look at that' gesture. 'And this has to be Alex! Gracious me, you are the image of Roger when he was your age.' Johan's voice had a light South African accent, pleasant on the ear.

Alex got up and shook hands. 'Pleased to meet you, Mr du Plessis.'

'Call me Johan. Uncle Johan, if you can manage it. I can't tell you how fantastic it is to finally meet you after all these years. I only saw you once when you were a baby before Roger barred to door to me. I feel like I am finally getting some family back.'

Uriel looked to me, still suspicious of the stranger. I nodded. Every word he spoke registered as true.

He is telling you the truth, Alex, I told my soulfinder.

Alex barely waited for my confirmation. *Thanks.* 'I didn't know about you at all, sir.'

'Really? When did your parents leave you?'

'When I was three.'

'So young? Then forgive me for not trying harder to discover what they had done with you. It never entered even my wildest dream that Miriam would leave you; she was such a devoted mother. I take it you're one of us?'

Alex nodded.

Johan gave him a proud smile. 'Of course you are. I can see it in you. My brother never accepted my gift. I didn't realize he passed it on to a child. And a very welcome surprise that is too.' He glanced over to the serving counter. 'I'll just get a drink and join you.'

Uriel stood. 'Please, let me get it. You take my seat. Coffee?'

'Oh, that's very kind of you, Mr . . . ?'

'Benedict, Uriel Benedict.'

Johan's eyes widened. 'Not one of the Colorado Benedicts?'

'That's us.'

'I've heard of you and your brothers. A very interesting family.'

'Interesting is one name for us. How do you take your coffee?'

'Black.' He glanced down at our drinks. 'Like my nephew, it seems.'

Johan sat down next to Alex and opposite me. His gaze now slid to my face. 'And who are you, young lady? Another Benedict?'

'Afraid not. I'm Misty Devon.'

Alex took my hand so our clasped fingers lay on the table between us. I was relieved he wanted to acknowledge me after the gap that had opened up. 'She's my soulfinder. We've just met.'

Johan shook his head, eyes sweeping me with renewed interest. 'Well, well. Clearly there is a huge amount for me to learn about you, Alex. I hardly know where to start. Tell me all about yourself: your gift, your school, your friends.'

I was grateful to Johan for giving Alex the excuse to talk about himself. We had begun to swap life histories but I had not had a chance to sit and hear it told like a story from the beginning.

'After my parents left me, I couldn't be adopted as my legal status was under question. The authorities weren't even sure if I had been abandoned—it was that confused. I was placed with some foster families—good people. Really I would've been happy to be adopted by any of them but the social services couldn't make up their minds. I'd told them some garbled tale that my parents had run away from the devil—I guess that's how they saw me. The authorities were still pursuing my parents to ask for an explanation but they'd done a good job covering their tracks.'

Johan sipped his coffee and winced. 'Need some sugar in that.' He dropped in two rough-cut lumps from the bowl. 'But they knew your name. I wonder why they didn't contact me?'

'Good point. I don't know. They couldn't trace my origins—all the documents hidden or destroyed; my past took a lot of deciphering and much of it remains a mystery. Clearly, I never mentioned you as I had no recollection of family. I guess I have no grandparents alive?'

'Not on my side. They died when I was a teenager, both quite suddenly. I think Roger was never the same after that. I don't know much about Miriam's family. I wasn't invited to the wedding. So what happened when you went to senior school?'

'I got a scholarship from a savant foundation to board at the International College in Cape Town. I was lucky to find Miss Coetzee had just joined the staff and she's been helping me ever since.'

'So you've been happy?'

'I have. I've got good friends and had a great education so I haven't done too badly.'

'I'm pleased. It would have made it so much worse to have found the last thirteen years had been a misery for you. So what's your gift?'

'I can persuade—people, things: I can usually get them to do what I want.'

'Excellent. So are you using it now to persuade me to be very proud of my nephew? Because that's what I'm feeling.'

'No.' Alex gave me a brief smile. 'Misty here is the spanner in the works when it comes to my gift. It switches off around her.'

'How interesting. So what's your gift, Misty?' Johan turned his pale blue eyes on me. They were a similar shape to Alex's but without the darker ring and lashes that gave Alex's eyes their intensity.

'I'm a truth-teller and, if I lose control, people around me can't lie. Even when I am controlling the scope of my influence over others, I can sense when someone is dishonest.'

'How extraordinary.'

'It's a pain in the butt, to be honest.'

Alex brushed a fingertip over my knuckle. 'And there's some deeper link between us thanks to our soulfinder bond. I've worked out that when she's controlling her zone so other people aren't affected, I still can't lie around her. It's as though I experience her gift in the same way she does.'

I hadn't realized that, I told Alex.

It came to me last night when I couldn't sleep. It's why you're my kryptonite.

'So, Mr du Plessis, tell us more about yourself,' said Tarryn. I was pleased to see that neither she nor Uriel were ready to let down all defences.

'I'm an investment manager, not married and I have no children of my own, so I couldn't be more delighted to find my nephew. But the good news is that you don't have to take that on trust as you've got Misty here. What are you getting from me, young lady?' Johan asked.

'I know you are who you say you are, Mr du Plessis. Nothing you've said has registered as a lie.'

'That clears up any doubt. How convenient. You have a very useful gift, my dear.'

'I'm glad you think so. There are quite a few people who prefer to steer clear of me.' And I was worried that in half his heart Alex was one of them.

'I guess that too much truth is more than some can bear. It's a sad world we live in.'

My phone buzzed. *Where are you?* Shoot, I'd forgotten about my parents. I jumped up and grabbed my jacket. 'I'm really sorry but I have to go. Nice meeting you, Mr du Plessis.' I hesitated then kissed Alex's cheek. Might as well act as if everything was OK between us until I knew for sure it wasn't. 'See you later after the debate.'

Alex only looked up briefly but I could tell he was

mesmerized by seeing someone who shared his family inheritance for the first time. 'Enjoy lunch.' His remark was offhand. I'd moved from being the centre of his attention.

'It has to be better than supper at least.'

Look out for Alex, I begged Uriel and Tarryn as I left the tea room.

We will, promised Uriel.

Mum and Dad were lunching at my school, catching up with my form tutor, who kept an eye on my personal life and academic progress. It was not the best idea I had ever had to be late for that meeting. I ran past the classical frontage of the Fitzwilliam Museum to my school campus just beyond. Set among fields near the Botanic Gardens, the Fens School had a beautiful location. There was something a little Harry Potter-ish about the buildings, though the health and safety record was way better than Hogwarts'. The classrooms had pretensions to be more like the Cambridge colleges down the road than the standard educational box of my previous schools: high ceilings, wood panelling, and fancy scrollwork plaster.

'Sorry, Mrs Huddleston, sorry Mum, Dad!' I called breathlessly as I tumbled into her office.

'Where have you been, Misty?' asked Dad. He showed no signs of an improved mood.

'I saw Angel and Summer off at the station and then lost track of the time over coffee.'

'I hope you remembered to sign in and out, Misty,' said Mrs Huddleston. A fifty-something woman with a sharp fashion sense, she never missed the details in lessons or in life.

'Um . . .'

'Go and do it now and I'll take your parents over to the dining room. Roast dinner today.' She sounded enthusiastic. I wasn't a fan of school cooking but the Sunday lunch was better than most meals during the week.

I returned to find my parents and Mrs Huddleston were already deep in conversation. I took a tray and joined the short queue. Most pupils boarded weekly so there were few of us around at the weekend. Having chosen my meal, I put my tray down next to my mum's.

You were with Alex? she asked.

Yes. It was amazing, Mum: his uncle has turned up. Alex didn't think he had any family who wanted to know him.

You must tell me about it later.

'So how is Misty doing?' my dad was asking.

'I think she's doing very well.' Mrs Huddleston deflated her Yorkshire pudding with her fork. 'We know she has a bluntness to her but most pupils make allowances. The head teacher said it was similar to other behavioural conditions. Have you thought of having her assessed? There's extra funding available to students with educational special needs.'

Assessed? Yeah, I was assessed as having a severe case of honesty. It annoyed me that she was trying to frame it as a medical condition.

'I don't think her directness will hold Misty back.' My mum leapt to my defence before Dad could go on one of his 'if only she were normal' digressions.

Mrs Huddleston didn't look convinced but decided against pressing her point. 'Academically, she is managing well. She's not in our top stream but we are still looking at a good university when she goes on to the next stage. Primary education, isn't it, Misty?'

'Yes, miss. At the moment, that's the way I'm thinking I'll go.'

'We think she'll make the grades she's likely to be offered, though I understand that you are finding maths a little challenging?'

A lot challenging. 'I'm doing my best.'

Mrs Huddleston patted my hand. 'And that sums it up: Misty always does her best so we can't ask for any more.'

That well and truly patronized me then. 'Thanks, Mrs Huddleston.'

Dad sniffed. 'There's a new development you should be aware of, Mrs Huddleston.'

Don't go there, Dad.

Too late. 'Misty has developed a relationship with one of the visiting debaters, one of the South African team. I'm concerned that it might make her take her eye off the ball of getting good exam results. That's what's important these next two years, not some high school romance.'

My mother made a noise suggesting she didn't agree.

'I'd like you to keep tabs on her, let us know if you think she's being distracted by him.'

'I am here you know, Dad,' I said.

'I know that very well. You can see that I'm not going behind your back on this, Misty.'

Mrs Huddleston smiled indulgently at me. 'Ah, what it is to be young and in love. Remember those years? She won't be the only one going through the ups and downs of a relationship—I could point you in the direction of a dozen girls in her peer group who are struggling with the same issue. These relationships don't usually last long at this stage in life—that's not to say they don't feel like matters of life and death to the young people involved. Please, feel free to come to me if you are upset, Misty. My door is always open.'

She means well, my mum said.

I know, but I don't think I'll be knocking on her door to tell her about being a soulfinder to someone who lives in the other hemisphere.

'Thank you, Mrs Huddleston. It's a great comfort to me to know she has someone with such common sense to turn to,' said Dad. By "common sense", Mum and I were to understand "a non-savant".

I said my goodbyes to my parents in the school car park after lunch. Normally I was sad to see them go; today I felt relief.

'Love to Grandma, Gale, Felicity, Peace, Sunny, and Tempest.' I gave Dad a kiss for each one and then hugged him, aware that for the first time in my life, we had had a serious disagreement and not resolved it before parting.

'Look after yourself, darling, and keep your priorities straight. I can see you are head-over-heels with that boy but you have more important things to focus on right now.'

I really didn't, but as Dad meant what he said sincerely, his words did not register as a lie.

'I'll try not to disappoint you.'

'This isn't about my feelings, Misty. It's about how you approach the next few years.'

It was really, though. Finding my soulfinder had opened up a chasm in the family and Dad felt he was standing on one side, my mum on the other and us children on a dodgy rope bridge between the two. It made me sad for him because none of us sisters and brothers could stop walking over to the savant side, our experiences ending up so different from his.

I offered him what comfort I could. 'It's early days yet, Dad. Alex and I both have a lot to sort out and neither of us wants to get in the other's way. That's not how it works.'

'Fair enough. Well, I've had my say. Stay safe.' He gave me a last kiss and got in the driver's seat.

Mum didn't need words to tell me what she was thinking: her expression said it all.

'I know. I'll not be cross with Dad. I get it—I really do.'

'It's so hard for him. Perhaps I should never have . . . '

I cut her off before she could voice regrets that should stay unspoken. 'No. This is not your fault. We'll work it out.'

She gave me a watery smile. 'Don't you sound the grown-up! I'm missing these moments of seeing you become the adult, what with you stuck all the way over here in Cambridge. I'm proud of you.'

At least I had the satisfaction of knowing that my relationship with my mother had travelled on to a new and satisfying stage, even if that with my dad had done a swallow dive off the high board.

'Thanks, Mum. Love you.'

When they left, I felt quite desolate. I could do with a hug but Alex was rehearsing his argument for 'This house believes that democracy is the best form of government'; he wouldn't want me to break his concentration. I'd have to face this one alone.

Wrong. Of course I want to give you a hug and you are most definitely not alone.

I turned round to find Alex standing behind me. 'What are you doing here?' My heart did a little skip to see him.

'I wanted to check you were OK. Miss Coetzee said I could come a little late to practice. She thought you'd need to see me.' He opened his arms. 'Hug?'

I ran into them, feeling like I'd reached a lifeboat from a sinking ship.

He cradled my head to his chest. 'Bad, was it? I waited until they left before coming out of hiding but I saw that you were still talking to them.'

'Mum's fine. Good, in fact. Dad's . . . not. He's put my form tutor on red alert about you.'

'Uh-oh. Does that mean I'm banned?' Like that would stop him, his tone suggested.

I flexed my fingers, feeling the soft wool of his jumper under his open jacket. 'No, nothing like that. Just don't be surprised if a Mrs Huddleston takes an interest in you.'

'I think I'll cope. After all, being charming is my strong point.' He smiled at my roll of the eyes.

I reminded myself that mine was not the only family drama today. 'How did it go with your uncle?'

Alex rubbed his knuckles down my spine in a light massage. I had an odd desire to purr. 'Really well, thanks. I can't tell you how lucky I'm feeling right now, what with finding you and then him turning up. Johan had a business meeting in Leeds but he's going to come back the day after tomorrow. He'll be here for the final if we get that far.'

'It must be strange for you.'

'Very. I look at him and I guess I'm catching glimpses of how my father must be. Johan says they look alike.'

I was relieved he wanted to share this with me. 'Did he say if any others in your family had a savant gift?'

'A grandmother definitely, and he suspected his own mother did but hid it because his father was violently opposed. He says that's where my father, Roger, got his attitude. That part of the family belong to a very strict sect that think savant powers have to be the devil's work. They couldn't deal with the idea that their own flesh and blood could turn out that way so they cut us off.'

'That's so sad.'

'But now we've met, so maybe he and I can start a new trend for the du Plessis family.'

I smiled, trying to ignore the sense that I was excluded from this new development in Alex's life. He was very optimistic about building a new family on the strength of one meeting. I hoped he wouldn't be disappointed. 'I'm sure you'll do your best.'

'Can I see you later, after the debate?'

Lessons again tomorrow and I had heaps of work to finish. 'I'd love to but I have to study.'

'I can help.' His eyes twinkled. I didn't think I'd get much done if he was around but he was irresistible.

'OK, come say goodnight later. I'll be in the library. They won't let you up to my room that late.'

He traced a finger down the side of my neck, causing shivers all the way down to my toes. 'In case we get up to no good?'

''Fraid so.'

'They know me so well.' His fingers danced over my cheek and tapped my mouth. It was flattering to find he liked exploring my face as much as I did his.

'Good luck tonight. I really wish I could be there.'

'I'll contact you as soon as we hear the result.'

'OK.' Reluctantly, I released my hold on his sweater. I'd be quite happy living in his pocket, but I had to be careful I didn't come across as clingy. I'd seen other girls do that and drive off boyfriends like they had a case of the plague. I so wanted to get this right. 'Later then.'

'Yes, later.'

Chapter 14

I spent the rest of the afternoon in my room studying, but my school friends Hafsa, Tony, and Annalise dropped by so not much work got done. They were understandably curious about my whirlwind romance with the South African team captain, demanding I spill the beans. I fended off their questions by telling them about the summer, how we'd met and spent some time together doing the sights. I let them draw their own (wrong) conclusions as to how the way had been prepared for Friday night. They didn't ask me if Alex had already asked me out in Cape Town—I let it hang there, a faint tingle of a fib, that he might've done—which meant no lie crisis interrupted them making sense of our rapid closeness.

After supper, I decamped to the library as my friends went off to the debate. They protested that I should support my guy but I muttered something about nerves. I didn't explain it was Alex who was unnerved by my presence, not me. Sitting in the study cubicle, I attempted to be diligent and not to watch the clock. My geography homework on population and migration refused to cross the border checkpoint at my brain. I flipped the pages, underlining things in a variety of colourful highlighters, but don't ask me what. As the evening progressed, the other students drifted off, leaving me the only person in the cavernous room and, to be frank, it was a bit spooky as half the lights were off to conserve power. I would have preferred to head back to my room but I'd promised Alex to meet him here. I began to notice how the building had its own soundtrack of clicks and creaks as the pipes expanded and contracted with the central heating cycles. The unwelcome thought came to me that libraries are perfectly adapted to serial killers as there are loads of places to hide and stalk your prey. And ghosts. Surely an old building like this must have a couple? I could just imagine them floating along the history section, turning nasty and chucking books at me.

That's poltergeists.

Shouldn't you knock before you pop up in my head? I asked. Alex was quickly developing the habit of slipping into my thoughts telepathically. I suppose his gift did still work on me because he was adept as persuading my mind barriers to let him past without me noticing. I'd have to work out what that meant, but not now.

Sorry. I'll cough loudly next time. But you were having such an interesting conversation with yourself, I didn't like to interrupt. I could feel the smile in the voice.

So, how was it?

We won.

I didn't seriously consider any other outcome.

The Amritsar team were really good. It was close.

My guess was that my golden boy had swung it in the favour of his team. *Well done you.*

Is it still OK for me to drop by? His debate had been taking place in our school theatre over the other side of the campus across the rugby pitch. He didn't have that far to come and find me.

I'm waiting up for you while trying to battle population statistics. They are winning. Come and rescue me.

Estimating he was about two minutes away, I got out a compact mirror to check I'd not done something Misty-ish, like scrawled on my nose with biro (it has been known as I chew pen tops and don't always remember which way round I'm holding them). I angled the mirror to inspect my cheek and caught a glimpse of someone behind me.

'Alex, how did you . . . ?'

But it wasn't Alex. The journalist from the news conference stepped out from behind the shelf. I got the distinct impression he wouldn't have emerged unless I had spotted him.

'Sorry to disturb you.' His voice was soft, oozing apology, but I wasn't buying it. 'I was looking for Alex du Plessis and I noticed he usually crops up where you happen to be.'

My heart thumped hard like the main stairs during lesson changeover. I quickly packed my folders away, not looking at him. 'I don't think you're supposed to be in here.'

'No worries. I have press accreditation.' He came up to the table. I think he was holding out his badge, or maybe asking to shake hands—I wasn't going to make eye contact. 'My name is Eli Davis. I work for a paper in Los Angeles.'

'What I meant was that this part of the school is nothing to do with the competition. It's private. Pupils and staff only.'

'Like that matters to you.' He laughed but I didn't sense any genuine humour. It sounded rather bitter. 'I've seen you and Alex du Plessis walk through plenty of locked doors—how do you do that, by the way? Or should I say, *who* does that?' Davis picked up the textbook from which I'd been working. 'Funny. I would have expected a spell book in a place like this.'

'I'm doing AS geography, Mr Davis, not living in a fantasy world.' I held my bag to my chest, debating if I should just abandon my book. My eyes flicked to the door. I hated the idea that he'd been spying on us in our first fragile moments of being a couple.

'Now then, no need to hurry away. I've spent days trying to talk to you and Alex. Don't spoil it now I've got you alone for a few minutes.'

Alex, don't come in here. That journalist has cornered me. Warn Uriel.

His reply zinged back like a boomerang. *You are joking, right? I'm not leaving you on your own with him.*

A little beeping alarm went off. Davis pulled a device from his pocket, about the same size as a phone. 'Interesting. You're doing telepathy.'

'That's . . .' I was desperate to deny it but I couldn't. I took a step towards the door but he slid into the gangway, blocking me in my study cubicle. '. . . None of your business.'

He turned his device round so I could see the display. It showed an image like a bar chart. 'I've had this tuned to measure psychic activity. Telepathy sends the levels way past normal and sets off the alarm. It almost got me thrown out of that first debate. I guessed your boy was cheating somehow, being in communication with someone outside the room. Was he talking to you?'

No, that had been Angel tweeting me. 'You're wrong. Alex doesn't cheat when debating.'

'But you don't say he doesn't use telepathy.' He gave me a long look, trying to guess my secrets. 'Now that I find fascinating as everyone else I've approached on this issue always denies it.'

That's because everyone else can lie. 'I don't even know what psychic energy is so how do I know if your device works?' No one knew exactly how our powers functioned.

'I would very much enjoy sharing that with you, young lady, but first I need some answers of my own.'

I heard feet running up the stairs and then the door crashed open.

'Ah, Alex! So delighted you could join us.'

He has a machine that detects telepathy.

The device beeped again.

'A little predictable. I suppose she was telling you about this?' Davis held up his sensor. 'I call it a savant detector. That's what you guys call yourselves, don't you? The knowledgeable ones; rather big-headed, wouldn't you say?'

Alex couldn't reach me the normal way because Davis was blocking me in. He vaulted the study cubicle and put himself between the journalist and me.

'Are you OK, *bokkie*?' He put his arm around me.

'I've had better study sessions.' I dipped my head against his chest, before pulling away. I felt we should keep our full attention on what Davis was doing.

'Alex, I hope you forgive me cornering you like this, but you are a very difficult person to get in to see.' The journalist had the intent expression of a hunting dog scenting prey. His gaze was fixed between my soulfinder's shoulder blades.

Alex didn't even turn round to face Davis, his eyes still on me as if I were the only one in his world.

'It's rare to find a young savant unguarded these days. I've had immense problems following up my leads.'

Did you tell Uriel? I asked.

The machine beeped.

Yes. He's on his way.

'Now that's just rude, talking behind my back. Though I suppose it's standard for savants.' That was rich: Davis sounded aggrieved when it was he who was pushing himself upon us! 'Exactly what my investigation is about: the abuse of power by a subgroup in society. You move among us without declaring your presence, manipulate the public so they don't even notice, swing competitions, elections, promotions in your favour. You name it: your side does it. Someone has to bring your behaviour out into the open.'

'Why?' Alex asked coolly, though I could sense the tension

inside him. With me in the room, he couldn't persuade Davis out of his dangerous investigation, but he sounded more calm than I was about this interrogation.

'Why? Because you are undermining democracy, of course! I just heard you very eloquently demolish democracy as a form of government, arguing instead for the rule of a benevolent and well-informed elite.'

Alex turned. 'Is that what this is about? You mustn't mix up debating positions with the truth, Mr Davis. I believe democracy is the best of the imperfect forms of governing available but if I had said that we'd be out of the competition. I don't think you get the point of a contest like this if you think we all believe what we say.'

But Davis wasn't open to reason. 'I had my doubts before today. It goes far beyond you, boy. The last election was manipulated by your secret society to put their man in the White House. His career will be over when I reveal him for who he really is.'

I had never heard that the president of America was a savant. We tended to go for low-profile jobs to avoid this kind of accusation and that was the opposite of obscure.

Alex injected a tone of derision into his voice. 'Help me out here, Mr Davis—what exactly is the connection between me and your president? I've never met the guy.'

'He started his career with a win in this competition, as you well know.'

'What? Thirty-five years ago? And that makes him one of these mind-manipulators, does it?' From the snap in his voice, I could tell Alex was afraid—for me rather than himself. He was stalling to give Uriel time to reach us.

'It certainly does! This extraordinary gift for manipulation is like the mark of Cain, passed down through the generations.'

A muscle ticked in Alex's jaw; fury mixed with his anxiety

but he was keeping tight control on his temper. 'And the fact that there's this mark, as you call it, gives you the right to creep up on sixteen-year-old girls doing their homework assignment to try to scare a confession out of them?'

Davis gave a contemptuous laugh. 'She's one of you too. I doubt I could scare her if I came at her with an axe!'

'No, believe me, that would scare me,' I said, shuddering.

'Don't kid yourself, miss. You'd just do that weird stuff you all do with your mind—take it from my hand with telepathy.'

'You mean, like this?' Uriel emerged from the shadow and flicked a finger. The detector flew out of the reporter's grasp and into his hand. He passed his fingers over it, reading it with his gift. 'I see you took one of Dr Surecross's inventions when you interviewed him and adapted it. Does he know that it's missing?' *Alex, get Misty away from him.*

Davis backed away, clearly much more terrified of Uriel than he was of either Alex or me. 'Now just you stop there—don't take another step near me!' The way to the exit was now clear.

Under orders from Uriel to get me away, Alex tugged my hand. 'Let's go.'

'He's got my text book,' I whispered.

Alex snatched the book from Davis' limp hand.

'Is that what you did? You just happened to find the detector in your possession when you left his office, like you did that book?' asked Uriel. There was a hardness to his tone that I hadn't heard from him before. 'I think you should come along with me and answer some questions.'

Davis opened his mouth to protest.

'Unless you want me to call the police? They'd be very interested to discover the theft and trespass.' Uriel folded his arms. 'This school takes a dim view of strange men approaching their female students. I'm sure your employers at the newspaper wouldn't approve.'

Davis wrung his hands nervously. 'I'll come with you if you promise you'll not harm me in any way—that includes using any of your powers.'

'Fine.' Uriel swept his arm towards the door. 'You go first. I'll be right behind you.'

Davis scurried out.

Uriel approached me. 'You OK, Misty?'

'Yes.'

Uriel brushed my shoulder. 'Did he say anything about the other savants who have been abducted?'

'No, he didn't mention that.'

Alex rubbed my upper arm comfortingly. 'He was going on about corruption and our secret society putting our man in the White House—standard conspiracy-theory stuff.'

'Thanks. I'll take it from here. Alex, make sure Misty gets back to her room OK and I'll ask Tarryn to find you. I don't want you walking back to your hotel alone.'

I swallowed. 'Should you be alone with him? He feels dangerous.'

Uriel gave me a direct look, revealing the steel core under the approachable exterior. 'I'm a Benedict, Misty. That makes me the most dangerous man in the room, trust me.' He left.

'That was scary.' I was shaking.

Alex hugged me closer, offering his warmth to my chilled skin. 'Terrifying. I couldn't get here fast enough. I don't think I've ever been so afraid.'

'I didn't feel threatened—not personally. He's focused on you. I think he sees you as a seedling president being grown for high office by us wicked savants.'

Alex smiled sourly at the image. 'But he knows I'm linked to you—that makes you a target too.' He picked up my bag and tucked the text book inside. 'Let's go back to your room. I don't like this place.'

I scanned the dark spaces between high shelves. 'Neither do I—not at night.'

We made our way across the school quadrangle to the accommodation block. The door to my part was protected by a punch-button code. Wanting to lighten the mood, I stood back.

'Go on. Do your thing.'

He tapped my forehead. 'You forgotten the code?'

'No, I just like watching you at work.'

Chuckling, Alex waved me to stand further back.

'By the way, what's *bokkie*?' I asked.

'Did I say that?' Alex smiled ruefully.

'Yep. In the library.'

'It means a little deer, but also means sweetheart.'

I grinned. Sometimes I didn't mind my gift.

Embarrassed, Alex turned away and wiggled his fingers over the control. The door clicked open.

'Was that finger movement necessary?' I asked, copying the motions with mine. No wonder Davis suspected spells were involved.

He caught my hands in his and kissed the tips of my nails. 'No, but I wanted to give you something to appreciate.'

'Oh, I do appreciate you—all the time. You are one big walking "like" button, Alex du Plessis.'

He laughed. 'That sounds really funny. Does it mean you want to press me all the time too?'

'Yes, please.' I pretended to click his shirt button. 'But not share on other pages.'

'Jealous, are you?'

'Yep.'

'And so am I. Come on, show me where you live before I get chucked out by whoever patrols your corridors.'

I led him up the stairs to my room on the second floor. We

passed a few of my fellow boarders. They gawped at Alex—not only was I breaking the rules, he was very gawp-worthy, so I couldn't blame them.

I opened the door to my room to let Alex go first. 'Here's my den.'

He stopped on the threshold. 'Misty, are you normally this messy?'

'I'm not messy!' I peered round his shoulder. 'Oh God.' Feeling overwhelmed, I clung to his arm.

My belongings were scattered everywhere—drawers upturned, wardrobe emptied, bags, purses and files tipped out. I tried to go in but Alex barred the door with his arms.

'Don't. Uriel needs to see this. The police too, I guess. You shouldn't disturb anything.'

I felt sick: it was like it had been done to me, not just my room. My private things were strewn about in full view— underwear, toiletries, photos, letters, mementoes. 'But who would do this? What's the point? I've nothing of value, no secrets.'

Really?

Apart from that.

And that is what it's about, I guess.

Hafsa came to find out why we were still standing in the corridor. 'Everything OK?'

I made space to show her the room. 'No, it really isn't.' My voice broke in a sob. Alex rubbed my neck in sympathy.

'Misty, someone's broken in!' she said, like I hadn't worked it out myself. 'Shall I get Mrs Huddleston?'

I glanced up at Alex. He nodded. This couldn't remain a savant-only matter.

'Thanks. She'll want to call the police.'

Hafsa pointed to her room down the corridor. 'Look, you can wait in there—I'll just phone and report this.'

'Thanks. I'd appreciate it.'

I closed the door to my room and took Alex along the corridor to Hafsa's bedroom. She had decorated her walls with posters of her favourite great authors—F. Scott Fitzgerald, Virginia Woolf and Maya Angelou (she has highbrow tastes). My walls by contrast had been a collage of my favourite actors from current film and TV shows and a slim collection of poetry books. I also had some personal touches, such as the picture of our family at Diamond and Trace's wedding in Venice. From what I'd seen in my glimpse of the interior, all of these were now in a smashed and tattered heap on the carpet.

'I don't understand. Why me? Do you think it was Davis?' I chafed my upper arms. I could imagine him crawling around in there like a cockroach but it seemed unlikely he would go unnoticed by my friends, who were in and out of their rooms the whole time.

Alex had a distant expression. He was talking to someone telepathically—Uriel I guessed. 'Uri wants to know when you were last in your room.'

'Until about seven. I picked up my geography books after supper.'

'If Davis is to be believed, he was in the debate then. I didn't pay much attention to the audience. Maybe Miss Coetzee did.'

'I'd prefer it to be him—at least I can put a face to the intruder. Surely there can't be two people creeping around the school?'

'He could've been lying about hearing my speech.'

'He wasn't, not that I could sense, but he might not have stayed for the whole debate so maybe he told us only half the truth.'

Alex relayed this to Uriel. 'He says to tell you that Victor Benedict is on his way but he'll be a few hours as he's in France. Uriel wants his brother to interrogate Davis.'

'Good idea. No one gets anything past Victor.'

'He has asked Tarryn to help you deal with the police and the staff. Then he suggests you stay with us at our hotel. Now you've been targeted, I don't want you alone here.'

I grimaced. 'Mrs Huddleston might not like the idea.'

'It's OK. I can be very persuasive.'

Tonight, I thought that was an entirely justified use of his gift. 'Go for it. She's a stickler for the rules. So without her permission, I'd have to stay here—and I know I wouldn't sleep.'

'Misty, before they come, just let me say how sorry I am.' He moved over to Hafsa's desk and picked up a book and put it down again, restlessness revealing his deep unease. 'I think it's my fault this has happened. Someone has found out about me and that's led them to you.' His eyes were filled with anguished guilt.

I put my arms round his waist to stop him prowling. 'Don't be silly; it's not your fault—and not mine. We're in this together.'

'Thanks, *bokkie*.' He brushed a light kiss on my lips.

'You're welcome, Alex.'

Our eyes met, his laser-blue and seeming to dip right inside me. At least there was one silver lining: I was facing this with a soulfinder by my side.

Chapter 15

The police found no fingerprints in my room, at least none belonging to a stranger.

'Gloves,' said the crime-scene processor. 'Most burglars know to wear them. And in a school like this it will be almost impossible to isolate any foreign DNA samples from your intruder. I suppose you're certain it wasn't one of your fellow students?' The local police made no secret of the fact that they were hoping to tag this an inside job, student prank that had gone wrong. A phone call from Victor Benedict had stopped them dismissing it without even turning up to look, but the officer dusting surfaces for prints did make me feel as if I were wasting her valuable time.

She stood up and repacked her bag. 'Nope, nothing. Your room is as clean as a whistle—apart from the mess.'

That reminded me of the killer's victims, who seemed to have died from no cause, and a murderer who left no trace. If she'd meant to be reassuring, she hadn't succeeded.

When she left, I locked the door from the outside, in no fit state to put the chaos straight. I promised myself I'd do it in the morning. I looked down the corridor. Tarryn and Alex were talking to Mrs Huddleston in the doorway to Hafsa's room. From the benign, enraptured expression on my form tutor's face, Alex's gift was in full flood. I waited where I was until he gave the signal that it was safe to join them.

He looked across at me and held out a hand.

'So you'll go with your friends tonight,' Mrs Huddleston announced as I approached, sounding for all the world as if it were her idea. 'I'll help you sort out your room tomorrow in the daylight.' She glanced up at the corner of the staircase. 'We really must see about getting CCTV installed in here. That would put off any would-be thieves.'

I suspected that ghost-intruders such as the one who turned over my room were too clever to register on digital either. I just wanted to get out of here. I had retrieved my wash bag and a change of clothes so I was desperate to go.

'Can we leave now, please?'

'Make sure she's back in time for registration at eight thirty,' Mrs Huddleston instructed Tarryn.

'Yes, of course.' Tarryn smiled reassuringly. 'Thank you, Maureen.'

We left by the night gate, emerging on to the Trumpington Road. Only a few cars passed as we walked to the city centre. Cambridge was alive with the rustle of leaves, a sound usually drowned out by human activity. It reminded me that we were surrounded by miles of flat countryside, seen from space as just a blip in the fields and fens of Cambridgeshire. I felt very exposed, prey trapped in the gaze of a hawk.

'Have we caught him?' I asked when we were clear of the school grounds.

'You mean is Eli Davis our killer?' Tarryn frowned. 'Uri doesn't know; that's why he's summoned Victor. There's a lot that doesn't add up about Davis, but murderer? We're not sure.'

'Uriel has no authority to detain him. Will he need me to persuade him to stick around for Victor?' asked Alex.

'He promised not to use savant gifts on Davis and so far the man's cooperating, so no, let's leave that for now. The guy's on fire to get us; you'd just be throwing fuel on the flames. According to Uri, Davis is relishing the confrontation, just waiting for Uri to put a foot wrong, but of course he won't. He is too good at what he does.'

This wasn't a peaceful stroll. I was unnerved but that was nothing to the tension pent up in Alex. With him walking between us, Tarryn and I were like bomb-disposal experts carrying an unexploded ordnance along the road.

'What if I persuaded him to confess?' Alex rubbed his hands over his face, trying to delete the stress of the last couple of hours.

'I don't think that's the right use of your power. Your strength is charm, not coercion,' said Tarryn. Thank goodness one of us was calm. 'Victor is a professional in the field; leave it to him.'

'But Davis went after Misty! He threatened her!'

'I know you want to get him for that, Alex, but that's hardly the right frame of mind for you to question him in. That's why we have due process. Victor can put the right questions in a legal framework—that's important if they end up prosecuting him.'

Alex gave a strangled, frustrated groan. 'How would you feel if it were Uriel he cornered in the library?'

'I'd feel very much like you do, but I hope I'd also know I had to step back so that the evidence is collected cleanly. You'd regret it more if you were the reason a suspect got away from us.'

Of course, she was right, but Alex was struggling to feel so detached. 'OK, OK, I get it. But I want to protect her from creeps like him.'

'Put your energy into making Misty feel better. I don't need Francie's gift to know that she must be really upset.'

'Yes, you're right. Sorry, Misty. I'm just finding this . . . hard.' Alex wasn't used to caring for someone. It was frightening him. I could see it in him: the desperation to protect, the dislike of being so vulnerable. 'What do you want me to do? How can I help?'

'Just be you.' I linked my hand with his. I didn't want to offload on him, not when he was carrying so much of his own baggage right now. 'You're doing fine.'

It was one in the morning by the time we got to bed. I was sharing Tarryn's room in a city-centre hotel on Parker's Piece, a grassy common that had escaped development. I drew immense comfort from knowing that she was only a short distance away in the twin bed and that Alex was just down the corridor. True to his promise to help me, he sent me to sleep with a soft chatter of telepathy, stopping me thinking too much about the violation of my private space.

But it had happened—and I couldn't understand why I had been singled out.

'Did he take anything?' Victor Benedict stood with me in the disaster area that was my room.

I stooped and picked up a jewellery box. 'Not that I've noticed.' The hinges had come apart on the casket. The box was painted in the colours of the South African flag but now only one side was still attached, the contents spilled on the floor. I didn't possess any trinkets of great value, just a few bits and bobs I'd been given over the years. I scooped them back into the broken box, having nowhere else for them.

Victor scanned the room. It looked like a whirlwind had pulled everything from the shelves, drawers, and walls. Only the bamboo-print curtains were still hanging. 'It wasn't a burglary but a search.'

'How do you know that?' I put the box on the empty dresser surface. From the scatter pattern of objects on the floor I could reconstruct how the intruder had swept his arm to push my stuff to the floor.

'The small items of value, such as the cash in your purse, weren't taken. I know you think you don't have much, but there are still many things here that could be sold if you know where to go and if you're desperate enough to stage a break-in. Your passport, for example, is worth quite a lot but he ruined it instead.' Victor plucked it from the top of a pile and put it in my bedside table. It had been torn in two, the page with my photo on it gone completely. 'Phone charger, iPod, laptop. None of them the latest model but there's still a market.'

'But if it's a search, then he wasn't very methodical.'

'No, you're right.' Victor gave me an approving look. 'I realized that a while back but I'm interested to know how you worked it out.'

'From the mess. I think a professional would manage to search my things without me even knowing he had been and gone. The way this person's enjoyed destroying my stuff suggests he was angry and mean as he did it.' I picked up the photo of Summer, Angel, and me which had been ripped in two. I could only find the half with my friends on; my side was missing.

'You got something?' Victor noticed that I'd gone very still.

I held out the half photo for him to see. 'The rest doesn't appear to be here.'

'And that part shows . . . ?'

'Me.' I turned over the frame that had held the wedding-party picture. Again, it had been torn up, this time into five or six pieces. I jiggled the bits free of the shattered glass and put them together. There was a gap on the far right where I had been. 'Victor?'

He took the pieces from my trembling hand. 'Maybe you should stop now, Misty.'

I'd never heard him be so gentle. I shook my head. Testing my new theory about this attack, I picked up my scrapbook. The pages fell apart from the binding. Shoving them back in, I could tell that any leaf with a photo of me on it had been torn out; even the baby photos if they had been labelled.

'This is sick. Why do this to me?'

'Come here.' Victor pulled me close and put his arms round me, forcing me to end the search. I don't think I'd ever seen him hug anyone before. He pretended to ignore the fact that I was crying. 'You have to stop now. I think we know what this guy was trying to achieve and you'll only drive his message deeper home if you carry on.'

'What message?' I wiped my eyes on my sleeve.

'He wants you scared.'

'Well, full marks then. He's saying I shouldn't exist—or he doesn't want me to exist, isn't he?'

Victor tensed. He would have preferred to have left that out. 'That's my reading of the situation. It would fit with a savant-hater like Davis.'

'What about the killer—if that's someone different?'

'It doesn't fit the pattern of the other abductions. There was no warning, nothing like this.'

'So it was Davis?'

'Possibly.' Victor's cool grey eyes registered his doubt. 'But he said he wasn't alone in his investigation. He's dreaming of a big exposé—winning the Pulitzer—the whole nine yards, so I can't see how room-wrecking fits. He's ignorant of the fact that many governments are well aware of our existence and that we have good reasons for not highlighting our presence in wider society. He's from the school of thought that there is no such thing as a justified secret.'

I was still stuck on the 'wasn't alone' part of what Victor was saying. 'There's more who think like him out there?'

'From what I've gleaned from Davis' rambling answers, there's a small group of like-minded crusaders against savants.'

'And one of them might have done this while I was sitting in the library and Davis was at the debate?'

My distress had reached the point where it was broadcasting on all channels citywide.

Hey, bokkie, what's wrong? Alex was supposed to be in a contest with my school team; he couldn't afford to have his concentration broken.

I wanted to say 'nothing' but couldn't. *Victor just filled me in about the anti-savant league and I got a bit upset. Sorry. Go back to what you're doing.*

Victor was eyeing me shrewdly. 'Misty, I think you need a break from this. I'll finish here. Why don't you return to classes?'

'Sounds good.' I reached for my maths folder, one of the few things that had stayed on a shelf. Drifts of confetti paper fell out. 'What?'

Victor took it from me and carefully opened it. Every page that had my handwriting on it had been destroyed. Photocopied sheets had been left untouched.

'My biology and chemistry coursework!'

He reached the files before I could and took a look inside. 'They're the same.'

Distress went off the Richter scale.

That's settled—I'm leaving this debate and coming to find you!

No! You can't let the others down. I'll . . . I'll be OK. Victor's looking after me. Stay, please. I'd feel worse if you came.

Alex agreed, but very reluctantly.

Victor piled the two files together. 'I'm really sorry, Misty. This is just cruel.'

'It must've taken ages to sort the things out into what was me and what wasn't.' I didn't want to be in this room ever again. The destroyer took a wicked relish in his work. 'That's all my coursework for three subjects. He didn't get geography but only because I had it with me.'

'I'll tell your teachers what's happened.'

'But the pages can't be replaced—they were my work, my notes.'

'I know—I'm sorry. Some things just don't make sense. There are people who are plain evil.'

My friends were shocked when they heard what had happened. In the vacuum of no sensible reason for the attack, they made up plenty of explanations, none of which were as scary as being the target of unknown savant-haters. My mind whispered that it could even be one of my peer group, someone in my school who thought like the journalist. Horrible though it was, I was beginning to suspect everyone.

But you know when they tell the truth, I told myself, and everyone is really unhappy for you.

Tony, Hafsa, and Annalise, whose subjects overlapped with my choices, immediately promised to photocopy their work. Hafsa stood over the machine in the secretary's office, feeding in her chemistry notes, while Annalise sorted out her maths and Tony his biology.

'Weird things are always happening around you,' Annalise mused, unclipping the ring binder.

'Never like this, I promise.' I sat curled up on the visitors' armchair, knees hugged to my chest.

'Maybe someone was upset by something you once said,'

suggested Hafsa. 'You know you can be . . . um . . . very direct.'

'Not that that excuses them,' Tony added quickly. 'You're not to blame.'

'Of course not. Just a thought.' Hafsa blushed and busied herself sorting out the subjects into order for me.

It was a thoroughly miserable week. I should have been on cloud nine in the days after discovering my soulfinder but instead I was in the dumps. My parents were muttering about bringing me home and only let me stay when I pleaded I wanted to stick it out in Cambridge. Alex was there; where else would I go? The only bright spells were the times spent alone with him, but even these carried with them the reminder that I couldn't be with him for the exciting final rounds of the contest. That small matter was assuming elephantine proportions for me because I was so upset about everything else.

On Tuesday night, his team had a free evening. Tarryn had the idea to take them to the leisure centre climbing wall as all the guys enjoyed the sport. Alex insisted I came too as there was no debate for me to derail and he could risk being seen with me in public. Even when not with me, he was making sure I wasn't left alone.

'I hate heights,' I warned as we walked across the grassy expanse of Parker's Piece to the modern sports complex. 'I'm just going to watch.'

'We'll see.' Alex gave me one of his heart-melting smiles. Oh lord, I could feel my resistance crumbling. I would do anything to impress him and I think he knew it.

Climbing harnesses are very unflattering, cradling those bits of you that no one usually straps in once you graduate out of a high chair. Alex seemed to appreciate the effect on me though, if the twinkle in his eye was anything to go by. He managed to kiss me several times during the process of strapping in.

'OK, guys, as you're experienced, take the red route,' said Hamish, our instructor. He had the beanpole stature of the serious mountaineer and had already won the boys' respect by his description of climbing in Yosemite.

'You got it.' Michael was off up the wall, using his long reach to grasp the next red block on the plastic rock face. Ropes hung down from the top like some bizarre maypole. I could not imagine myself going up there. What was the point?

Oh yeah, I wanted to show Alex I'd try to fit in with his life and climbing was one of his favourite hobbies.

'Misty hasn't done this before,' Alex told Hamish before I bolted.

Hamish's eyes swept my black Lycra-clad form, gauging my abilities. 'You're looking a bit pale, lass. You sure you want to do this?'

'Um . . . '

'What's the easiest route?' asked Alex. His attention wasn't really with me now as he was watching Hugo make a great move to reach the next ledge. My stomach turned over.

'Yellow. You'll find it child's play. Nothing too challenging.'

'Hmm.' Words were no longer possible.

Alex put my hand on the first position. 'There you go. Take it slowly.'

'Hey, Alex, what are you doing? We're getting old up here,' called Phil. He'd already reached the top and was looking to abseil down when the rock face was clear.

'Coming.' Alex boosted my butt in a 'get going' gesture and began climbing next to my spot. He was soon several metres over me. I listened as if my life depended on it to Hamish's patient instruction.

'The next one's to your left. No, not the green. You're doing yellow, remember.' He didn't know that half the time I had my eyes shut.

About a third of the way up I made the mistake of looking down.

'Misty, are you stuck?' asked Hamish. 'No need to panic, love, the next handhold is only a little stretch away to your right.'

But my hands would not release their grip. Why was I even doing this? I thought I'd be with Alex but he had zipped up the wall like a gecko and there was absolutely no reason for me to carry on as I certainly wasn't enjoying myself. I'd go back down—when I remembered how to make my arms and legs obey me.

'Hey, Alex, your girl's frozen,' Hugo called helpfully, monitoring me from the top. 'C'mon, Misty, you can do it. *After all, you're my wonderwall.*'

The guys picked up the song. '*Today is gonna be the day . . . *'

The other people in the leisure centre paused to listen as the quartet serenaded me, stuck on my not-so-wonderwall. Now everyone knew I was stranded.

'Cute—but not helpful!' I called up, my muscles beginning to shake with fatigue.

'You'd better go back for her,' Phil told Alex.

Did Alex huff with impatience? 'OK, Misty, I'm coming.'

Sorry for stopping you reaching the summit, Edmund Hillary, I thought sourly. I was getting very tired just holding on. Humans aren't made to stick to rocks; that was the province of insects and reptiles. And lichen. I tried to distract myself by thinking of all the various natural world creatures that would be happy clinging on here. Nowhere on the list was Misty Devon.

A familiar hand appeared beside mine—strong, capable.

'Problem?' Alex was grinning at me—that was until he saw my expression. 'You really are stuck, aren't you? I kinda thought you were pretending because you just wanted my company.'

'That would've been nice.' I looked up. No way. I glanced down. Oh crap. I was going to be caught on this climbing wall for the rest of my life and all because I thought I'd impress him and he didn't even hang around to see.

'It's really very simple.'

'Says the guy with double my reach.'

'The yellow route is for children.'

'You're not making me feel better here.' If I'd had a free hand I would have hit him.

'OK, sorry. Look, I'll help you find the next handhold.' He scanned the wall around me, then swung round so he was blanketing me, his arms either side of mine. He put his lips near my ear and began to sing just for me alone. '*I don't believe that anybody feels the way I do about you now.*'

Somehow he had found the one thing that would make me laugh.

He prised my fingers off the yellow lump and rubbed them to release the stiffness. 'Now put it there. *By now you should've somehow realized what you gotta do.*' He guided it to the next step up. His knee nudged the back of mine. 'Bend your leg and lift it—yes that's it. Find the grip with your toes.'

'*Maybe, you're gonna be the one that saves me,*' I sang back.

'*And after all, you're my wonderwall.* That's it: you're doing it.'

With him beside me, I was able to continue with my snail's-pace ascent. I had ropes and a harness but it was really his steady encouragement that kept me going.

'That's good. See, you're getting there, *bokkie.*'

We were almost at the top.

'OK now?'

'Yes, thanks.'

He leaned closer, on the point of kissing me.

'Hello? Alex, is that you up there?' called a voice from below.

Kiss postponed, Alex looked down. 'Johan! You're back! Excuse me, Misty.' Without further ado, he abseiled down, leaving me to my own devices again.

Hugo, Michael and Phil talked me up the last few holds so I reached the platform next to them. I couldn't stand, only sit with my head on my knees murmuring 'never again'.

'Do you want me to show you how to abseil?' asked Phil, the best of the four at climbing.

I shook my head.

'I don't think it's worth waiting for Alex. He's talking to that guy, his uncle. Great, isn't it? I'm so pleased he's got family now.' Phil crouched beside me.

I nodded. I shouldn't feel sore that I'd been abandoned for Johan. I had had plenty of people to help me and Alex probably had no idea how scary I found heights.

'So you'll let me demonstrate?' asked Phil. I think he got how upset I was, unlike my soulfinder. We'd had that sweet moment on the wall and then he'd just abandoned me. 'There's no other way down, you know.'

'And I'd been hoping for wings,' I said, a little shakily.

'It's much easier than climbing up.'

'Yeah, it's simple.' Hugo helped adjust my ropes. 'Just keep straight or you get off alignment and end up swinging like a pendulum.'

Michael rubbed my neck consolingly. 'And think: you never have to climb this damn wall again once you get down.'

Now that was a good thought. I stood up, kept my eyes fixed on Phil, who was letting out my rope, and walked slowly down the wall. No showy slide for me.

I got to the ground without mishap. Phil gave me a thumbs-up as Hamish unclipped my gear.

'Want to try that again?' he asked.

'Not in this lifetime,' I replied earnestly. I looked round, expecting Alex to at least congratulate me for overcoming my fear of heights but he was at the drinks dispenser with Johan, feeding in coins. 'Thanks, Hamish, but I'm done here.'

The guys zipped down the ropes like Special Forces ending a hostage crisis.

'Got anything more challenging?' asked Phil.

I left the other three to their climb as they tried the black route.

'Hey, Alex,' I said softly, approaching him and Johan. 'Hi again, Mr du Plessis.'

'Misty.' Johan nodded.

'So, Misty, you got down OK?' asked Alex.

He hadn't even watched.

'Yes.'

'Easy, isn't it?'

I swallowed and looked away. 'I think I should be getting back to school.'

'Already?'

'Homework.' I hadn't been intending to do it tonight but it was true that I did have some.

'Uncle, do you mind if I just walk Misty back?'

Johan smiled apologetically at me. 'That's fine but I can't stay long. My car's only got an hour left on the meter.'

'Oh, I see. Misty, maybe Hugo could go with you? Hey, Hugo, come here a moment!'

Holding on to the wall with one hand, Hugo waved that he was on his way.

I didn't want to be passed round like a parcel. 'No need. Tony's got a jujitsu class here this evening. I'll text him and ask if I can walk back with him. He finishes about now.' I got out my phone and sent the message.

Alex smiled distractedly. 'Great. Problem solved. Hugo, request cancelled.' He brushed a kiss on my cheek, lacking its usual spark.

'I hope you don't mind me monopolizing Alex like this,' said Johan, 'but I'm only in the country a few more days.'

So was Alex.

'It's not every day you discover a nephew.'

Or a soulfinder.

'Of course, it's fine. I'll see Misty later.' Alex stepped in before I could say something blunt. He had to sense I wasn't happy but I could tell he thought I was being selfish. Was I? I didn't know if it was that or even more ugly resentment that I was being edged out. I'd told him I'd put him first in family things but he wasn't reciprocating, was he?

'Actually, Alex, I'm busy tonight.' Washing my hair.

He didn't sound too bothered. 'OK. Tomorrow then.'

'If you can fit me into your busy schedule.'

'Very funny. See you.'

Finding myself dismissed, I headed for the women's changing room, seething.

Arriving back in my bedroom after the climbing wall incident, I reached for my phone.

'Hi, Summer?' I could hear classical music playing in the background. 'Can you talk?'

'I'm not supposed to but hang on.' There was a fumbling and a muttering at the other end, then Summer came back on line. 'OK, escaped from that deadly concert. I have a few minutes before they notice. How's things with your gorgeous soulfinder?'

I couldn't help myself: I just poured out all my woes—my feelings after the trashing of the bedroom, my exclusion from the debates, Alex's preoccupation with his new relative. 'Am I being really selfish and horrible?' I ended.

Summer paused before answering, choosing her words with care. 'I think anyone would feel like you, Misty. It's a difficult time for you both.'

'Funny thing is that Uriel once asked me not to dent Alex's confidence but Alex is doing a brilliant job dismantling mine.'

'Oh, Misty.'

'Yeah. I know you and Angel think that finding your soul-finder is the passport to eternal happiness but I'm finding it a one-way ticket to feeling bad about myself. Surely this isn't right?'

'Have you talked to Alex?'

'He knows there's something up, but he's finding excuses: the attack on my room, the threat of the killer, the journalist creep. He says sod all about his failure to provide what I need right now.'

'And what do you need?'

'What I need . . . is to feel that I'm as important to him as he is to me.'

'Does Alex realize that?'

'I don't know. I guess he thinks we'll have time to sort things after the competition and when this Johan person has left. He's distracted.' Anger flared. 'But do you know what? Alex is breaking his promise to put my happiness first. He won't even allow me in to see the final and I so want to be there.'

'You've got to tell him. How else is he to know?' I heard a sigh. 'Look, I've got to go. Promise me you'll try to explain this to him. Don't hide how you feel.'

'I'll try.'

'Love you.'

'Love you too, Summer.' As I ended the call, I realized I wished Alex would just say he loved me.

Alex's team won the final but it was really hard for me to join in the rejoicing. Tarryn and Uriel had seconded Alex's opinion that I was too dangerous to have in the room so I hadn't been there to see them triumph over the Danes. We went to a pizzeria to celebrate the victory, square tables shoved together for our party. Hugo, Phil, and Michael were down the other end with Tony, Annalise and Hafsa. My friends had cheered for the South Africans and they couldn't understand why I hadn't turned up to support them. I said something lame about not being good for Alex's concentration.

Dismissing my explanation with a shrug, Annalise turned back to Phil. 'You were so funny! Your joke about bankers really floored the Danish team.'

'And Alex really crushed them in the summing up. There was no coming back from that,' added Hafsa.

'Yeah, it was way more fun than I expected,' said Tony.

I fiddled with the fat pepper grinder. 'You know, Alex, all I need is a bell and a sign saying "leper".'

'You're in quarantine for my sake, not because there's something wrong with you,' Alex pointed out, topping up my lemonade from the little bottle it had come in.

'There's a lot wrong with me when I can't even be there for my soulfinder.'

'Sssh, *bokkie*, you're getting upset.'

Calm and reasonable did not help. '*Getting* upset? I am upset! I've been upset all week.' Oh no, I was going to lose it, here in the middle of La Dolce Vita.

'I know. I understand.'

He didn't. 'I'm such a crappy soulfinder. I just want to be there for you—to hear you, see you do your speeches.'

'Maybe one day we'll work out how to do that, but today you would've ended our winning streak. I didn't want to do that to my friends.' Alex's eyes went to his mates who were having a great time with mine at the other end of the table. 'Winning meant so much to them.'

'You let Johan listen.' Alex's uncle had been to all the debates, positioning himself proudly in the front row. Johan was now sitting next to Alex but was caught up at the moment in his conversation with Tarryn. If he heard our quarrel he was too polite to show it. Tarryn was reminiscing about Alex at school; Johan liked to soak up all the little growing-up stories he had missed. I heard snatches of 'top of his class', 'amazingly mature for his age', 'valued member of the school community'. The differences between us had never been starker.

Alex's attention turned to his uncle, a small smile appearing. 'Of course he can listen. He doesn't have the same effect on me as you.'

I already knew that. 'But Alex, I feel a total dead loss.' I wanted to be better, more selfless than I was. I massacred my pizza crust and gave up on the meal. 'No wonder someone wants to get rid of me—even I want to get rid of me.'

'Don't talk like that!' I'd made him cross but I didn't care; hopelessness and recklessness surged through me. At least he was now paying attention. 'You're my soulfinder—perfect for me.' He squeezed my hand, almost punishingly. 'We are just going to have to work at things.' His blue eyes blazed with sincerity.

'Work at things? Like we can do that with you living on the other end of the world! I barely have a week with you and you're spending it with other people.'

Why was I doing this? I knew I was being self-destructive but somehow I couldn't pull myself back.

Alex released my hand and sat back in his chair, expression a great deal cooler than normal. 'You know something, Misty, it sounds to me like you're having second thoughts.'

Not for the reasons he was thinking. I felt as if I were competing with Johan and losing.

Attack seemed the best form of defence. 'Why am I the problem here? What about you? What about you trying to get by in public with me there?'

'Misty—'

'No, you listen. Why do I have to be exiled? Can't you learn to cope? Why not give me some of your precious time and try that?'

'I can learn, but I don't think the international debate competition is the place to road test, do you, what with you forcing the unvarnished truth out of me if you're there?' His tone was cool, even a little patronizing. 'And I won't apologize for wanting to get to know my uncle: that's natural.'

'When will there be a good moment for you to learn if you can always put it off?'

He shook his head in a don't-be-silly-Misty way that drove me over the edge.

'And what is it that you think you're going to say if I force you to tell the truth? That's how you put it, you know: me forcing you like . . . like a slave driver cracking a whip behind you.'

'I don't say it like that.'

'Yes, you do!' I had counted the occasions even if he didn't keep score. 'You make me hate myself when you say that about my gift. It's always "Misty made me . . . " or "the truth was forced from me". What's so wrong with the truth? What if I'm the one in the right and everyone else is wrong to spend their whole lives lying to each other to smooth the way?'

Then it hit home. I had thought that, of those I was close to, only my father didn't accept me as I was, but he wasn't alone. Human society hated honesty. Savants differed only in that they saw my truth gift as a condition to be handled carefully, a handicap that needed therapy. Being Misty wasn't enough, not even for my soulfinder. Not even for me.

'Hey, Misty,' Hugo called, 'your friends say you sat in your room during the debate.'

My new room. It was empty apart from a small case of new clothes as all my possessions were spoiled.

'Yes, I did.' I didn't look at Hugo. My gaze fixed on the black blob of olive sitting on my uneaten pizza. It looked like a mini car tyre had got mired in yellow mud. Wheels come off a relationship.

'Now that's just mean. I thought you were our friend.' His tone was jokey but it came out as an accusation. 'We needed all the support we could get as most guys were on the side of the glamorous Danes.'

'Hugo,' warned Alex. He was worried about my dark mood, I could tell, but hadn't twigged how deep my despair had become. 'I asked Misty not to come.'

'Why? You ashamed of her or something?' Again Hugo meant it as a jest but it didn't come out as being funny; his tone was too serious. My gift at work.

I got up. Alex had said right from the beginning I embarrassed him. I was proving him right.

'Misty, I'm not ashamed . . . ' Alex stopped; he couldn't complete the sentence, telling everyone in the room exactly how he regarded me. His embarrassment. His burden.

'I'm going home.'

Alex rose to follow me.

'Not with you.' I couldn't bear to be with him right now.

He sat down, his hurt clear to read in his expression. *Why not?*

I just can't be with you right now.

'You can't go alone.'

Uriel started to rise but Johan got up, waving him to sit. 'I've got to move the car from its two-hour slot so I'll take her back for you, Alex.' He patted his nephew on the shoulder.

'Thanks.' Alex nodded to his uncle but didn't glance at me. He was in 'licking wounds' mode.

Hugo opened his mouth to add something but Phil elbowed him in the ribs.

'See you later, Misty!' called Hafsa. I could hear the subtext: she would check on me when she got in.

I nodded and walked out, shoulders hunched. I had been rude but it was better than bursting into tears and spoiling everyone's evening. Exile at least had that benefit.

Johan caught up with me on the pavement outside. A bitter wind was blowing. 'My car's just round the corner.'

'Thanks. You don't have to do this.' Part of me hankered after a quiet walk back to put my scattered thoughts in order. My head felt like my room after the intruder had been through it.

'It's fine, Misty. In fact, it's a pleasure. A lift will save you a freezing walk across Cambridge and Tarryn explained why none of you should be alone.' He pointed his keys and the lights on a black Toyota flashed, wing mirrors moving out to drive position. 'Jump in. I'll have you back in no time.'

Settling into the passenger seat of his hire car, it took me a moment to register we were heading for the ring road.

'It's quicker this time of night if you cut through town. Do you want me to direct?' I massaged my temples. My head felt like I was suffering from a bad cold, congested so that it was hard to hear and breathe. Lights flashed by, people distorted by shadow and speed.

'That's OK. I can find my way with the satnav.' He angled the little dashboard machine towards him and glanced at the screen. 'I see what you mean. But now I'm on this route we might as well follow it. Are you feeling any better?'

Actually I was feeling worse.

He didn't wait for an answer. 'My nephew is quite something, isn't he?'

'Yes, you can be very proud of him.'

'Do you think he'd like to make a home with me during his college breaks?'

'Probably. Ask him. He wants family more than anything.'

'Not more than you, surely?'

After our argument? We'd find that out in the morning. 'I don't know, Mr du Plessis. Sorry, I've a headache.' I closed my eyes, head back against the rest.

'You have? I'm good with curing that kind of small problem. Do you want me to get rid of it for you?'

'That's your gift?' I couldn't seem to open my eyes.

'Yes, I can take it away. It's really very simple.'

He was telling me the truth. 'Well, if it won't distract you from the road, I'd be grateful.'

'No problem. I'm just going to touch your forehead. You won't feel a thing.'

'Useful gift.'

'I think so.' A cool fingertip brushed my eyebrows. 'Right, on the count of three, you will be gone. One, two . . .'

Chapter 16

There was a twig under my cheek.

It took me a moment to make sense of that. Hang on, it still didn't make sense. I opened my eyes. I was lying face down on a leafy patch of ground, not in my bedroom.

'What the heck . . . ?'

Someone was walking away from me, leaves crunching under boots. I felt sluggish, my arms and legs slow to obey my order to get up. I was also freezing. As sitting up was too much just at the moment, I rolled onto my back. Bare branches networked overhead, only a few bone-dry leaves hanging on but half-heartedly as if they knew they wouldn't survive the next brisk wind. I registered that I was still wearing the clothes I had worn at the pizzeria but that night had passed and it was dawn. The next day or some other day? Chilled birds sang their distress from a tangle of brambles.

Making a huge effort, I sat up. The dew damp had gone right through all layers of clothing. A small campfire had burned down to ashes a metre away. Someone wrapped in a sleeping bag with his back to me was stirring it with a stick. His face was hidden so I couldn't tell if I knew him.

Too exhausted to move, I let myself explore the possible explanations. A dream. Sucking the scratch on my palm—how had I got that?—filled my mouth with the taste of blood and earth. No dream could do that, not with such intense reality.

I'd gone on a camping trip and lost my memory? Got really drunk for the first time? This seemed the best explanation. But why wasn't I in a sleeping bag like the other person? It seemed cruel to leave me shivering even if I'd passed out in a stupor.

OK, so maybe I'd hit my head and wandered into this camp by accident? That would make the sleeper a stranger. I'd ask him for help.

But what if one of the anti-savant people had abducted me? I had a vague recollection of being roused in the pitch dark to walk here and falling asleep again immediately. If that was the case and not some random dream, it was likely to be my kidnapper over there.

Desperate now, I looked about me, trying to get a clue as to where we were. I was lying in a clearing surrounded by tall, ancient-looking trees. In the distance I could hear a road but it sounded very far away.

Alex, are you out there somewhere? My telepathy fizzled out, stopping just a little way from my brain. I'm not sure how I could be so convinced of that but it was like knowing how far your voice would carry; my telepathy was down to a hoarse whisper.

Someone had heard though. The man turned round.

Johan.

He didn't look threatening wrapped up snugly like an Indian papoose in his sleeping bag. His expression was—well, *exulting* was the word that came to mind. He gave me a 'good morning' nod and shrugged off the cover. I really didn't want him to emerge—I wanted him to stay huddled over there for ever while I made a run for it. That was if I could get rid of this sensation of being weighed down by concrete.

'You slept well, Misty?'

His question was bizarrely inappropriate to someone who had 'slept' sprawled without cover on a bed of old leaves.

'What am I doing here, Mr du Plessis?' I brushed my hands on my jeans then brought them up to my face to blow on cold fingers. I was scared to the bone but guessed it was safer not to show this.

'I thought after some breakfast we'd make a start. There's some business to deal with in Cambridge, then we can get on with it.' He poked the fire, frowning at the dead ashes. 'We could do with Yves Benedict—I hear he's good with flame. I decided he was too complicated—and a little too old. I don't suppose this is one of your hidden talents?'

I shook my head, dislodging leaves caught in my hair.

'Shame. Still, you have some gifts that will prove rewarding, I'm sure.' He took kindling from a pile he had made a little way off. He painstakingly built a tepee structure, then struck a match. I watched in silence, debating if I could outrun him. I'm small and light on my feet usually, but I had woken up with the sensation of being weighed down by manacles. I rubbed my ankles. He glanced at my hands. I stopped moving and tucked my fingers back under my arms.

'I'm afraid breakfast is going to be very basic as this was more an impulse outing than a well-planned expedition.' He threw something at me. I was too slow to react and it hit my curled up knees and fell onto the ground. A cereal bar.

'The service station didn't offer much in the way of choice. I've water, if you want it.'

Now he mentioned it, I realized I was ferociously thirsty. I nodded.

'Come now, what have you done with your manners?' His expression was taunting.

'Yes, please, I'd like some water.'

This time I was ready and caught the little plastic bottle. I unscrewed the blue lid and took a gulp.

'There, you see, we'll get along fine. I can't abide bad behaviour. If you are quiet and obedient, we might even be together quite pleasantly for some time to come.'

It was no comfort to know that everything he said was a truth as far as he understood it. That still left me confused: what could possibly be the point of this?

'Mr du Plessis . . . '

He held up a hand. 'Uncle Johan. We are practically family, after all.'

The idea of calling him 'uncle' made me want to vomit but his expression warned that he would take anything else as a sign of rebellion.

'Uncle Johan,' the questions jostled in my mind—where, why, who—I settled for the one I thought the least offensive, 'where are we?'

'Epping Forest.' He looked around at the stands of elegant beeches. Their trunks shone faintly in green and silver streaks of smooth bark. 'Pretty, isn't it? I do like how you British preserve old places despite the pressure of your population. There are far too many of you on this small island. Surely you aren't all necessary?'

'Why are we here?' I checked my watch. It was seven in the morning. 'I'm supposed to be at school.' I had the sudden random thought that I would be missing breakfast if I didn't get back by nine when they stopped serving, but a second thought followed immediately that I had far more serious worries than that.

'I thought I would liberate you from a situation that you found intolerable.' That was only a partial truth. He gave a half-smile as if recalling that he couldn't lie to me. 'I find your gift interesting, and I can't say that I like your link with my nephew, so I thought it would be good for the two of us to spend time together so I could get to know you better.'

He was speaking honestly but there was some hidden meaning that he was concealing. He had had us all fooled in Cambridge but now I suspected I knew who—or at least what—he really was. Hoping I was wrong, I latched onto one part of what he said that hinted at a less frightening motive for his actions.

'Why don't you like my link to Alex?' We had hit a rough patch but I hadn't been that bad, surely?

He opened his own bar and gestured to me to copy. I didn't dare refuse, though food was the last thing I wanted.

'To be frank, you're inconvenient. Soulfinders make their partners so boring. I don't have a family that acknowledges me and I want Alex to be mine. He won't be while he is focused on you.'

So there was some weird kind of jealousy at play. Maybe that was the only reason—maybe he wasn't the person I feared. In any case, he was wrong about the attention being for me.

'But didn't you see how eager he was to get to know you? I don't get in the way—he has made room for both of us or, at least, was attempting to.' I'd been unfair to Alex, I realized. He had been trying.

'No, he puts you first.' Johan stated it as if there was no doubt on the issue. 'I did think about it for a day or two but came to the conclusion that you would always have his loyalty before me. That is unacceptable.'

'And it's not unacceptable to kidnap me and drag me off to the middle of a forest?' I couldn't contain my anger a moment longer—but I wish I had.

'Careful.' His tone was searing. I flinched even though he made no move towards me. 'You're not to question me. I'll tell you only those things I want to share with you. You can't understand the greater plan that is at work here or your part in it—you are just one small immature savant, but I am so much more.'

The clues that he wasn't sane had been there since the waking-up-in-the-forest moment; that speech clinched it. If I was dealing with someone so unstable, I would have to keep him calm. I remembered Sky and Phoenix's advice. My one advantage was looking small and unthreatening, so I would use it.

'I'm sorry, Uncle Johan. I just don't understand, that's all.'

He got up and approached me. I tried not to cringe. He leaned down and patted my hair. His mood had shifted again to something more benign. 'Don't worry your pretty little head about the whys and wherefores, Misty. Thinking has never been your strong point, has it?'

I guess it hadn't as I had ended up here with him. I looked down rather than risk an answer.

'Unfortunately, I have to get back to Cambridge so I can be there to comfort Alex when they discover you're missing. You were sleeping in the car when I went back to the restaurant but I told them I dropped you safely at school. They'll want me to confirm my story.' He said all this as if it were entirely reasonable. He was leaving and by the sounds of it I wasn't. 'I can see that you think I'll do something drastic to you but don't worry, there's plenty of time left for you and me to work together. I'm going to put you into nowhere for a while as I deal with the fuss, but I'll be back for you, never fear.' He looked at my blue-tinged nails. 'I think I will leave you the sleeping bag. Can't have you freezing to death now, can we?'

I tried to leap up but the weights-that-weren't-there on my legs kept me down.

'Now, now, none of that. Just get in the sleeping bag. I'm going to hide you here so no one will stumble over you.' He dropped the sack on my lap.

There had to be a way out of this but I couldn't think of one. Heroes in the books I read were always immensely resourceful, having some secret weapon or plan to foil plots against them. But maybe I was only a minor character—another victim that falls about halfway through. With my track record, that seemed far more likely.

'W-what do you mean, nowhere?'

'If you get in then I'll tell you.'

Seeing nothing else for it, I wiggled inside, disgusted at myself for not putting up a better resistance. It smelt of his overpowering pine-scented deodorant, which made it even worse, like accepting a hug from him.

He crouched beside me, his expression friendly again. 'There's a good girl. You're much quicker than the others to know that making a fuss is unproductive.'

The *others*? Oh God.

'My gift is to make a void. I suppose you can say it is the reverse of my nephew—he fills people up with his charm; I can make them blank, register as an empty space. I can do it to myself as well, which I must say has proved most useful.' He looked as though he wanted me to congratulate him.

I could feel tears pricking my eyes. 'And you are going to make me disappear?'

He nodded, pleased at my quick grasp. 'Yes, exactly. For today at least. I'll be back to fetch you when I can reasonably leave Alex. I'm anticipating that he might be a little distressed that you've dropped out of his life as suddenly as you fell into it.'

Johan didn't understand. Soulfinders can't be only a 'little' distressed at such a thing. 'But you'll be back?' I wasn't sure I wanted Johan to, but suspected he was the only one who could make me return from nowhere.

Johan smiled. 'Absolutely, Misty. I promise. You won't feel a thing. It's just like passing out under anaesthetic.'

I tried sending out another telepathic distress call but it went no further than the nearest tree.

Johan reached out his finger and touched my forehead. 'One, two . . .'

Chapter 17

'Misty? Misty?'

It took me a while to rouse myself. I woke feeling like I'd just had a heavy dose of flu. I didn't want to open my eyes. The voice belonged to the man I most hoped—most feared—to see.

'I'm sorry you've been out so long. It took more time than I expected.' A bottle was pushed against my lips. I could feel that they were cracked and dry. I gulped.

'How long?' I croaked.

'Two days. You must be hungry and in need of a bathroom break. Let me help you out of the sleeping bag.'

Limbs as wooden as the fallen branches around me, I staggered to my feet as Johan pulled me up. He was right; I did need a visit to the bushes. That added a slick of humiliation on my ocean of fear.

'Where can I . . . ?'

I didn't need to say any more. He took me to the other side of the tree, showed me a low branch I could hold and left me to it. After some clumsy fumbling at my jeans, I managed to sort myself out, refasten my clothes and stumble back round the tree. He held out a little bottle of handwash. He then helped me sit on a log he'd pulled near the fire.

'Feeling better now?'

'Yes.' Apart from the fact that I was stuck in a forest with a madman.

'You'll be pleased to hear you are much missed. Alex is very distressed.'

I was supposed to be happy about that? 'My parents?'

'Out of their wits with worry. And your friends.' He smiled and passed me a filled baguette. 'There you are: lunch.'

Wiping my eyes, I registered that it was broad daylight.

'Go on: eat.' He nudged my hand nearer my mouth. Remembering how quick he was to anger, I took a bite. The taste reminded me that I was hungry; if he wanted to kill me, I wasn't going to do the job for him by starving.

'You'll be flattered to know that there's a huge hunt under-way for you. They've flown in your aunt Crystal. Now there's a fascinating gift. She's using your link to my nephew to track you.' He didn't sound worried. Instead he got out a flask and poured himself a cup of coffee. He held the drink out to me. 'Would you like some? Best Arabica beans.'

I shook my head. 'I'd prefer water.'

'It's by your foot.'

I looked down to see the bottle resting against the log. We continued our bizarre picnic, me wondering why he hadn't killed me yet and him . . . well, I don't know what he was thinking. I wondered how close a rescue party might be.

He answered my question before I had to ask. 'Of course, Crystal can't sense you, thanks to my gift. She is getting a rather distressing nothing in response. I'm afraid they think you are dead. Everyone's hugely upset.'

I twisted to be sick behind my log. I didn't have much in

my stomach so it hurt my abdomen. I grappled for the water to rinse my mouth.

'I did wonder maybe whether Uriel and Victor Benedict suspected me but I allowed Uriel to touch me and trace my history; he got nothing except an impression of a blank blameless night spent in a Cambridge hotel. They're focused on that idiot, Eli Davis, who helpfully didn't have an alibi for the time you disappeared.' Johan crossed the campfire clearing and helped me to another log away from where I had been ill. He didn't mention that, neither to tell me off or apologize, just ignored what he didn't want to notice. 'Alex was very upset with the Benedicts for suggesting I had anything to do with it. He's a fine boy.'

I could imagine that Alex was massively confused. If I had vanished, he wouldn't want his only family to be taken from him as well.

It was going to kill him when he learned what Johan was.

Alex? I didn't expect to succeed but my telepathy still had no way to escape Johan's influence. I needed him so much it hurt.

'You'll feel better if you eat something.' Johan gestured to my sandwich.

'Maybe later.' If there was a later. I wrapped the clingfilm back round the end I had bitten. Mozzarella and tomato. One of my favourite flavours until today. I'd only just noticed.

'I imagine you want to know what happens next?' Johan drained his coffee.

'Yes.' He raised a brow. 'Please.'

'I for one don't like sleeping in a forest.' He smiled as if I should get the joke. 'My tastes are more *evolved* than that. I've told Alex I have to go on business but will be back next week to aid with the search if you haven't been found. I was his only comforter, you know, as I suggested that you'd probably just run away, thinking yourself not worthy to be his soulfinder, and that you'd be back when you had had a chance to consider things in peace.'

'How does that work with them thinking I'm dead?'

His thin mouth curved in a smile. He was enjoying this. 'Well, I refused to believe it, naturally. I said that Crystal was letting fear blind her, that Alex would know if you were dead and he's convinced you're still alive.'

Because I was. I felt a little comforted by the fact Alex hadn't given up on me.

Johan put the top back on his Thermos flask. 'He was very encouraged by my faith in his instincts.'

Snake.

'I promised to hurry back but had an unavoidable meeting in America to attend. As do you.'

'Me?'

'Yes. I've brought you a change of clothes. You are coming with me to Oregon for Thanksgiving.'

His shift of direction was as erratic as the path of a tornado, twisting one way then the next. 'Why?'

'Why? Because Thanksgiving is a family time, don't you know that?'

He was making no sense. I took some hope from the fact that if he tried to take me abroad we'd have to leave the forest. Questioning him to make him see the pitfalls in that would probably end up with me left here dead. Cooperation seemed the right course.

'Let's go then.'

He pulled a carrier bag from his backpack—all new clothes bought from some supermarket. 'There you are. I'll get you some more things when we get to America.'

So he was serious about this going-abroad notion. I didn't have my passport on me as that had been destroyed. He'd never get me through border control.

I took the bag and went behind another tree. I was relieved to see he had put in some thick layers, including gloves, scarf, and coat. I dressed rapidly. Somehow being warmer made it a little easier to think. I had to keep him happy, give him no cause to decide he should kill me and be done with it; but I also had to escape. His wild idea of going to Oregon—where was that exactly?—sounded like it could end in a showdown at the airport. I had to keep as far from him as possible. He could put me out with a touch; I guessed he could kill with a fingertip too.

That was probably what happened to the others.

We had to hike a long way back to the car. He had parked by the side of a minor road and we passed no one. I tried to work out what day it was. Wednesday? Americans always celebrated Thanksgiving on a Thursday, didn't they? That meant he planned to be across the Atlantic very soon.

When we reached the car, he gestured to me to get in the back.

'I'm afraid I can't risk having you up front,' he said in his hateful let's-be-reasonable tone. 'You might be seen.'

The rear had darkened windows and he had put up a grill, the sort used to contain dogs in the boot.

'Now you have a choice: I can put you out or you let me secure your hands and feet. I won't gag you: there's no one to hear.'

Until we reached the airport.

I held up my wrists.

'Good choice.' He quickly fastened them with plastic ties. Once he was content that I was immobilized, he got in the driver's seat and started the car. He put on the radio to fill the silence. When the news came on, we listened to the emotional appeal from my parents promising me that I wasn't in any trouble for running away if that was what I had done and begging me to come back.

Please don't think I did this to you on purpose, I pleaded, wishing for a chink in Johan's blackout to send my message through to them.

The announcer quickly moved on to war in the Middle East. Johan searched for another channel, settling for local radio with its almost continual travel announcements. I looked out of the window. I didn't know this part of England very well but the road signs changed to the blue of a motorway. The plane icon pointed to Stansted as our destination—London's third airport. We didn't go in the main entrance but took a detour round to a gate for a private aviation company. The barrier folded back for Johan without him having to announce his arrival. My hopes of a public showdown were diminishing.

'Don't be surprised, Misty, when people don't notice you,' Johan said cheerfully. 'I'm going to expand my gift to cover you so you won't register on any of their senses. It takes a lot of effort for me to do this so I trust you won't give me any trouble?'

I was fully intending to be as much trouble as I could so I said nothing.

He parked in front of a little glass building. 'This is the terminal for VIPs and those with their own planes.' He emptied out the glove compartment of anything connecting him to the car. 'I won't be long.'

I watched as he went into the building. The moment his back was turned and he was talking to the official at the reception, I tried the door. Locked. I tried to move the mechanism with telekinesis but I didn't know how the catch worked and I lacked Alex's gift to persuade doors to do what I wanted.

Johan was coming back. I sat very still.

He opened my door and cut the ties at my feet. 'We're good to go. Again, you have a choice: cooperate and remain conscious or do this the hard way.'

'Conscious.' I got out. There would be a crew, surely, people I could appeal to on the plane if nowhere else?

'Good girl.'

He gripped the back of my coat to stop me trying to make a run for it and led me across to a plane—an executive jet of some sort. Beautiful, slender, and white—it was the kind of aircraft I'd only ever seen in films. A stewardess waited at the door.

'Welcome, Mr Smith. So pleased to see you back with us.'

Johan gave her a broad smile. 'Hebe, great to see you too.'

Now or never. 'Please, won't you help me?' I shouted.

Johan poked me in the ribs, finger a threat, reminding me what he could do.

Her eyes slipped right past me. 'Is there any luggage to bring aboard?'

'No, it's already loaded.' He prodded me to go up the stairs.

'Then I'll inform the captain you're ready to fly.'

She stepped inside. Johan pushed me over the threshold and into the main cabin. We walked past the row of four seats to a door at the back. He opened it and propelled me inside. It was a private cabin with a bed and a seat by the window.

'Sit there.' He buckled me into the seat. 'The door will be locked. If I hear you making any noise to attract attention to yourself, I'll be through that door first and that will be the last thing you know.' He pinched my chin. 'Do you understand?'

I nodded, tears filling my eyes despite my resolution not to show him any emotion.

He patted my head. 'If you behave, I'll bring you some food later. The flight takes about ten or so hours depending on the headwind.'

He left, locking the door from the outside.

Once alone, I sprang up to explore my prison. There was a little bathroom with sink, toilet and tiny shower. Other than soap and hand towels, there was nothing. The bed was made with a tightly stretched blanket and sheet. I could rip up the material but then do what with it? The seat by the window was fixed; the lighting was wall-mounted—no handy heavy-based lamp to turn into a weapon.

Come on, Misty, be realistic: you're a smallish girl and he's a tall man. You're unlikely to do anything but annoy him if you attack.

But neither do I want just to fall in with his plans.

What other option do you have?

My inner dialogue stopped at that point as the engines started.

'Mr Smith, on behalf of First Officer Finlay and myself, Captain Hussain, I'd like to welcome you aboard this flight to Portland, Oregon. We have been given our slot by air traffic control and expect to take off in five minutes. The weather forecast looks good at this time. Please be seated, buckle up, and enjoy your flight.'

The plane started to move. Johan had forgotten, or perhaps not intended, to remove my wrist ties. Having no immediate escape plan, I took my seat and grappled for the seatbelt. Gazing out the window, I had a last fleeting hope some airport employee would see me but the field was deserted as 747s lumbered along the taxiways like sleek white dinosaurs. We turned to the start of the runway, paused and then the aircraft moved with more determination. The front lifted, then the rear. We were airborne, climbing steeply. Johan had managed to get me out of England without even a hint of difficulty.

The captain came on again. 'Mr Smith, in a few moments it will be safe to remove your seatbelt. Hebe will then serve you a selection of light snacks and drinks, followed by lunch when we reach our cruising height. Thank you for flying with Executive Manoeuvres, the world's premier airline for business charters.'

As I had begun to piece together, Johan had hired his own plane. It sounded like he made a habit of it. It must cost a fortune. Where had he got the money?

The answer came quickly. His last victim had been a treasure seeker, and there had been others with similar skills—the Australian girl, the American trio with their stocks and shares. I had to assume money was no obstacle in my enemy's plans for me.

The seatbelt light went off so I released the buckle. The door to my cabin opened and Johan slipped in.

'I'm pleased to see you haven't tried anything foolish.'

Only because I couldn't think of what to do.

'I'll reward your cooperation by releasing your wrists. You may shower—I won't need to use this bathroom.'

'I'd like to get clean.' Lying in the forest had left a layer of grime no handwash or clean clothes could remove.

'I'll bring you some lunch in an hour.' He left, locking the door again.

There was a 'call attendant' button by the seat. Did I dare? Hebe did not expect anyone else to be aboard so would she even check? And if she did, what then? Would it endanger her and the crew? I guessed that was likely. Until I had a better idea what to do with that button, I'd leave it alone. Picking a fight with Johan while in the air was like releasing a swarm of killer bees in the cabin: dead stupid.

So, shower it was.

I stripped off in the little cubicle and stood under the spray. I let tears I'd been holding back fall with the water now there was no one to see. The ugly truth was that I was unlikely to survive this adventure. Johan had killed before, easily and with no regrets. For the moment he had a use for me but I was an obstacle to him monopolizing Alex's love. That thought made it even worse: if he succeeded in killing me, he would also ruin Alex's life, forcing him in his grief to rely on the very one who caused it. I wanted to scream at the obscenity of that.

My inner voice piped up: so you accept that Alex does need you for his life?

Yes, I did.

You were an idiot to make such a fuss at the pizzeria.

I knew that at the time, thanks. I just . . . just don't feel enough for him.

Then you'd better fight for what you want—if you want him.

To the death, I promised myself.

As I had dismissed the idea of putting up a struggle on the plane, I decided to wait until we got on the ground and Johan was lulled into thinking I was going meekly along with his plans.

My teeth ached. Now was not the time to have a truth attack. Meek wasn't a lie: I would be passive until the moment arrived for resistance. And my chance would only be one very brief second, I was sure of that. There were various things to look for. I needed to be conscious and out of his range. How far was that? I didn't know. So far he had kept me by his side when he wanted to hide me from others. Taking my own truth gift as a guide, my influence spread to a room; beyond that they were free to lie without interference. I needed to get that distance before I tried.

And appeal to whom? I knew some of the Benedicts lived in the west of America—Yves and Phoenix were in California.

How far was that? I cursed the fact I'd never paid attention to the map of the States, which surely I had to have seen loads of times. I had a vague memory of something called the Oregon Trail, one of the last settler routes, which is why I knew it was over the far side of the country. Biting my nails as I regretted my rubbish grasp of geography, I noticed an inflight magazine in the seat pocket. Pulling it out I turned to the page showing international airports. The pilot had mentioned Portland. Even though the map did not show state boundaries I now had a fair idea where we were headed: north of San Francisco, south of Seattle. The scale suggested the distances were still huge. I couldn't speak to my mother from Cambridge, a journey of about a hundred and twenty miles, so I guessed that I'd be very unlikely to reach Phoenix or Yves.

OK, I'd just have to scream an appeal for help and hope a local savant was listening. At the very least I wanted Alex to know it was Johan, even if I couldn't save myself.

Not that I was giving up. At the bottom of Misty 'Screwup' Devon, I discovered I had a deep and firm foundation of stubbornness. Johan had had it easy from me so far only because I had been more scared than angry; in Oregon he was going to find I was one pissed off savant.

Phoenix and Sky had advised me what to do, little knowing I'd need their words of wisdom so soon. Look for anything to be a weapon and use it. OK, I had my truth gift, some telekinetic powers, and ace hand-eye coordination. That had to add up to something. I was not going like a lamb to the slaughter.

A line from a favourite Dylan Thomas poem came to mind: 'Do not go gentle into that good night.' Though written for old age, it felt appropriate for what I faced. Johan's method of killing was oddly gentle: obscene but without violence. I was going to rage against it.

Chapter 18

When we began our final descent into Portland, it was still daylight. We'd been travelling with the time zones in our favour, making Wednesday stretch like melted mozzarella. I'd taken advantage of having a bed and made sure I got enough rest. I hoped Johan was sitting up in his executive seat and getting a crick in his neck, not able to sleep a wink in case I tried something. That offered a little satisfaction. I buckled in for the landing. As I watched the ground get closer, it dawned on me that I had been so caught up with strategies for escape that I had given little thought to the reason for Johan's visit. He had said something about family time. None of my family lived here and I thought Alex was his only relative.

Only relative who acknowledged him, I corrected.

But Alex's dad, Johan's brother, was last heard of in South America, wasn't he? Maybe we were catching another flight. Johan was covering his tracks.

Don't get taken aboard another plane, I told myself. At least here you speak the same language. Going south will not improve your situation.

Wheels touched down.

Johan entered the cabin. 'Right, Misty. Same deal as before and this time I hope you are convinced of the futility of shouting for help?'

I nodded.

'I'll just speak with the immigration authorities then we'll be out of here. Something of a drive ahead, I'm afraid.'

So at least we weren't catching another plane.

'OK.'

He took out a new set of ties. 'If you don't mind.'

Of course I minded. I held up my wrists.

'This gift of yours—it's pretty awesome.' I wondered if flattery would get him to spill a few more hints about how it worked.

'Thank you, my dear. I've found it useful.' He gently tugged the ties and I got up. 'People just don't see what I want to blank out. I'm like the invisible man, except I can make others disappear too. You can't imagine what that has allowed me to do over the years in my long search.' He opened the cabin door.

'Feeling better, Mr Smith?' asked Hebe, hovering in the aisle.

Johan rubbed his stomach. 'Just a touch of something. I feel much better already.' So that was how he explained his frequent trips into the cabin.

But he was lying. That gave me the first chink. I purposely let go of my control. It was like letting go of your breath after holding it in for as long as possible: instant relief.

'I hope it wasn't something you ate?' Hebe handed him a briefcase.

He opened his mouth to say it was exactly that but instead out came, 'No, I just had someone to check on in the cabin.' He looked shocked at what he had admitted.

Hebe's face registered her confusion.

Johan quickly raised another topic. 'Well then, I'll see you next time I fly. Saturday.'

His odd remark was replaced by thoughts of giving the company script to a frequent flyer. 'Indeed, sir, it will be my pleasure to see you on board again. You are a most undemanding passenger.' Hebe frowned, surprised that she had admitted this.

Johan's grip on my wrist tightened painfully. He had worked out who was to blame. 'See you then. Goodbye.'

He pulled me with him out of the plane. The air outside was like a dash of cold water in the face.

'One more trick like that and I'll be forced to kill,' he hissed.

'You're going to kill me anyway,' I replied stubbornly.

'I meant I'd have to kill that stewardess and the pilot. Do you want that on your conscience?'

Like this was my fault? I wasn't the one doing the kidnapping here.

A black limo waited at the bottom of the steps. Johan opened the rear door and pushed me inside.

'To the terminal building, please,' he ordered the chauffeur.

As at Stansted, VIPs did not have to queue with ordinary people. Johan left me in the car as he went to complete his immigration papers. He tied my plastic handcuffs to the door handle. I hoped for a brief moment that I would still be able to appeal to the chauffeur but he got out and accompanied Johan across the sidewalk into the terminal building, hand tucked in his jacket in an armed-and-dangerous stance, giving away that he acted as bodyguard as well as driver.

But Johan had left his briefcase.

I scuffed it closer with my feet, straining to hitch it up from the floor to the seat. When it touched my thigh, I bent over it and used my chin to scoop it onto my lap—not an easy move. Sweating with fear that I would be discovered, I glanced over to the terminal. Johan was close, just the other side of the glass chatting with the official, giving every impression of being a relaxed, innocent traveller. There was very little give in my hands, but by jiggling the case, I managed to get the front clasps within reach. This would all be for nothing if he had set the combination. Click—the first clasp sprang up. Click—then the second. I lifted the lid, shoving my fingers in the gap. It was nearly empty, just a few sheets and photos inside. I quickly scanned the ones on the top. The photo showed a family outside a blue house with a white fence: a couple and a son who looked about my age or a little younger. He had a baseball cap on so I couldn't make much out about his face but the father was distinctly familiar—a mixture of Johan and Alex. Roger. It had to be Alex's dad. So that was Alex's mother—the pale-faced woman with a haunted expression and long brown hair. So maybe the boy was another son? From what Alex had told me he didn't even know he had a brother.

The top sheet of paper was from a private detective agency and gave an address and map. A street in a place called Florence, Oregon. From the map I could see that it was on the Pacific coast. I now knew where we were going but no idea why Johan thought I should be along for the ride. He already knew what his brother thought of him; there had never been any lying there. This was no friendly holiday get-together.

A quick look up and I saw time was running out. Johan and the bodyguard were heading back to the car. I closed and fastened the briefcase, then kicked it back to roughly where he had left it. Now all I had to do was look innocent.

Johan got back in the car. He glanced once at the briefcase to check it was in place but, if he thought it had shifted, he appeared not to connect it with me. He rapped on the window between us and the driver; the limo began to move. With a satisfied huff, he pulled the case onto his knee, opened it and put his passport inside. I noticed that it was an American one.

I suppose that identity fraud was nothing to a man with his talents. He might even have American citizenship for all I knew. If I was to anticipate his next step, it would be helpful to know more about him. Silence wasn't gaining me anything. I thought a natural question from someone in my position would be to ask where we were going, even though I knew the answer.

'Uncle Johan, where are we headed?' I made myself as trusting as I could manage without my gift defeating me.

'I've invited myself to my brother's for Thanksgiving.'

'Does he know I'm coming?'

Johan chuckled. 'He doesn't know I am coming so he certainly doesn't know about you. If he were a decent man, he would be interested in his son and the people in his son's life, but there you are: that's Roger du Plessis for you.'

And that measured up against killing how exactly? I bit back the acerbic comment.

'So you want to convince him to change his mind about Alex?' Please let it be something as innocent as that.

Johan curled his lips in distaste. 'He doesn't deserve a second chance with his son. He abandoned a three-year-old: that is all you need to know about my brother. My own parents were so proud of him; I bet they would've cheered him doing even something like that to his own flesh and blood.'

'It was very cruel of Alex's parents.' I could at least agree with him on that.

'Roger is just like our father: a cold-hearted, prejudiced man. It's time he was shaken out of his complacency. He thinks he rules his family but really he's never understood the first thing about it.'

'And you're what? Going to shatter that complacency?'

Johan shook his head. 'No, my dear, you are.'

The car skimmed over the miles of freeway, soon shrugging off the suburbs of Portland and out onto the open road. I bit my fingernail as I gazed out at the fields, woods and hills of Oregon. It was beautiful in its winter dress of leafless trees and frosted grass.

'An interesting place, Oregon,' said Johan conversationally, following my gaze. 'Exports a huge percentage of the world's turf and grass seed. My brother works as an agent for a large seed company. I should have guessed sooner where he would go to ground after so many moves around the world; he was always keen on plants as a child.'

'And what were you interested in, Uncle Johan?'

He gave a flick of a grin. 'Nothing.'

Dangerous topic. 'And his wife, Alex's mother, what does she do?'

'Miriam? She hides.'

'Do you mean she hides out in the home?'

He put a finger up between us, warning me to stop. 'Enough questions.'

The threat was sufficient to make further words wither. I was so tired—tired of being terrified rather than physically weary. I curled my knees up to my chest.

'Feet off the seat.'

I put my legs down. I turned slightly so my head rested on its side away from him and closed my eyes. I would make myself unobtrusive so he had no call to use his powers on me. I hated that sensation of absence. He took away my basic right to life with his control over my consciousness. One nudge further and I'd never wake up again.

Many hours later, the car drew up outside a motel.

'I've made a booking for you as you requested, sir, for the largest and best-equipped cabin,' said the driver over the intercom. 'Your hire car will be with you at nine tomorrow morning and the keys will be left under your door.'

'Thank you, Chandler.'

'Thank you for choosing Silver Fleet. Enjoy the rest of your stay.'

'I have every intention of doing so.'

Johan gave me a look, not even specifying what he expected from me as I already knew. I nodded. Chandler opened the door on his side and Johan got out, tugging on my bound wrists to signal that I should follow. The bright lights of the motel spilled out into a foggy night, stopping only metres from their source. The motel was a series of large cabins with a parking space in front of each. It was possible to go straight in and out of your room without passing through any public areas—no doubt why Johan had chosen it. If Chandler thought it odd that a rich man like Johan had picked a three-star motel over a luxury hotel, he made no comment.

'I'll fetch the key for you, sir. I called ahead to warn them of our arrival; the door is unlocked.'

'Excellent.' Johan gave him a crisp nod, waited for him to set off for reception before opening the door of Number Five. 'Make yourself comfortable in the bathroom, Misty, while I say goodbye to our driver.'

I hesitated, wondering if this was another chance for me to run. Only my wrists were bound.

Johan anticipated me. 'Remember that any resistance on your part will only get other people killed.'

I walked into the bathroom and sat on the edge of the tub. It had recently been refurbished: dark slate floor and tiles, shiny vanity unit, and pure white basin and bath. The grouting was bright chalk-white; the place looked barely used. Little soap wrapped up in fancy lavender cellophane. No windows. The ceiling fan hummed, drowning out the brief conversation between Johan and our driver. The cabin was very big so they were quite some distance from me in any case, even without the motor noise.

Johan tapped on the door. 'It's safe to come out now.'

I emerged to find that he had drawn the curtains. Two double beds divided by a shelved unit, and a kitchenette completed the spacious facilities. A picnic dinner was spread on the circular table by the window.

'Wrists.'

I lifted my hands and he sliced the ties. My skin was raw after wearing the plastic for so many hours. Johan tutted as if that were my fault.

'I suggest you bathe those in cold water.'

I returned to the bathroom and stared at myself in the mirror in a vacant way. I felt empty. My face was paler than normal, grey eyes wide with a permanent state of shock, hair in a wild tangle. I splashed some water into my face to stimulate my brain. I had to keep my wits, keep looking for that weakness.

I felt a faint hiss at the very edge of my mind.

Bokkie?

Alex? Relief flooded me.

Thank God—finally! You're still alive. I knew it. His voice was faint but even so he had to be close enough to talk to me, else I was hallucinating. But I was at the back of the cabin, Johan up by the window: maybe that was far enough to get away from his influence. Even at the terminal buildings he had only just been on the other side of glass as he had parked so close; we'd never been this far apart. His desire for a grand accommodation here had proved the first flaw in his scheme.

Is it really you?

Yes, really. Where are you?

Oregon somewhere.

We know that. I'm in Portland. We landed an hour ago.

How do you know that?

I sensed him falter. *Tarryn.*

How did Tarryn know I was here?

Her gift. She saw you with my parents. Victor traced them to Oregon.

'I see a person's fate,' Tarryn had told me in Cape Town. Cold lodged in my stomach. *Am I going to die then?* I asked but my mind was already screaming.

No. I won't allow it.

Lie.

'Oh God, oh God.' I collapsed to my knees. I couldn't feel Alex in my head any more. The reason soon presented itself: Johan was at the door.

'Hurry up, Misty, I want to eat.'

'Coming!' I croaked. I had to get him back down the other end of the cabin and return to the bathroom without him suspecting me. I came out.

'You don't look well,' he said solicitously.

'Are you surprised?'

He patted my arm but that only made me tremble twice as hard. 'No, I suppose not. You're doing very well, considering.' His face brightened. 'And I'm sure it's nothing that a meal and some sleep won't put right.'

He really believed his own words. He couldn't understand how someone under a death sentence imposed by him might suffer. But then, he had given hints he didn't see what he did as bad; he thought it painless. Now you're here, now you're not. A kind of game.

I made an attempt to eat. I couldn't swallow anything solid so toyed with a yogurt. Banana flavour. It didn't taste anything like the fruit, more like those sweet chews in the shape of one. Johan tucked into an overfilled roll with pastrami and salad falling out. He held it out to me.

'America,' he said happily, thinking the sandwich was illustration enough.

I dabbed my lips with a napkin, hoping this read to him as impeccable manners. 'Would it be OK with you if I had a bath? My wrists are really aching.'

'Fine, fine. Don't take long. I'd like a shower before going to bed.' He got up and moved to the kitchenette to make some coffee. Damn. That put him much nearer the bathroom. 'There are more clean clothes for you. I've put them on your bed.' He indicated the bed furthest from the door. 'Use the T-shirt to sleep in.'

I grabbed the items he described and closed myself in the bathroom.

Alex? Alex?

Nothing. Johan had to be in the middle of the room outside. I kept calling Alex's name while I bathed but Johan remained stubbornly too close. Drying off, I dressed and emerged from the bathroom to discover why: he had stretched out on his bed and was reading a newspaper.

'I'm finished,' I said.

'I'll grab that shower then.' He took off his reading glasses and dug inside his case for his wash bag.

I tried not to look too pleased. I wandered over to the table and began tidying.

'Leave that. It's what I'm paying for. You don't need to do it.'

Giving him a faint smile, I got into my bed, trying to signal that I was intending to go to sleep.

'Good night, Misty.' He closed the bathroom door behind him.

I leapt out of bed and hurried to the opposite end of the cabin.

Alex?

What happened?

Johan stops me communicating. There's only one spot in our room where I'm far enough away.

He wasn't surprised to hear me mention Johan's name so I guessed that Tarryn's vision had included him. I wanted to comfort him for this betrayal but there was no time.

Listen, we need to know exactly where you are.

He's planning some kind of confrontation with your parents using me. They live in a town called Florence on the coast.

Victor traced where they live and we've got their house under surveillance and there's no one home. We have to stop you reaching my family.

I'm in a motel. I think it's called Harbour Inn.

He was repeating the information to someone else. *That's a chain. Do you know which one?*

No, but we're heading for the coast—I saw signs to the coastal road when we left the airport.

That's great—that should be enough to find you. Whatever you do, Misty, don't let him take you to my family, OK? We'll get to you first.

How exactly can I stop him? He can kill with a fingertip.

Just do your best. Alex couldn't disguise his anxiety. It shivered down our connection like a chill breeze. He wasn't sure how long I had.

If this was to be our last conversation, there was so much to be said. *Alex, I'm sorry I got upset at the pizza restaurant.*

And I'm sorry I didn't handle things differently. I was too caught up in meeting an uncle and winning the competition to imagine how you felt being left out. I was a jerk, taking you for granted, just as your father said I would.

Who's with you? If something went wrong, I didn't want him to be alone.

Everyone—your parents, Uriel, Tarryn, Victor, Crystal, Xav. More are coming. We've called in every law-enforcement agency we can. He's not going to get away with this, Misty, I promise you.

I'm sorry about your uncle.

Yeah, well, with a family like mine, I'm better off adopting yours, aren't I?

I wondered fleetingly what my father was thinking, because this was his worst nightmare. I couldn't imagine him giving Alex an easy ride. If I were gone, my family would be a mess, unable to look after Alex. He'd need someone. *I saw a photo. I think you have a brother.*

I do? Really?

He looks about our age—or a little younger.

I don't remember him. He sounded sad now on top of anxious.

And I bet he doesn't know about you. You'll be able to start fresh.

Misty, you're so sweet—worrying about me when this is about saving you.

I rubbed hot tears away. *Just don't blame yourself, OK?*

It's not going to come to that. Tell me what I can do for you now?

Just be with me.

He must have sensed I desperately needed the comfort because he began to sing very softly one of my favourite songs:

'Are you afraid of being alone?

'Cause I am, I'm lost without you.'

Oh, Alex.

'I'm lost without you,' he whispered.

As I was without my soulfinder. His song was like a gentle stroke, dulling the edge of my terror. I could hear sounds at the bathroom door. *He's coming back. Find me. Love you.*

I signed off quickly before Alex could reply. There was no time to cross to my bedroom so I decided it was better to be caught trying the front door rather than standing suspiciously quiet by the window.

'I suppose I should've expected that,' sighed Johan, seeing me with my hand on the doorknob.

'I just wanted some air.' It wasn't a lie. I wanted to run outside as far away from him as possible.

'So not thinking of escape?'

'Of course I'm thinking of escape.' He knew I couldn't lie.

'And you're not hoping to get help from people outside, are you?'

'At this motel? No.'

He rubbed his newly shaved chin. 'Maybe I should put you out, just in case. I want to sleep well without worrying about you sneaking off.'

'I won't sneak off,' I promised. I was hoping for a rescue party battering down the door.

He shook his head. 'I know you can't lie but you may be twisting your words. Better safe than sorry. I suggest you get back in your bed. It doesn't bother me if you spend the night as my doorstop but I think you'd prefer the alternative.'

If he put me out, there were no guarantees he'd wake me up again if the others did arrive. I'd be a dead-alive hostage. I couldn't think of a way of stopping him. My rescuers had to be warned.

'Can I just visit the bathroom again then?'

He shrugged. 'Fine, but hurry up. I want to sleep.'

I had to get him over by the door so I could send my warning. On the bedside table, he had his phone and reading glasses. Using a touch of telekinesis, I yanked the glasses off the bedside table and dragged them over by the window at floor level so he didn't see the movement. I made his phone follow. Hopefully, he'd want to find them before sleeping.

'I won't be a moment.' No, I'd be several long moments. I dashed into the bathroom and closed the door.

Keep calm. Panic bubbled inside me.

Alex? Alex?

Nothing. How long would it take Johan to notice he was missing a few items?

Alex?

Misty?

I've seconds. Johan is putting me out again. When he does that, only he can bring me back. If you bust in, there's no guarantee that he'll do it.

O—

The rest of the OK was cut off. Johan had found his phone and glasses. I flushed the toilet and came out. My mind morbidly suggested that these cream motel walls and brown curtains might be the last things I saw. I slipped into the bed and waited. *Oh God, help me.*

Johan nodded, paused at my shoulder, fingertip raised. 'Sleep well. Tomorrow it will all be over.'

That was supposed to be a comforting thought?

He's mad: don't tell him where to go even though it's what you want to do.

Screaming inside, all I could do was edit my words. 'Please, Uncle Johan, you will wake me up, won't you?'

Johan just smiled. 'One, two . . . '

Chapter 19

'Rise and shine!'

Johan was horribly chirpy. That meant no one had broken down the door overnight, that I was still his prisoner, but also that he had woken me up. The last was the good news.

'Happy Thanksgiving.' He put a cup of coffee on my bedside table.

'Thanks.' I sipped the bitter brew. The taste confirmed that I really didn't like coffee this early.

He slapped my leg through the cover in a matey gesture. 'Hurry up and drink it. We'll have a quick breakfast then head on out. We have to reach Roger by lunchtime.'

'OK.' My fear roared back from its hiding place during the night's oblivion. Was this how the mouse felt when the cat played with it: glimmers of hope alternating with despair?

Forcing myself to keep going, I picked out some clean clothes from the ones he had bought me and went into the bathroom. I knew he was too close but that didn't stop me constantly trying to reach Alex. When I received no response, it was hard not to imagine that was because there was no one there, that rescue had been a delusion.

Stop it. I splashed water on my face, cold enough to be a kind of punishment. You didn't imagine those conversations last night.

Neither had I dreamt up Tarryn's prediction of my fate.

The most likely time for my rescuers to strike was on the exit from the cabin. Surely by now they had had plenty of opportunity to stake out the motel? Alex wanted to stop me getting to Florence so this was the only chance before we hit the road. I had to keep a lid on my panic and make sure Johan opened the door to show I was awake; they wouldn't move before then.

My mood more positive, I left my refuge and returned to the main room. I even managed to eat half a bagel, listening to Johan talk about American Thanksgiving customs. It occurred to me, listening to him and watching emotion breeze across his waxen face, that he was a really lonely man. Pathetically, the foundation under the killer was a man in search of love. He was aiming to emerge from this with Alex as his family; those like me who fell by the wayside in that hunt were collateral damage, not really of any significance to his drone attack. I wondered if any of it was personal to me.

'Did you break into my room, Johan?'

'Oh yes.' He smiled as if he had paid me a huge compliment. 'I had come to the decision that I needed to clear you out the way so I was looking for more information about you.'

'You destroyed any trace of me.'

'That was a double message. I was hoping that Victor Benedict would assume it was one of Eli Davis' people, but there's a level on which it will make sense later, when all is revealed.' He said the last like a magician running a trail for his best trick.

'If all is revealed, you don't really think Alex will still want to live with you, do you?'

242

He appeared genuinely surprised I doubted this. 'Why not?'

Because you will have killed the other half of his soul. 'I don't think he'll like some of the things you'll have done.'

He slathered peanut butter on his bagel, gluey tan bumps scattered on the dry surface with a slick pass of the knife. 'He'll come round. He'll understand I did it for his own good. Soulfinders are an irrelevance, a distraction.' He took a bite and a third of the round disappeared. 'I've managed fine without mine.'

There were doctors for psychiatric cases like him who would beg to differ.

I brushed the crumbs from my lap. 'I'm ready.'

'Good.' He devoured the last bagel in three gulps. 'You're very brave, Misty, bearing up better than I expected. Not much longer now.'

I wasn't brave; I just didn't have a choice. Johan tied my wrists for what I hoped was the final time. Opening the door, he led me out. The hire vehicle, a cherry-red Chevrolet, waited on the forecourt.

Come on. Now! I willed my rescue to arrive.

'In you get.' He pushed the small of my back, urging me to climb inside.

Perhaps they'd come while he fetched his case. That would be even better as he wouldn't be able to touch me.

He went back into the cabin, our foul umbilical cord of restraint snipped, freeing me.

Alex, it has to be now!

Misty, where the hell are you?

We're leaving the motel—surely you can see me? Isn't the rescue party ready?

We've searched every motel on the Pacific coast near Florence and you're not in any of them.

But . . .

Jonas was back. He threw the case in the boot then slid into the driver's seat.

'All set?' he asked. He put the automatic in reverse and backed out onto the forecourt. I scanned the surroundings frantically for clues as to where we were.

'When are we going to reach Florence?' I asked.

'So you know about Florence, do you? I did wonder. You've been too cooperative not to have tried a few things behind my back.' He pushed the stick to drive. 'We turned off that road a long time ago. That's one of the traditions I didn't mention. My brother and his family have hired a chalet in the mountains for the holiday.'

I swore silently. I'd sent Alex to the wrong place.

'I don't see that it makes any difference to you, so no need to look so disappointed.'

I looked out the window instead. If my face was telling him so much, I had to make it blank before I let him see my reaction to his news. There was still hope. Alex wouldn't give up; the Benedicts were shrewd; everyone would be looking for me. Johan might think he passed undetected but he'd used a motel, a car, and a plane so there was a trace somewhere if they searched. Had to be. Oh please God, let there be.

From the tumble of my thoughts, I knew I was close to meltdown.

Anger welled, far more welcome than panic. Who was he to think he could merrily go round the world deleting lives and enriching himself? I weighed up the odds of surviving a crash if I grabbed the wheel. We were travelling at seventy miles an hour. Probably best to slow down before I tried anything that desperate. There was also the possibility he would be so caught up in the drama he planned with his brother that I would get my chance then.

Stick with it, Misty. One failed rescue hope was not the end of the road.

We climbed higher and higher in the mountains, leaving behind the coastal zone and heading into a region of logging tracks and woods. Disturbed by our engine, birds bloomed from the trees, circled and returned to roost.

'Good hunting country,' observed Johan.

He was not alone in thinking that; the few other vehicles we passed were open-backed trucks with lockable gun boxes in the rear, Ore-gun bumper stickers, driven by men with granite faces, plaid shirts, and baseball caps. They weren't interested in us, eyes beady with anticipation of blood sport, a hound dog's greed in the way they glared at the road.

We turned off the tarmac onto a crunching stretch of gravel. Looping around a cliff bottom, we came out into a highland meadow. There were some patches of snow from an earlier fall, white heaps making random erasures of ground like missing puzzle pieces. A waterfall tumbled over the steep slope of the mountain, edges silvered with icicles. A black wooden chalet with a pitched roof and yellow trim stood in fairy-tale isolation in front of the falls. A car was parked out front, mud splatters on the blue paintwork. We pulled up alongside, positioned to block in the vehicle.

'This is it. Lovely, isn't it? And you'll just love the name: Misty Falls. Could've been named for this day, couldn't it? Such a shame Roger and Miriam never wanted to share. All this could have been avoided if they'd just been better people.' Johan sighed like a teacher opening disappointing exam results for a promising student.

Time was running out. I had to avoid Alex's family as they were involved in whatever it was that Tarryn had foreseen. I was getting desperate for rescue.

But Tarryn never claimed that fate could be changed—that was why her gift was so awful.

I told that weasel voice in my head to shut up. I wasn't giving in.

'Look, please, there's nowhere for me to go. Why don't you leave me in the car while you talk to your brother?'

'Because, my dear Misty, your services are required inside. No ducking your destiny.' He gave me a long look. 'I don't want to drag you in, so are you coming willingly?'

Sick flutters in my chest. My body felt like it was disintegrating, buckling under the unbearable weight of fear. 'It can't be willing if you don't give me a choice.'

'I apologize for my imprecision. I meant are you coming without me having to force you?'

What to do? If I resisted, he'd compel me which might mean I had even less freedom of movement.

I got out of the car.

I paused for a moment, breathing in the cold thin air of the mountains. Part of me knew I was going to die but the majority was screaming to resist.

My seesaw brain changed its mind. Not even aware that my body had made the decision for me, I bolted for the nearest crop of trees, bound hands held up to my chest like I cradled something precious—hope, maybe. Thin-soled plimsolls were not ideal for mountain country; I could feel every stone under my feet. The suddenness of my race for cover had surprised Johan; running away from the waterfall, I made it to the edge of the copse, stones replaced by twigs and pine needles. There was a kind of track; my feet fell in with it naturally. The ground rose; breath sawed in my chest, ribs ached. I would run until I burst. I would outpace my fate.

Turning a corner I almost collided with a man and a teenage boy returning down the path, firewood stacked on a sledge behind them. They were laughing, cheeks reddened, woolly hats pulled over their ears, perfect picture of a happy family. I skidded to a stop, stumbled and practically fell into the arms of the man.

'Whoa!' He was still chuckling. 'Slow down, sweetheart. No need to panic the wildlife, hey?'

'Let me go, let me go!' I tried to free myself from his grasp. I recognized the older man's blue eyes and the line of the jaw in the boy: this was Alex's dad and brother.

The man lifted his hands warily, noting my bound wrists for the first time, his alarm registering. 'Look, now you just take a breath, honey. What's so bad that you are tearing up the path like the devil is after you?'

The thud of boots reached us. Johan appeared at the bend in the trail, slowing as he saw I had already been caught. I dodged round Roger and took off down the track.

'Misty!' Johan shouted. 'If you run, I'll kill the boy!'

I tripped over a root and landed on my palms, scratching the path deep into my skin and chin. Rolling over and scrambling up, I glanced back. Johan had his finger aimed at the boy's forehead, his threat immobilizing father and son.

He'd kill us all anyway.

I took off at a run again, stopped only by a father's anguished cry. Looking behind, I saw the boy on the forest floor in his father's arms.

'I won't revive him unless you get back here on the count of five! One!'

Oh God, help me. *Alex, please this is really bad. You've got to get here!*

'Two!'

Where, Misty?

Mountain cabin. Misty Falls. High near snow line. Your family's holiday place.

241

'Three!'

I'm coming. Keep running.

'Please, Miss!' begged Roger. 'He's only fourteen!'

I took a step back towards them. *Can't. I'm doing this for your brother.*

No!

'Four!'

I was back in Johan's range, no chance to say goodbye.

'You'd better hurry.' Johan's temper was fraying, his eyes lit by a feral gleam.

I ran, reaching him just as he announced 'Five.'

He leaned over the boy and touched his cheek. Hazel eyes flickered open. Roger sobbed and clutched him to his chest. 'Jason, Jason. Thank God. Thank you, Miss. Thank you.'

Johan stood over the couple on the ground and pointed to a spot at his side. 'Stand there. You do not move unless I give you an order; understand?'

I nodded. The short walk to his left felt like the retreat of a whipped puppy into the shadow of the master. He was itching to punish me but for the moment had other more pressing matters on his mind.

'Hello, Roger. Happy holidays.'

Roger groaned and rocked his son, pressing Jason's face to his coat so he didn't have to see his uncle.

'Now this is what is going to happen next: you are going to walk back to your cabin with me and my little friend here and we are going to enjoy the delightful dinner Miriam is no doubt preparing. Then we are going to have a frank discussion about the past and our future.'

'Please, Johan, leave Jason out of this. Let him go!' Roger wiped tears from his cheeks; his arms were trembling.

'Like you left your other son out of your life? I think not. I believe in including everyone in the family celebrations.'

Roger got shakily to his feet and helped his son stand. Jason was taller than me, though a little younger. He must have been warned about his uncle because he moved to the far side of his father.

'No, no, Jason. Come walk with me, your uncle Johan.' Johan was shifting on his feet, a prize-fighter eagerly warming up for a championship bout. 'Your father will pay much more attention to my wishes that way. I wouldn't want you to get any wild ideas of escape like Misty here. Look where that got her. I hope you appreciate the irony of her name. Which reminds me.' Johan struck suddenly, viciously, backhanding me. I ended up on the ground. My right cheek stung; my lip felt fat where it had mashed against my teeth.

'Johan!' exclaimed Roger. He moved to restrain his brother then backed off, afraid to make contact with him.

Someone knelt beside me and touched my face gently. I looked up to see Jason crouched over me. It was oddly comforting to be helped to my feet by this younger, darker version of Alex. The hazel eyes were different but Alex's features were echoed in the fourteen-year-old's face, softer, rounded but still family.

'Don't sound so shocked, Roger,' said Johan. 'She deserved it. It's no more than dear old father did to me while you looked on and never protested.'

Roger bit his lip and looked away, face grim. 'You had to be disciplined but the demon consumed you anyway.'

'And maybe you'd be less concerned about the girl if you knew she is one of the demon spawn too?'

'Step away from her, Jason.' Roger reached out for his son.

'Pa, she's just another kid. Her lip's bleeding.'

'She's one of them.' Roger beckoned, empty fingers scratching the air.

'I see there's hope for your son.' Johan nodded his approval.

'Yes, you stand by Misty, Jason. That's what your father failed to do for me and for your brother, Alex.'

'What brother?' Jason's eyes flicked to Roger.

'Oh, how interesting. You don't know? Well, nephew, you have an older brother, a fine young man by the name of Alex. He and Misty are, how do you say, close? Very close.'

Roger knew what he was referring to even if Jason had no idea. 'Is that why she's here? She's his soulfinder and you want to throw her in my face?'

'Ah, if only it were that simple. Come, I'm getting cold. Let's go back and introduce the most important member of this affecting family scene into the mix.' His pointing towards the cabin was both threat and urging. We all knew what that finger could do.

Jason took my hand and gave it a squeeze. 'You OK, Misty?'

I tried to smile my thanks but tears came instead, my face a war zone of emotions. 'Not really.'

Johan took Jason's elbow and led him down the path, chatting happily about the beauty of the trees, the falls, the silence of the mountains after city living, a parody of family chitchat. Roger and I followed, me limping, but Roger did not offer an arm to assist.

'What do you do?' he whispered.

Perhaps he was hoping for some superpower that would allow me to take out Johan single-handed—as if I wouldn't have done that already.

'I tell the truth.'

He hissed, condemning me as useless. 'If you harm my son— or my wife—I'm coming after you. I won't rest until you pay.'

Hadn't he noticed that I was a victim just as much as he? 'I'm not your enemy here.'

'You all are.' He increased his pace to catch up with his son, taking a protective stance on his other side.

I let my steps lag, hoping Johan wouldn't notice.

Alex, you'd better get here quickly. It's really bad.

Misty? Tell me what's happening.

Johan has your dad and brother. I think he's going to mur . . . I couldn't say it, *get rid of some or all of us.*

I won't let him. Alex did feel closer, his voice more definite in my head. *Look, Misty, I haven't had a chance to tell you but Johan contacted me earlier this morning after you left the inn. He guessed you were communicating with me from something you said or did and he wasn't surprised we'd tracked you to America; he knows what our friends can do. He doesn't want them there though so I'm coming alone. Stay away from everyone if you can.*

No, please. You need backup. I don't think you can stop him. I only wanted Alex here if he had a team with him.

Delay—keep him talking—spin it out.

What do you think I've been doing ever since he took me? I sounded a bit hysterical even to myself.

Sorry. You're doing really well. You've been so brave.

Johan turned at the steps up to the cabin, noting that I had fallen behind. I let him see my limp and continued slowly towards him. About five more paces and I'd be out of contact again.

If you can't stop him, please know I don't blame you.

I will stop him. I've been given this gift of persuasion for a reason—for you. I could hear the steely determination beneath the words.

I was out of time. *You never needed it to persuade me to love you.*

I could feel his pleasure at my words tingle down our line of communication.

I love you too. That's the truth.

The next limp closer to Johan cut him off.

'Hurry up, Misty, our hostess is waiting. You'll be able to

chat to Alex later—yes, of course I know what you're doing. Roger, help Misty up the steps.'

Reluctantly Roger steadied me as I ascended the stairs. 'Johan, is it necessary to keep her hands bound?'

'Necessary? Maybe, maybe not. But I am learning not to take Misty for granted, Roger; I suggest you do the same. There is more to her than meets the eye.'

Roger let go of my elbow. Johan shark-smiled and pushed open the door.

'Hi, honey, we're home!' he trilled, towing Jason over the threshold. Their feet left muddy tracks on the wooden floor as Johan ignored the mat and boot room. The hallway smelt of roast turkey, transporting me back to my own parents' house and our family Christmases. I felt horribly homesick, just wanting my mum to hug me, my dad to stand between me and this man.

There was a scream from the kitchen and the sound of a plate smashing. Miriam had spotted their unexpected guest.

'Hello, Miriam, you look beautiful as ever.' Johan sounded gleeful.

I followed the voices into the kitchen. Miriam was standing by the sink in the last stages of preparing the meal. The turkey was already out, sitting on the wooden table, crisp caramel skin. Three places had been laid. Green beans sat in a casserole dish next to creamed potatoes. Two plates remained in her hands, one lay in shards on the floor. A tall woman with a little weight on her hips, Miriam had the air of a competent cook, apron snugly tied, surfaces neat and cleaned between stages. Her long dark hair was caught back in a ponytail; her wide eyes were hazel like her younger son's.

Johan took command.

'Hmm-hmm—that smells good. Please do sit down and I'll carve. Jason, get another three plates out please; I'm sure you know where they are kept.'

Miriam collapsed onto the nearest chair. 'Roger?' she said weakly.

Roger rubbed his face. 'Let's just . . . just do what he says.'

'Dear brother, if you don't mind.' Johan held up a plastic tie. 'Hands behind your back.'

Roger hesitated.

'Either that or I repeat my touch on Jason with no guarantee I'll bring him back.'

Roger put his wrists together. Johan secured him, pulling the binding tighter than needed.

'Miriam? If you would be so kind.'

Glancing once at her husband, Miriam let him bind her wrists. She couldn't stop her shudder when he brushed an affectionate hand across her neck.

'Don't touch my mom!' said Jason, thumping three more plates on the table.

'And last but not least, our brave Jason.' Johan jiggled the tie tauntingly.

'P . . . pa?'

'Just do what he says,' Roger whispered. He sounded defeated. 'He's got something he wants us to hear so let's give him his chance. Then you let us go, right, Johan?'

'I suppose you could see it like that,' mused Johan, tying Jason so his hands were in front of him like mine. He prodded him to take the third seat then brought a chair over for me. Once we were all seated, he took his place at the head of the table. 'For what we are about to receive . . .'

'Don't you dare blaspheme!' hissed Roger, looking as if he was going to head-butt him from his position at Johan's left.

Johan quirked a brow. 'I suppose it is a little much from me. I never had much time for fathers, heavenly or earthly, did I?' He stuck the carving fork deep in the breast. Clear juices ran out. 'Done to a turn, Miriam. Perfect.' He smiled at the unappreciative cook sitting on his right. Johan carved a slice, white gash against orange-gold skin. With sickening care, he served us all, piling our plates with food none of us could eat. 'I hope you didn't use any of that pre-prepared stuff Americans are so fond of?' He took a wary mouthful of potato. 'No, made from scratch. I applaud you, Miriam.'

The woman's eyes were skittering from her son, to husband, briefly to me, then back to Johan. 'Why are you here, Johan?'

'Excellent question.' Johan poured himself a glass of wine. 'First, to enjoy this very fine meal in the bosom of my family. Second, to set a few things straight.'

'What things?'

'I do love family celebrations. Misty here comes from a large and loving family—no abandoned sons in your family, are there, Misty?'

'No,' I whispered, as he appeared to want a reply.

'And that despite the fact her father is no savant and not that keen on us or our way of life. See, there were other choices.'

'If you want us to apologize—' began Miriam.

Johan rapped the end of his fork on the table. 'Stop! Too late for that. No, Alex is mine now. Don't worry about his future. I'll make it up to him. In fact, it's about the past that I am here, not the future. Isn't that right, my dear?' He looked straight at Miriam.

Chapter 20

'Miriam, what's he saying?' Roger's gaze swung between hated brother and much-loved wife.

'Remind me, when is your birthday, Miriam?' Johan asked.

'April twelfth.' Miriam was staring at her plate, finding the cranberry relish riveting.

'And how old are you exactly?'

She opened her mouth but the words failed.

'I should explain at this point that little Misty here has a very useful gift. She cannot lie and, if she's not controlling her power, those around her can't lie either. Now, as I've made her life fairly unpleasant recently, my guess is that she has no control over what her power is doing at the moment. Is that the case, Misty?'

I hadn't even thought about controlling my gift. It would be rippling out as far and wide as it ever had. I nodded.

'So that means we all will be brutally honest with each other. I already know that Roger hates me so I'm not interested in what he has to say, but you, Miriam, I think there are some home truths that you've never told him, aren't there? Things you've kept hidden.' He folded turkey and beans on the end of his fork, compacting them savagely. 'Returning to my question, when were you born?'

'April twelfth,' she repeated.

'Yes, yes, we all heard that. I'm asking how old you are. Roger here thinks you are forty-six, the same as him, when you and I both know you've been lying.'

'I'm forty-eight.' Her voice was a thread of sound, stretched like a spider's web.

'The same age as me. In fact, we were born within a week of each other, weren't we?'

Miriam nodded.

'How do you know this?' asked Roger, his expression bewildered. 'Miriam, honey, I don't care you're older than me. Is that why you didn't say: you were embarrassed?'

Knowing I was unwillingly aiding Johan's cause, I tried to rein in my truth-zone, remembering what Zed had told me. There was so much emotion in the room, secrets and lies, that it was impossible, like trying to pitch a tent in a storm-force gale.

'Now we've got this far, I think you should finish, don't you, Miriam?' Johan sounded disgustingly pleased, a schoolboy ripping the legs off an insect to see it stagger.

She shook her head.

'Then I'll do it for you. Roger, meet my soulfinder. Your savant wife was destined from the moment of our conception to be mine. We met when we were in our twenties but she turned away from me and chose you instead. There: now you know the truth about the woman you married, despite my pleas not to do so. She has been able to hide it from you as that is what she does best.'

He chewed his forkful with taunting pleasure.

'I turned away from a monster! I hated you from the moment I knew what you were!' spat Miriam, her control fracturing. 'You were already a murderer and your brother would've been next to die if I hadn't saved him!'

Johan smiled amicably. 'Ah, so you worked that out, did you? Yes, I did kill our parents. Father gave me one beating too many and mother never raised a hand to stop him. The world did not miss them. I think Roger suspected what I had done but couldn't prove it.'

Roger was swaying between gut punches of truth. His wife a savant, a soulfinder to his own brother; confession that his parents were murdered. 'Is this true, Miriam?'

Her face creased, new lines ribboning across her forehead in her distress. 'I thought I would love him but by the time I found him your father had twisted him into . . . into this.' She flicked horror-filled eyes at Johan. 'I knew then my task had to be to save you from my broken soulfinder.'

'You're one of them?' Roger's gaze swept to me and Johan. I didn't very much like being put in the same category.

Miriam shook her head. 'I'm nothing like him. I'm your wife. Every choice was made to protect you, and to protect Jason and . . . and Alex.'

'Even Alex?' Johan raised a finger to rub the bulb of his wine glass. 'Oh do tell. How does abandoning him equal protection? I'm all ears.'

Miriam swallowed. 'Roger hated savants. I understood— I did; your father had made sure of that. I was afraid Roger would become like him if Alex stayed with us and he would create a second monster in his son.' She sobbed. 'Oh God forgive me but I couldn't stand between Alex and Roger all the time and keep you away as well—my gift does not stretch that far. I'm just not that strong.'

'Your gift. Mom, what gift?' asked Jason.

She pressed her lips together, unwilling to admit this last proof of her savant identity.

Johan stepped in. 'Miriam hides things, Jason. Very effectively, I might add. It took me years to track you down after you fled South Africa.'

'I knew when I saw you standing over Alex's cradle that we had to go—had to make you believe we'd taken him with us. And it worked. It worked.' She repeated it to herself, as if reminding her heart that the sacrifice had been worth it. 'It took years to organize but I managed to hide him for a long time—out of your clutches. You never even suspected that I would leave him behind, did you?'

'True. I looked for you, not Alex on his own. You loved the boy too much for me to suspect you'd abandon him.'

'It was the most difficult thing I have ever, ever done.' Miriam's eyes were fierce. 'I just hope you'll be too late to warp him. How did you find us?'

Johan sipped his wine. 'Through no fault of yours, Miriam. I'm afraid you were defeated by pure chance. A business acquaintance remarked on the similarity between me and a man he'd met on a plane, a South African involved in the seed trade. That conversation gave me a direction and then the rest was simple.'

Roger was still caught in the earlier revelation. 'You lied to me—all these years?' He stared at Miriam as if she had become a stranger.

'Yes. I had to.'

'Mom?' Jason's voice trembled.

Miriam turned to her son, chin quivering as she held back her tears. 'It doesn't change anything, darling. Not all savants are as your father has taught you; some of us care and use our gifts for good.'

'I can at least absolve you of stealing my soulfinder, Roger,' Johan said calmly, sketching a mocking cross in the air. 'The blame for that rests on Miriam's shoulders alone as she hid that truth most closely of all her secrets. I was only angry for about a decade. Recently I've come to see that a soulfinder is a burden that I am happier without. Alex will come to know that too. I'll explain when he arrives.'

'No, please, don't involve him!' My protest was out before I could stop myself.

Johan winked at me—conspiratorially, jokily. 'He's in this right up to his neck, my dear, so of course he should be here.'

Roger breathed heavily, trying to master his temper. 'Look, I know we've had our differences over the years, but I've never harmed you, Johan.'

'Ha-ha-ha!' Johan's laugh rang cruel—jagged. 'Oh, I beg to differ, Roger. You harmed me by taking all our parents' love. I think our mother might have been a savant, a minor one, or maybe she never understood her gift; whatever her true nature, she had it beaten out of her by our father and became a shadow—a nothing. You made no protest when he turned his fists on me, called me the devil's own child. Instead, you echoed him, added your own kicks with his blessing—or have you forgotten?'

'I was young—I was only copying what I thought was right.'

'And he taught you too well. You, Roger, do not deserve to live any more than that evil man deserved to draw another breath. I killed Mother first with no fuss, but him I made suffer. I explained in great detail my plans for our family, how I would eliminate the haters and rear the gifted children to know their superiority and take pride in it. You too will know what that feels like by the end of the day.'

'All right, Johan, kill me if you must . . . '

'Roger!' exclaimed Miriam.

'Pa, no!' protested Jason.

'But let Jason and Miriam go—they're not part of this.'

'Does Jason have a gift?'

Roger shook his head.

'Oh well. Pity that. And I see you don't beg for the girl here. What about Misty?' Johan pierced Roger with his gaze.

Taking an awkward gulp, Roger glanced at me; I had no more significance than a piece of furniture to him but he understood that I was a kind of test. 'I wish her no harm. She's useful to you—spare her too.'

'Ah, so you can learn. Before now you would've called for the eradication of any savant, claiming we were demons. I intend to show you what eradication feels like. I think you'll find it a most memorable lesson.' Johan's bitter gaze slid back to Miriam, a snake twisting invisibly through long grass, enjoying seeing us all flinch and try to guess who he would bite first.

I sensed he was coming to the end of the showdown part of the agenda and would soon move to the killing. I couldn't bear the thought of Alex walking in on a room of corpses. There was nothing to be gained by continuing to be silent. It would probably be the stupidest of my Misty moments but I was going for it nevertheless.

'No.' I stood up. 'You won't kill these people. I won't allow it.'

'And how do you intend to stop it, little girl?' Johan also rose.

Giving no warning, I flung the carving knife at his throat with telekinesis. He deflected it with a sleeve but not without earning a cut to his forearm. The long-pronged fork I sent to his eyes but he ducked and it stuck in the wall behind. Jason grasped that we had to fight and swept the plate and glasses towards Johan with his bound fists. Roger lunged to head-butt his brother; Miriam bolted for the back door, trying to kick it open. I sent missile after missile hoping something would get through. Johan knocked his brother down and stamped on his stomach until shoved sideways by Jason. I rushed to help him, tripping over Roger in my haste.

In the commotion none of us noticed the rumble of a motorbike engine cutting out and someone entering through the front door.

'What the—!'

'Alex!' My cry slammed the brakes on the tussle. We staggered to a halt, Miriam with shoulders heaving in wrenching sobs, Roger sprawled on the floor, creamed potatoes smeared on his face and chest. I had ended up on my knees between Johan and the kitchen counter. Looking up, I saw that Johan had got Jason in a strangle hold, using him as a shield.

'Did you come alone?' asked Johan urgently. 'Remember, with Misty here you can't fool me.'

'Yes, I came alone. I persuaded some guy to lend me his bike.' Alex's voice was rich with steady sincerity. Fists clenched at his sides.

'No tricks, no notes left behind; you slipped away without them knowing what you intended?'

A muscle ticked in Alex's cheek, a sign he was biting back words. 'I promised I would.'

Johan pointed a finger at Jason's neck. 'But did you?'

'Yes.'

Johan mistook this for loyalty to him. 'Good boy.' He swept a triumphant look at the wreckage of the Thanksgiving dinner and his unwilling guests. 'Welcome to Misty Falls. So pleased you could join us. I believe the main course is beyond saving but maybe we can have pie? You made pie, didn't you, Miriam?'

The woman nodded but her eyes hadn't left her oldest son's face.

'Then I suggest we all take a seat.' He thrust Jason in a chair beside him. 'Alex, maybe you'd like to greet your soulfinder?'

Taking that as permission, Alex crossed the room and helped me to my feet. He clutched me to his chest, burying his face in my hair. 'Oh God, Misty, I thought I'd lost you.'

Just to put my head against his heart, scent his safe, warm Alex smell, was heaven amidst this hell. I wanted to climb inside him and escape. Mentally, I placed a little bit of myself in him with a kiss. My refuge.

'I'm sorry—so sorry. Why did you come?' I whispered.

'He gave me no choice—he told me he'd kill everyone if I brought the police with me.'

'How did he contact you?'

'Telepathy. He guessed we were using telepathy so reached out to me after you left the motel.'

After I'd asked my question about Florence.

'I'm sorry.'

'It's not your fault.' A rub on my back seconded his words. 'It's better that I'm with you. I feel whole again.'

'Now, now, Alex, that's quite enough. Please, sit at my right. Have you met Jason? No, I don't think you have.'

'Is it really necessary to have everyone's hands tied?' Alex was looking at his brother. It was too much for him to take in—a family after so many empty years. Jason was equally fascinated and appalled. No one could have predicted this macabre reunion.

'Oh yes. See what your little soulfinder provoked a moment ago.' Johan pointed to the plates that had upended on the floor. 'She's quite the spitfire—fought me every inch of the way, tried to lull me into thinking she was cooperating but I could see the cogs in her mind whirling. You should be proud of her.'

'I am,' said Alex quietly, holding my eyes.

I love you, I thought, wishing I could use telepathy but Johan was still nulling any attempt.

'I'm beginning to wonder if she isn't worth keeping alive. You'll want your own children one day and she's got the mettle to make a fine mother—protective, not like Miriam here, who, as we all know, proved inadequate.' Johan turned his cruel attention on the woman trembling at the other end of the table from him. 'Alex, I don't think you'll remember her, but this is your mother. She claims, by the way, to have left you for your own good, so that Roger didn't try to beat your gift out of you in a mistaken attempt to save your soul. I suppose she may have a point; you did splendidly alone, as I have.' His eyes slid back to me; he was reconsidering my usefulness after reminding himself of the virtues of being isolated. 'I won't bother to introduce you to your father—he is beneath your notice, no more than a piece of gum on the sole of your shoe. But your brother, Jason, shows some signs of decency. He helped Misty when I got a little angry with her. She just won't do what she's told.'

Alex swallowed. My cheek was probably bruised, and my lip was definitely split. He would be able to guess what form that anger had taken. 'Thanks, Jason.' His voice had a rasp I'd not heard before.

'It was nothing . . . er . . . Alex,' whispered Jason. I reached out and touched Jason's thigh with my bound hands, adding my gratitude. He was holding up well considering how terrifying this situation was for all of us.

'You may wonder why I've brought you all here today,' said Johan, then laughed. 'Listen to me, Alex, I sound like Hercule Poirot, don't I? Well, I suppose that is fitting: this is a kind of denouement, a revelation of wrongdoing. Here are the suspects: the faint-hearted mother, the abusive father, the rejected brother, the favourite son, and the abandoned one.'

'And Misty,' added Alex. 'The girl caught up in this through no fault of her own. Surely you can let her go now she's served her purpose? She isn't your family.'

Johan considered it for a moment, hovering yes-no, yes-no. 'But she's yours, isn't she, Alex, so that makes her part of this. You missed the bit where I revealed that your mother was my soulfinder.'

Alex jerked back in his seat, gaze swinging to Miriam. 'I didn't realize.'

'Only she and I were party to that secret. I tell you now so you understand that being a soulfinder isn't enough for happiness. You may think Misty is integral to your future but she really isn't necessary—not worth twisting your life out of its true course.'

'And what do you think is my true course?' Alex's eyes were telling me he did not agree with a word Johan was saying.

'To be the best you can be—conquer whatever field you choose to go into.'

'And if I choose Misty as my first priority?'

'I'm afraid I'll have to step in. She lives only so long as she doesn't get in the way. I'm doing this because I love you, you understand. I have your best interests at heart.'

It was chilling to hear Johan talk of love; he didn't know the meaning of the word.

'I want you to listen very carefully to me, Uncle.' Even though I was in the room, Alex was trying to use his gift. If ever we needed a charmer, this was the moment. Think, Misty, how can you stop your gift messing with his? It had always been in conflict before now.

But then Alex had been debating for fun, not meaning what he was saying. Now he was a hundred per cent sincere. Surely my gift for truth could augment that, not diminish it?

'Alex?'

'Misty, please, let me talk to my uncle.' Alex was keen to keep me out of Johan's attention.

'I just wanted to say that as it's true, I can help you.' I kept my voice low, hoping only he would catch my words.

His face creased then cleared as he got my meaning.

'Uncle, I know you had a cruel start to life. I know enough about my grandparents to understand that they mistreated you.'

I could feel the waves of sincerity sweeping through his words; I let my power give them a push. I hoped that, like a rip tide, Alex's and my gift combined were enough to pull Johan from his murderous goal even as he swam towards it.

'And you came here to punish my parents for abandoning me,' Alex glanced at his mother and father, puzzled by the signals he was getting from them—Miriam longing, Roger defensive. 'They copied your own parents who rejected you.'

'They were never there for me,' agreed Johan. 'Our father only cared for Roger.'

'Over the last few days, I feel as though I've experienced some of the pain you've felt. You loved them but they turned from you. I love Misty and I thought I'd lost her. The pain is . . . is huge. Beyond bearing.'

Johan was listening, really listening for the first time.

'But, please, the ones who started this are long dead. Everyone in this room is a victim of their cruelty. Jason has never been allowed to know his brother; that woman over there I don't even recognize as my mother; your brother was taught to hate his own blood—and Misty just because she got tangled up in my life.'

Johan's face softened. 'I'm doing this for you, Alex. I've been looking for this family—for you—for so long so I could save you from them. Everything I've done, the money I've gathered, has been for you.'

'I see that—you've done so much. But I'd like a chance to talk to my parents—judge for myself.' Gift at full flow, Alex's voice rang with sincerity, sweeping away objections.

Johan could not resist him. 'Yes, yes, you should have the opportunity to question your parents. Then I'll dispose of them for you.' Johan made his callous announcement sound so ordinary, like putting out the rubbish for the bin-men on the allotted day.

Miriam moaned softly, praying, I think, under her breath.

'But what if I think it they deserve to live?'

'I'll consider it. Sometimes it's a better punishment to live with loss. I regret now my father did not last longer. Roger has to know what it's like to suffer.' Johan leaned forward, his fingers resting close to Jason's bound hands on the table. I got a hint of what he intended a second before Alex. 'Sadly, sacrifices are needed to drive the lesson home.'

His hand struck out for Jason.

'No!' Alex dived at his uncle a fraction too late to stop him.

But I was close enough. It was not Jason's hands Johan touched first.

Chapter 21

This was not like before. The other times Johan had touched me with his power, I had slipped from waking to unconsciousness in a blink; now I felt myself . . .

Fade.

Misty going misty.

Ha.

Like a drowning person finally taking the breath of water that would kill.

Or hanging single-handed over an abyss, finding it easier to let go than bear the screaming pain in the muscles and joints.

My mind flicked through the images, the last pages in the book before it shut. Story over. Blank leaves.

Leaves.

'You will bring her back right now!' The conversation was very distant, voices heard on the street, not my business, fragments of another life.

But it was Alex—he was *my* life. My soulfinder had turned his persuasion on my killer—not the easy charm of the debates but a raw demand, visceral, impossible to refuse, hooks in the chest dragging out compliance. Even I could feel its power and I was dead.

So how could I hear this?

'Calm down, Alex. I'm sorry about that . . . that accident, but I can't bring back those I touch that way.' Johan sounded so reasonable, offering nothing more than an 'Oops, my bad'. 'They become nothing—and nothing comes from nothing.'

I was not nothing.

'You have to!' I knew somehow that Alex was shaking him, crazy with desperation. 'She's not going to die.'

'But I can't reverse it. There are limits.'

Limits. I had reached one now. I knew that my body really was dead, the heart stopped beating, lungs no longer demanding breaths be taken. Part of me didn't much mind. Sinking. Accepting. Falling.

But one tiny part of my soul refused to depart. It would not spin down the drain like a spider under the spray of the shower. That piece was the fragment I had entrusted to Alex, our soulfinder bond. My flicker of consciousness was with him, seeing what he saw. He was clutching our bond, bitterly determined not to let it go, screaming in his heart not so much persuasions as orders that I damn well better listen because he was not giving me up.

But how could he win against the dead weight of death dragging on me?

'You can't save her? Then damn you, Uncle!' Alex launched himself at Johan.

Suddenly, Johan's blanket barrier on telepathy vanished, and messages burst in on all sides. It had to be deafening to Alex but I only caught the echoes, the burble of a radio left on in a neighbour's empty house. Nobody really at home.

Alex, where the hell are you? That was Tarryn.

I've followed your history as far as the mountain road—I know you're here somewhere, called Uriel.

I've got him! Oh God, Misty—it's Misty! We've lost Misty. I recognized Crystal's telepathic distress call.

Report, Alex—I need you to hold yourself together. Victor's demand shuddered through everyone else's cries.

She's not dead; I refuse to let her die. Alex sounded closer to me. I was seeing what he was seeing because that was the only fraction of me still here: the part that was his. He was cradling my head in his lap. Johan was stretched out beside my body, a lump on his jaw where Alex had knocked him out.

Good one. I wished I could reach Alex to let him know I approved of his right hook but I wouldn't now get the chance.

Time to go. The rest of me—and now I really was confused—the me that had accepted death was tugging at my sleeve, saying it was time to go.

Do not go gentle into that good night. Remember that?

Give me a moment.

Jason knelt beside Alex. 'I learned CPR at scouts, Alex.'

'Yes, yes, what am I thinking? Yeah, I know it too.' Alex laid me flat. 'You get ready to relieve me. We must keep oxygen getting to her brain. There's nothing wrong with her—nothing.'

That was the problem—Nothing was what was wrong with me. Johan's nothing.

'I've called for the paramedics,' said Roger. He had freed his hands on the fallen carving knife and quickly cut the bonds on his wife and son. 'I'll tie that up.' He didn't even give Johan a name.

Alex tipped my chin up and leaned over my face to give me the kiss of life.

I loved his kisses, but this one I couldn't feel. I was in him, not in me.

Hey, Alex, look inside! I shouted but I was trapped. He didn't realize I was there. He hadn't let me go but he had no idea that he was the only thing keeping me alive. My life support.

Keep doing the first aid. My team will be with you in five. Victor sounded furious—angry with Alex for going off, angry at me for dying. Victor didn't like losing.

Sorry, Victor.

Miriam cut my hands free. That was sweet of her. I hadn't liked seeing myself lying there too much like a medieval tomb effigy.

'When you're tired, let me take over,' she told Alex, her hand resting for a butterfly touch on his neck.

And so they carried on, doing it by the book: chest compressions alternating with mouth-to-mouth. If I'd been inside that body, I'd have come back, no problem, but I'd moved on. Even that little bit that Alex had was almost ready to go. He would give up soon and I'd slip away. I didn't even feel scared any more. We all die. I was glad I'd saved Jason. I'd not done much in my chaotic short life, but I was proud of myself for that.

Ain't that the truth.

Summer and Angel were going to be so cross with me for dying. Dad and Mum—oh please, don't let this drive them apart. And Alex—hold it together like Victor ordered you, I beg you, darling.

The front door burst open and a medical team ran into the room, pushing Alex away from my body. They had one of those electric things to shock the heart. A defibrillator—the word bounced into my mind, frilly like a sea anemone. The medics clustered around dead Misty doing their thing, talking their code.

Alex crumpled against a wall. Jason tentatively put an arm round him. Miriam's hand hovered at his shoulder then rested lightly on it. Roger stood over Johan, ready to knock him out again if he revived.

Uriel, Tarryn, Victor, Xav, and Crystal hurried into the chalet. Xav peeled away to join the medics. Victor took charge of Johan, feeling for a pulse in the neck, then adding cuffs to the flex Roger had used to secure him. Tarryn took over comforting Alex. I could hear her:

'I'm sorry, Alex. I wish I'd been wrong. How I wish I'd been wrong but I saw this—so sorry, so sorry.'

'You are wrong.' His voice was low, a kind of chant against death. 'You have to be wrong. She's not dead.'

Crystal stood as close to my body as she could without interfering with the doctors. Her knuckles were pressed against her mouth, looking down rather than at Alex.

Hey, Auntie Crystal, you've got your back to me!

But like everyone else, she thought I was in that girl on the floor—or not here at all.

I was being ignored at my own deathbed—a funny kind of irony that.

The lead medic sat back on her heels and shook her head. 'I'm sorry but there's nothing.'

That's what I was trying to tell them—there was nothing in that body because that was how Johan killed. But I was still something. If they just stopped and listened they'd hear me. Alex would hear me.

Alex, don't give up. You are all that's keeping me here.

'Time of death,' the woman looked at her watch, 'fourteen twenty-two.'

Xav gently buttoned up the shirt that had been moved for the defibrillator pads.

Alex turned and punched the wall. I felt that even if he hadn't—pain shooting up the arm. 'No!' he roared. 'She is not dead. Crystal, you find her. She's my soulfinder—you're a soulseeker—you damn well find her!'

Crystal wiped tears from her face with the heel of her hand. 'Alex . . .'

'No, just do it. I'll believe you if you say she's gone but I know she isn't. Seek her out.'

Against her better judgement, Crystal crouched down beside Xav, touched my limp hand, dipping in for her inner sight. She started to shake her head, then her eyes opened and she turned back to Alex, letting go of my body.

Finally, someone understood.

'Alex, she's not there . . . she's in you.'

'What?' Tarryn moved to protect Alex.

'I know, it doesn't make sense. But I can see your soulfinder bond as clear as anything and there's a little thread of it still in you. Somehow, God knows how, Misty hid something inside of you before Johan killed her.'

Alex pressed his hands to his chest as if trying to keep me inside. 'What do I do?'

Crystal's eyes darted to Xav. 'I don't know. I've not met this before. Can we put her back in there?'

Xav beckoned the medics to return from where they stood by the door. 'Guys, keep this body viable. There's some weird shit about to happen here but she'll need it.'

The head medic looked on the point of protesting.

'Do it,' snapped Victor.

They jumped to obey.

Crystal thrust her fists into her hair and pulled. 'OK, OK, how do we do this?'

Uriel touched her shoulder to get her attention. 'Let me try with Tarryn—together we can trace her history from her last moment. Tarryn can see that—I can do the rest. We'll lay a path.'

'You think I can do this?' asked Tarryn doubtfully.

'I know you can, sweetheart.'

Tarryn knelt beside my body and covered with her palm the splayed fingers that had felt Johan's death touch. She took a deep breath, closed her eyes and sought out my ending. Uriel crouched beside her and put his hands over hers. It reminded me of 'Rock, paper, scissors'—his hand engulfing hers, covering mine; their 'paper' trying to defeat the rock-death of Johan.

'Rock, paper, scissors,' murmured Alex. He clutched his chest. 'I can feel her—hear her very faintly. She's thinking of the game.'

Victor stood close to Alex. 'That's good—really good. Keep talking to her.'

I wouldn't play against Victor. He'd pull my next move from my head before I knew it.

'She's thinking you'd cheat so she won't play you,' Alex said, eyes blazing with fierce pride.

'Tell her I challenge her to a round and I promise not to cheat if she gets back to us.'

You're on.

'She agrees. I should warn you, she's very competitive.' Tears shone in his eyes.

You bet, partner.

'Oh God, Misty, just hang on, hang on. I'm not letting go.'

Then the atmosphere changed again. A little cold wash of doubt flowed over me; I'd been technically dead now for almost fifteen minutes. Death felt like the moon, pulling me with its gravity to turn tide. I had been in the slack water of indecision for too long.

'No. Forget death, Misty. I've got you.' Alex collapsed and curled up on his knees as if he could hold me there, like a ball just barely caught by a fielder.

'We're losing her again,' warned Victor.

'I've got her history—I can make the path,' said Uriel. 'Crystal, come here.' He held out his hand and gripped my aunt's fingers tightly. 'Can you see it?'

'Yes, but how do we use this? Damn it. I wish I knew more about how my gift works!'

Poor Crystal, feeling responsible again.

'Alex, you've got to persuade her to reverse her course,' said Victor. 'Her mind has set course for the horizon; she thinks it's inevitable. You have to bring her back to port. Crystal will pilot her in.'

Alex nodded. They all shifted to telepathy, sharing a common space in their minds. He took Crystal's hand, the third in the chain starting at Tarryn and my hand. I couldn't quite see what they were doing; they were fading. Victor was right. I was travelling on despite my wish to stay. Wind in my sails.

Misty, don't you dare take another step away.

Where was the smooth talker who could charm the fish from the sea? I had an angry soulfinder hot on my heels.

Too damn right. You get the sweet talk when you get the hell back here and inside that spectacular body of yours.

I took a little moment to preen with pleasure—he thought me spectacular.

Yeah, I do, so don't waste it.

But it's too late.

You can't let that loser defeat you. If you do, you're not the girl who came all the way to South Africa to kick this champion's butt on the ping-pong table. Come on, bokkie, it's your serve. Time to get back in there and wake up.

It's too hard; life only goes in one direction.

Says who? Not me. Reverse course now or I'll lie and tell everyone you were rubbish at table tennis and I let you win.

You did not!

I felt his heart leap. He really could hear me this time, not just catch the impression of what I was thinking.

That's right, bokkie, come closer. Without you to set me right, I'm gonna lie and swear you couldn't win even if I had my arms tied behind my back and held the bat in my teeth.

The image made me laugh. After the creeping cold, I began to feel a little warmer.

But you can't play from inside me—that's kinda weird even for us—so hop back in there and prepare for a rematch.

Where? I was still lost in the fog.

Misty, come home. That was Crystal. I couldn't see her but I could sense a trail, a line of shining white stones laid by Tarryn and Uriel; Crystal was holding them up for me to follow.

I came nearer. Uriel and Tarryn's fists still covered mine. One potato, two potato . . . I remembered playing that silly game with my little brothers and sisters, seeing who would come out on top of the pile. Not Johan. Not that Nothing Man. Alex was right; no loser would beat me.

But how to get back inside yourself? All very well for everyone to tell me I had to do it, but it was like un-peeling an orange, or putting peas back in a pod.

You fit so naturally in me, bokkie; just slip back inside yourself that way. Look, I'll show you. Alex remembered kissing me on the bench in Cambridge, that sense of completeness, flying with the stars. Magic dust.

Glide in through the nursery window. Landing on the rug. Between the sheets.

I was back.

I opened my eyes—my own, not Alex's.

The head medic swore, holding up the pads of the defibrillator, hands raised in surrender. I felt like I'd been kicked in the chest by a horse.

'Crap. Don't use them on me,' I whispered hoarsely. Not stellar first words, but then I'm not the kind of girl who has 'first words on escaping death' ready written.

'Yeah, she's back,' grinned Xav, throwing his arms around Crystal.

Alex broke down and wept, clutched me to his chest. It hurt, but I didn't care. He deserved a hug.

Chapter 22

'I am not going to hospital.' But no one seemed to be giving me much choice. The paramedics were loading me on to their ambulance, Alex holding my hand as he walked next to the stretcher.

'Yes, you are, *bokkie*.'

'I'm fine.'

'No, you're not fine: you were dead.' The paramedics pretended they weren't listening to our argument but I could tell they were all fascinated.

'But I'm not now. Xav says I'm good to go.'

'Good to go to hospital to get checked out.'

'He's already mended the broken rib.' My resuscitation had been a little over enthusiastic and someone had cracked a bone with their chest compressions. To tell the truth, I was still feeling a bit sore but I didn't want the fuss. 'All I need is a lie-down.' With you keeping me safe, reminding me that I had left that cold foggy place between life and death.

'What you need is an X-ray and a brain scan with a team of doctors to check everything is functioning OK. Misty, you were gone for half an hour!'

'Twenty minutes,' I grumbled.

Alex raised a brow.

'Oh all right then! Take me to this completely pointless hospital check-up. I don't even have insurance.'

'It's OK—the FBI is picking up the tab.' Alex had looked away over the waterfall to the mountain tops, a sure sign he was smiling at my expense.

'Waste of American taxpayers' money.'

'I don't think that's true.'

'Well, I do.'

Alex sat down beside me as the medic strapped the stretcher in place for the ride. 'Think about your dad. Do you really think he'd be happy with only Xav's say-so that you're OK?'

He had a point. Dad probably bracketed Xav with witch doctors in his scale of reliable medical personnel. 'I'm going, aren't I?'

Returning from the dead had not sweetened my character a jot. I was still the same little bit grumpy, little bit absurd Misty. It was a relief to discover I hadn't changed; even my gift felt welcome. I would not be me without it.

Xav poked his head round the door of the ambulance just before it closed. 'We'll see you down at the hospital, Lady Lazarus.' He disappeared and then bobbed back into the frame. 'I don't mean that in the depressing Sylvia Plath sense, of course.' He slammed the door. Given the size of the van, it was a little like sealing me back in a tomb.

'Sylvia Plath?' Alex asked.

'She wrote a dark poem of that name.' Wow, I knew something Mastermind Alex did not!

'You like poetry?'

'I love poetry.'

'You'll have to share it with me. I don't read it very often.' He must have seen my surprised face. 'What?'

'I'm so used to thinking of you as perfect, I'm just taken aback that you have a weakness.'

He grinned, blue eyes twinkling. 'You think I'm perfect?'

'No.'

'Ah.'

'I *thought* you were perfect and now I know you're not. It's a huge relief. Are there any other flaws you wish to share with me to, you know, make me feel better?' I waggled my eyebrows.

He hummed in thought.

'That's another: you hum!'

'Do not.'

'You just did.'

'Oh. OK. I hum. And I don't like garlic bread.'

'How can you not like garlic bread! Oh my, that is a serious failing.' I began to laugh but it hurt my ribs.

'You could think of it as more for you.'

'True. But if I eat garlic then I'll get garlic breath and that's not fair on you.'

'Why is it a problem for me?' he asked innocently.

'You know.' I looked at his lips.

He dipped down and kissed me. 'Yeah, I do. And, Misty, I'll kiss you even when you have garlic breath, I promise. I'll just peg my nose.'

I tried laughing again. Ouch.

'Sir, would you please let the patient rest,' interrupted the medic.

'Yes, sorry.' Alex sat back, trying to look chastised but it was a miserable failure. He was so euphoric that I had survived, nothing could dent his mood.

I reached out so we could keep our hands interlaced. 'Thank you.'

'For what?'

'For keeping hold of me.'

'I'm never letting go. I'm lost without you, remember?'

The medical experts at the hospital in Eugene, the nearest big city, insisted I be kept in observation overnight. They couldn't find anything wrong but apparently a prolonged period of being dead could not pass without at least an overnight stay. No visitors apart from my parents were allowed. Alex ignored that. I added rule-breaker to his other imperfections—or maybe it should be in the other column?

Victor Benedict didn't let regulations bother him either. He arrived for my debriefing at eight in the evening.

'Misty, I didn't have time at the chalet to tell you but all I can say is "thank God".' He nodded amicably to my dad, who was glaring at him, and kissed my mother on the cheek. 'How's she doing, Topaz?'

My mum gave him the rundown of my test results. I think Victor knew these already but was diplomatically giving my parents some control after being helpless for days after my abduction.

'That's great. Take all the time you need, Misty.'

I'm ready to leave now, Victor.

Take all the time your father needs, Victor corrected. 'So I suppose you might want to hear what happens next?'

'Exactly.'

'I'm getting you a temporary passport so you can fly home. Until then, you can stay here or with one of us if you feel you need a little longer.'

'I think Misty would prefer to recuperate at home,' my dad said severely.

'Of course. Her brothers and sisters will be worried until they see her,' Victor said smoothly.

Dad was finding it hard to be angry with us savants when we were all being so nice to him.

'Alex, your uncle.'

Alex's face darkened. 'What about him?'

'He came round shortly after you left with Misty. His gift is still functioning so he can very easily slip away unless we keep him under restraint.'

'You won't let him escape?' I asked anxiously. I would never feel safe if I knew Johan was at large.

'No, I promise. I've had to deal with difficult prisoners before and we've got a system in place. He'll be tagged so we know where he is even when he does his disappearing thing. No, my biggest problem is that I doubt Johan du Plessis is fit to stand trial.'

'You mean because he's as crazy as a loon? I kinda gathered that when I woke up in the forest.'

'As Misty so succinctly put it: du Plessis is insane. It is likely he will serve his sentence in a psychiatric ward, not a cell.'

'He did kill those people—and more,' said Alex quietly. 'I'm not sure that's enough.'

'I know, he has a lethal combination of a high level of organizational ability and severely stunted emotional functions. He killed thirteen people in his obsession to find your family. The psychiatrist's early assessment is that du Plessis has no understanding of the gravity of what he did and shows no remorse. Other people's lives aren't real. I suppose that will be up to the doctors to decide, but I think they'll recommend he be given a secure placement for his own safety and that of everyone else.'

'How will you stop him killing more people, Victor?' My mother rubbed her upper arms, still scared even though I was safe. 'He only has to touch them.'

'He'll have to be isolated, sedated when anyone needs to treat or move him. I can't see any other option.'

'That's worse than a prison sentence,' said Alex.

'Good.' My dad folded his arms. Johan had taken his little girl and he was not feeling very European Human Rights convention at the moment.

'I think it's unbearably sad,' I said. 'Alex, please, we should at least see him. He was already isolated: this is going to be even worse.'

'Misty, my uncle killed you.'

'But I came back. Look, I know he's killed others but he's also been rejected all his life. In some twisted way, he cares about you. Don't add your rejection to the pile. Who knows what that'll do to him? He's dangerous enough as it is.'

Alex closed his eyes, then nodded. 'OK, if you need me to do this, I will. We'll see him if Victor can arrange it.'

Victor smiled at me, eyes warming a little from their Arctic cool. I realized I had impressed him. 'I can do that. If you're sure?'

'Misty!' My dad was gearing up for one of his interventions.

My mum put a hand on his. 'Let her do it, Mark.'

They held each other's gaze, not needing telepathy to communicate.

'All right, Topaz. Misty, just be careful.'

'When am I not?' I asked brightly.

For some reason, the other four occupants of the room laughed.

Johan had been allocated a single room off a psychiatric ward. It was pleasant, furnished with homely pieces and pictures on the wall of Table Mountain. Someone had been thinking about his needs. The only things that gave away that it was a cell were the bars on the window and the thickness of the locked door. A television burbled in one corner but he didn't seem to be paying it attention. He was looking outside at the bare tree beyond the pane.

Victor, who was accompanying us on this visit, paused, communicating with Johan telepathically.

'He has promised to stay in the chair, arm's length from all of us,' he reported. 'I can paralyse him with a mind-strike if he makes any sudden moves. You OK with that?'

Alex nodded but I had a cold sweat running down my back. The terrifying few days as his invisible prisoner rushed back. It was easier to be courageous when Johan wasn't near.

'You can stay out here if you like, *bokkie*,' said Alex.

This had been my idea. 'No, I'm going in.'

Alex smiled wryly. 'Sometimes you are too brave for your own good.'

'Says the guy who walked in on a hostage situation,' I finished.

Victor gestured to the nurse to open the door.

'Hello, Johan. I've brought you some visitors.'

Johan didn't look round. 'I don't want to talk to any more doctors. I'm perfectly sane. None of you have the wit to understand me.'

'Uncle, it's me. And Misty.' Alex stood a little in front of me, alert and protective.

Johan looked round swiftly, a delighted, almost childish smile on his lips. 'Alex! How kind of you to come. And Misty. You know, I'm pleased that for once my gift failed. I hadn't intended to take you out of the picture so soon.'

I noted he hadn't said that he never intended to kill me, just that it was too early. 'Yes, I'm OK, as you can see.'

'But, Alex, you have to persuade these people to let me go. I'm fine. I don't need drugs or doctors.'

'But you killed at least thirteen people we know about,' Alex said quietly.

Johan waved that away. 'It's not so much killing as stopping—yes, stopping. They were all pointless people. The world doesn't miss them.'

'I think the parents of Mia Gordon, Jody Gaspard, and eleven other victims wouldn't agree,' said Victor.

'Mia who?' Johan looked puzzled.

'The last girl you killed.'

'Oh yes. She'd served her purpose; I couldn't keep her alive after that. She didn't feel a thing, I assure you. I put her away.'

'You dumped her in the Thames.'

Johan's blankness was outrageous. I wanted to shake him—make him feel something for his victims—but it was hopeless. He just did not understand. He certainly wasn't interested in going over his crimes. 'So Alex, you see, you have to tell them to let me go,' he said earnestly.

'I can't do that, Uncle. You're not well. You can't be trusted to respect life, so you have to stay here for our safety and for yours.' Alex was using his gift to push the message home.

'You want me to stay here?'

'I do. It's a good place. They'll look after you.'

'You'll come and see me?' Johan appeared so hopeful that Alex couldn't refuse.

'Yes, I'll return.'

The door opened again and Miriam du Plessis walked in. 'You won't be the only visitor, Alex. I'll keep an eye on Johan too.' She brushed a lock of hair away from her face, the gesture betraying her weariness. My first thought was that she was the last person I'd expect to visit, but then I realized that she wouldn't be able to stay away. 'He's always been my responsibility.'

'Miriam!' Johan looked from Alex to his mother. 'This is another unexpected pleasure. How's Roger?' His expression turned malicious.

'He's . . . he's upset.' Miriam touched my arm, conveying silent thanks to see me up and around.

Johan chuckled. 'Excellent. Why don't you tell him to visit me? I have something for him.' He laced his fingers together and bent them back, cracking his knuckles.

'Johan!' warned Victor.

'I was just joking.' The lie made the breath hiss between my teeth.

'There is no way you'll persuade Roger through that door,' said Miriam, 'but I'll come if you promise to behave. No more kills, Johan. You're done.'

'Done?' Johan suddenly looked lost and confused. She must have touched him with telepathy to reinforce the message and the impact had shaken him. 'Why did you reject me, Miriam?'

Her eyes were anguished. 'Because I couldn't reach you. You were too far gone.'

'But I'm here.' He pounded his chest. 'I'm here.'

'No, you're not—and that's the saddest thing. You killed the person you could've been before you started on the others. I'm sorry, soulfinder.'

Johan began to sob. The sight was shocking; he'd always been so sure of himself, his sufficiency without Miriam. 'I'm nothing,' he whispered. 'That's what my father said—and he was right.'

I could feel his resolve building in the face of that truth. *Alex, do something. He's going to turn his gift on himself.*

'You're not nothing, Uncle. You're a man whose life was twisted out of shape by the people who should've loved him as he was. You need help. Miriam and I—we're here for you. Hold on to that.'

'But you don't love me—neither does she.' Johan was swallowed up in black clouds of despair. No grief or regret for his victims, only for himself, but somehow that made him even more pitiable.

'We both cared enough to come this afternoon,' argued Alex. I lent my power to his words to break through the clouds. 'You can make something of the rest of your life if you decide to do so. No one is stopping you now.'

'I don't know, Alex; I don't know.' Johan rocked himself to and fro.

'Misty's here so you know I'm not lying. You've just got to trust in us. In family.'

'What am I? What have I done?' Johan brought his knees up to his chest, looking like a little boy hiding in a corner. I had a sudden vision of him as a child curling up against the blows and the hatred. I wept inside for his victims—and for him.

I weep too, whispered Alex.

Before any of us could stop her, Miriam crossed the distance and put her hand on Johan's shoulder. She turned pain-filled eyes to us. 'Leave us, please. He's mine—he's always been mine.'

Obeying the authority in her tone, we retreated. Once out in the corridor, I turned into Alex's hug.

'He won't hurt her, will he?' Alex asked Victor, his voice ragged.

'No, I don't believe so. You and your mother are the only ones he never contemplated hurting. In a way, with Roger, the three of you are the only real people in Johan's world. His mind is a mess, large blanks where he refuses to look, emotions stunted.' Victor sighed. 'His parents did a number on him, that's for sure. You know, I usually get some satisfaction from putting the bad guy behind bars but with him I just feel depressed. There's no justice for the victims—no way back for him.'

Jason and Roger were waiting in the car park. I imagine Roger had no idea what his wife was doing or he wouldn't be sitting there so quietly. He saw us but his eyes moved away. Jason, however, was out of the car before his father could stop him.

'Alex, Misty! I didn't expect to see you here!' He bounded over to us with puppyish enthusiasm. 'You feeling OK, Misty? 'Cause you looked rough last time I saw you.'

I gave him a hug. 'I looked rough because I was dead, you muppet.' Alex flinched; he didn't like the reminder even when I made it a joke. 'But I'm fine now, Jason. How are you?'

'Oh, you know.' He shrugged. 'It's been a bad couple of days.'

Victor tapped my shoulder. 'I'll just go have a word with the doctor in charge while you catch up.' He swept us all with one of his 'don't do anything stupid' looks before striding away.

Jason gave a pretend shudder as Victor left.

'I saw that, du Plessis!' called Victor.

'Eyes in the back of his head,' explained Alex.

'He's a really scary savant, not like you.' Jason grinned at his brother. 'I was wondering, Alex, if we could, you know, keep in touch or something?'

Alex punched him lightly on the shoulder. I could tell he was pleased. 'Yeah, of course. Your father OK with that?'

'Our father,' corrected Jason. He shot a glance at Roger, who was still studiously looking the other way. 'I think he's not exactly wild about the idea but Mom says it's going to be different from now on. We don't have to hide any longer. Pa's just got some adjusting to do, according to her.'

He sounded like my dad but much worse. We'd have to make sure the two of them didn't meet for a long, long time as they'd only reinforce each other's prejudices.

Funny how we have that in common, isn't it? I remarked to Alex, showing him the comparison I was making.

You're right, but Roger makes your dad look very mild. Jason's great, isn't he?

Awesome. 'So, Jason, are you going to visit Alex and me then?'

'You live together?' Jason zeroed in on our weak point.

'Um . . . '

'Yes, we'll be together,' said Alex firmly. 'I'm going to persuade Cambridge to take me if I can't get in on merit. I won't risk letting her get too far from me again; I don't do well without her.'

I tugged his sleeve. 'But Alex, that's cheating—and I'd make you confess.'

He smiled and ruffled my hair. 'True—you'll keep me on the straight and narrow.'

'Anyway, there'll be no need for underhand tactics. They'll love you. You're a debating champion, future leader material, aren't you?'

Miriam came out of the hospital looking very shaken. Roger leapt from the car and hurried to her side, enfolding her in his arms, talking softly to her. His relief to see her back safely was clear for anyone to read.

Jason smiled, pleased to see his parents returned to a more even keel. 'I'm sorry you never knew them, Alex. Pa can be crazy about savants but he's an OK guy about everything else.'

That was a massive character fault in my book, but I held my tongue as Miriam was towing Roger in our direction. I made a move to leave.

Stay, urged Alex.

Roger won't want me around.

I want you at my side.

Miriam stopped a little way from Alex. 'I . . . ' she cleared her throat. 'Oh Alex, there's so much to say, to explain. I know you must hate me but I truly thought I was doing the only thing I could to keep us all safe.' She used her wrist to dry her eyes. 'I'm a pathetic mother—I couldn't stretch my gift far enough. Maybe I should've stayed with you—but then he would've got to Roger and Jason. And if I had taken you with us, then Roger would've never understood. I didn't want Roger to make the same mistakes, turn into the cruel man that his father had become. And what would that have done to you?'

Alex let her speak, neither forgiving nor condemning.

'So . . . so I took the idea from the story of Moses in the bullrushes, letting someone else care for you so you could grow up and be the man you should be. Did I do the right thing?' She shook her head, annoyed with herself. 'No, that's stupid. There wasn't a right thing—only two wrongs to choose between. Do you forgive me?' She held out her hands in a beseeching gesture.

On the surface calm, Alex was experiencing an emotional blizzard inside. He turned to me. *What do I say?*

Say what's in your heart.

OK, then. 'I think I understand, Miriam. You had an impossible choice. You didn't spare yourself pain, did you? You could've kept me and let others suffer. I guess that took courage so, yes, if it matters to you, I forgive you.' Alex looked across to his father, wondering—hoping—that a similar appeal was forthcoming. Roger glanced away. I could feel the sadness well inside Alex.

You have me and Jason and now your mother, I told him. *Try to make that enough.*

Miriam noted her husband's stiff-backed stance, her expression reflecting her disappointment. 'I don't ask for you to think of me as your mother but I'd like for us to build something between us.'

I could feel a truth within Alex that he couldn't express himself—it was buried too deep. 'But, Mrs du Plessis, Alex needs you to be a mother as much as you need him to be a son.'

'Misty . . .' Alex began to disagree.

'No, it's there in you; it's the truth.'

He closed his mouth—possibly another first for Alex, to be rendered speechless by someone else.

'Then I'd like that,' Miriam sniffed, 'I'd like to begin again.'

'OK.' Alex's face broke into one of his gorgeous smiles. 'Mom.'

Chapter 23

Christmas at our house was always a fantastic mess of family, presents, and food. I had warned Alex to be prepared for an attack on his senses: amazing decorations made by Hazel and Willow, helped along by my sisters, Gale, Felicity, and Peace; the shrieks of Brand, Tempest, and Sunny in the little boys' bedroom, ankle-deep with Lego and animal toys; Dad's superb cooking making taste buds zing; the smells of the fir tree in the living room and roast goose in the kitchen. Alex and I had vetoed turkey after Thanksgiving.

'You forgot the sense of touch,' Alex told me, an appreciative little smile curving his mouth. He ran his fingers down my neck to play with the necklace he had given me on our one-month anniversary—two interlocking hearts. I hadn't yet opened my one for Christmas but it was small and ring box-shaped. I was guessing it would match.

I shivered, feeling his caress all the way to my toes. 'I think we've got that sense covered.'

'We certainly do.'

Our kiss in the conservatory was broken up by a loud cough from Sky and a laugh from Zed.

'Hey, Misty, do you want us to go?' she asked, eyes sparkling with mischief. Zed and Sky were spending Christmas with her parents in Richmond so we were all sharing lunch together.

Uriel and Tarryn appeared behind them, carrying a huge stack of presents.

'She can't reply,' said Tarryn, 'because the truth would be rude.'

Alex hid my blush against his chest. 'Remind me why I wished for more family?'

'Because you love us,' said Crystal, emerging with a plate of mince pies from the kitchen.

Xav followed with a tray of steaming spiced apple juice. 'When you're not wishing to strangle us,' he concluded. 'Misty, have a drink, then you can blame your red cheeks on the fruit punch.'

We helped ourselves to the glasses sitting in little filigree metal holders, a present from Alex's family in Oregon. There weren't enough chairs for us all in the conservatory so we had to double up, girls on boys' knees, though Crystal did try arguing with Xav that he should sit on her. He won. The living room was given over to the children disembowelling their gifts. Out of the corner of my eye I could see Pest batting Brand over the head with an inflatable Rudolf and Brand lion-roaring back, but as the encounter appeared to agree with both of them, I decided not to intervene. Sunny's hair was looking suspiciously short at the sides. The younger girls had their heads together plotting something but I wasn't sure what. As Felicity and Peace were showing a gift for getting into mischief (after all, I had set them a very good example in that department), I anticipated the afternoon would turn interesting at about five o'clock when their plans matured. Gale had an anticipatory smile as she sat back and let them plot. Mum, Dad, Auntie

Opal, and Uncle Milo were oblivious to the trouble ahead, singing away to Christmas carols in the kitchen as their team prepared the feast.

Just as well I'd organized for Alex and I to meet up with Summer and Angel about then to go for a walk along the Thames. It was one of our traditions ever since we found out that Angel could do really cool things to the river water—a little fountain show to round off the festivities. It also got Summer out of her less-than-happy home.

'I have to thank you,' Tarryn said, tapping my knee to gain my attention.

'Me? What for?'

'For teaching me that my gift could be used to save lives, not just predict their end. Uri and I have realized that together we can bring some soulfinders back from the brink. On some rare occasions, if they haven't completely passed on, we can lay a trail home.' She grimaced. 'We can also combine our gifts to see how someone died, which is very useful to Uri and Victor in their work—not that I'm so thrilled about that part of my gift.'

'You will be when you get justice for those who've been the victim of crime,' said Uriel gently.

'And you might stop the wrong person being convicted. Think what that would mean to someone's life,' added Zed.

Tarryn shrugged in surrender. 'See, there's more to my gift, as you predicted. Thank you, Misty, for starting me down this track.'

'Just a shame you had to die to do it.' Xav winked at me.

Alex opened his mouth to tell Xav he didn't find that crack very funny, but I put my finger against his lips.

'I'm not intending to repeat the experiment, but I'm glad it worked out well for you both,' I told Tarryn and Uriel.

Sky giggled. 'That's so sweet.'

'What's sweet?'

'The way you get Alex to shut up. When I first met him, I thought no one would dare stop him as every word he speaks is so . . .' she wriggled on Zed's lap, '*mesmerizing.*'

'Watch it,' growled Zed, 'or I'll have to have words of my own with him outside.'

'Power down those macho boosters, bro,' broke in Xav. 'Haven't you noticed that when he's with Misty—which is nearly all the time as far as I can make out—he is as foot-in-the-mouth as the rest of us.'

'Unless they get their gifts together, combining truth and persuasion, then we are all doomed to do what they say,' added Sky.

Alex laced his fingers with mine. *So we are an unstoppable combination?*

Too right, partner.

You make me humble; I make you . . . ?

Happy.

Good one. I make you happy. And together we can rule the world. The last was said with a cheeky smile as it wasn't quite a lie.

Just as well I have no ambition to rule.

Aw, spoilsport. Alex pushed me up from his knee. 'Talking about facing your doom, I believe you owe me a game.' He gestured to our family ping-pong table set up on the veranda undercover.

'Cool!' Sky jumped up. 'I'll play!'

'I'll take you on next,' I promised, 'but Alex and I have something of a grudge match to settle. I thrashed him in Cape Town and he's been waiting to get his revenge.'

'Thrashed? Hah, hardly,' Alex scoffed.

'Grudge match?' Xav rubbed his hands. 'Nice.'

'I'll umpire,' offered Crystal.

'I'm keeping well out of it,' said Tarryn swiftly. 'Uri, if you value your life, stay put.'

'Prepare to have your excellent butt well and truly kicked!' I warned Alex, tying back my hair, readying for table-tennis battle.

'You're on.' He picked up the bat and ball resting on the table at the far end, rolling his shoulders to loosen up. Oh my, it was hard to concentrate: he looked so gorgeous—and he was all mine.

The first serve whistled by me.

'Oh, weren't you ready?' he asked with that smile that told me he knew exactly what I was thinking.

'I am now,' I replied, getting serious.

'Don't get mad, get even,' counselled Zed.

'I'm on it. Stand back everyone: this is about to get bloody.'

And the result of the match?

In the end, it didn't matter as the prize to the victor was a kiss.

Win or lose: we both won.

Joss Stirling lives in Oxford
and has always been facinated by the idea
that life is more than what we see on the surface.

You can visit her website at **www.jossstirling.com**.

BOOKS BY
Joss Stirling

COMING SOON ...

What if the one person you love is the one person you shouldn't?

Stung

Joss Stirling

The best-selling author of Finding Sky

OUT FEBRUARY 2015

eBook
Available